EX LIBRIS

VINTAGE CLASSICS

T0315591

A LONG TIME AGO

Margaret Kennedy was born in 1896. Her first novel, *The Ladies of Lyndon*, was published in 1923. Her second novel, *The Constant Nymph*, became an international bestseller. She then met and married a barrister, David Davies, with whom she had three children. She went on to write a further fifteen novels, to much critical acclaim. She was also a playwright, adapting two of her novels – *Escape Me Never* and *The Constant Nymph* – into successful productions. Three different film versions of *The Constant Nymph* were made, and featured stars of the time such as Ivor Novello and Joan Fontaine; Kennedy subsequently worked in the film industry for a number of years. She also wrote a biography of Jane Austen and a work of literary criticism, *The Outlaws of Parnassus*. Margaret Kennedy died in Woodstock, Oxfordshire, in 1967.

OTHER NOVELS BY MARGARET KENNEDY

MARGARET KENNEDY

A Long Time Ago

VINTAGE BOOKS
London

Published by Vintage 2014

2 4 6 8 10 9 7 5 3 1

First published in Great Britain by William Heinemann in 1932

Vintage
Random House, 20 Vauxhall Bridge Road,
London SW1V 2SA

www.vintage-classics.info

Addresses for companies within The Random House Group Limited
can be found at: www.randomhouse.co.uk/offices.htm

The Random House Group Limited Reg. No. 954009

A CIP catalogue record for this book
is available from the British Library

ISBN 9780099595472

The Random House Group Limited supports The Forest Stewardship
Council® (FSC®), the leading international forest-certification organisation.
Our books carrying the FSC label are printed on FSC®-certified paper.
FSC is the only forest-certification scheme supported by the leading
environmental organisations, including Greenpeace. Our
paper procurement policy can be found at
www.randomhouse.co.uk/environment

Printed and bound in Great Britain by Clays Ltd, St Ives plc

TO LAURENCE AND BARBARA HAMMOND

Prologue

SUNDAY MORNING

SUNDAY MORNING

I

ELLEN NAPIER came downstairs with a piece of brown paper in her hand. From time to time she paused, for she was trying to remember where it was that she had secreted a particular piece of string which she had taken off a parcel of Parish Magazines.

It was not in the hall drawer, for she had looked, but it might be in the ginger jar on the dining-room mantelpiece. The whole thing would come back to her if she could only remember where she had been when the magazines had arrived. Was it the day before yesterday? What else had she done that day?

She came to a standstill on the half-landing and began methodically to live her life backwards, minute by minute. Yesterday evening, yesterday afternoon, yesterday morning . . . no magazines or string occurred in any of them. Well then, Friday evening . . .

Her daughter, who had just come into the hall, looked up at her and laughed.

"You ought to have your portrait painted like that, Mother. You ought to have your portrait painted standing on some stairs, just like that, holding a piece of brown paper. I wish I could paint!"

"What, dear?" said Ellen. "Was Friday the day before yesterday? Which day did we have kedgeree for breakfast?"

"Kedgeree? I wasn't here. . . ."

"No! That's all right. I remember. I put it in the top drawer of the lacquer cabinet."

She came down the rest of the stairs and vanished into the drawing-room.

Hope, who knew the workings of her mother's mind, reflected:

"Now what . . . oh, string, probably! But why kedgeree? Because they always have it for breakfast on Saturdays, because they have fish on Fridays, because Maggie is a Catholic. . . ."

She looked up again at the empty staircase and thought of the picture which she would have liked to paint. The idea had been conceived in a sudden rush of affection, of admiration for her mother's character. For such a portrait there could be no better background than the hall at Cary's End, which was large and square and lighted by a long north window. The colouring would be a trifle austere, for the walls, the doors and the banisters were all painted white. Twelve broad and leisurely stairs led to the half-landing, where Ellen had stood, and twelve more went up, at right angles, to an upper gallery. In spite of all the dog baskets, gardening scissors, newspapers and walking-sticks which littered the hall, there was a general effect of whiteness, space, and straight lines. The cold, prosaic northern light distributed itself impartially over the whole scene.

But it would not be a cold composition because the central figure would give it warmth. Even in her still pose, as she mused on the landing, she had been full of vitality and purpose. And the piece of brown paper in her hand would provide the final clue, both to character and to composition. It would make a pattern, breaking up the column of her black dress, seen against the whiteness of the walls. It would tell the beholder who she was and what she did: that she was a widow, living in the country, and that she had children and grandchildren to whom she was continually sending parcels.

"As good as bread!" thought Hope, as she went upstairs for her library book. "It would be a great picture, if anybody could bring out just that quality of goodness."

Ellen had found her piece of string in the top drawer of the lacquer cabinet. She did up her parcel and wrote the address, clearly and firmly, in two places. Then she put it on the hall table in order to remind herself to have it posted on Monday morning.

Straightening herself, she pushed the untidy grey hair out of her eyes. What was the next thing to be done?

"Dick is dead," she thought.

She looked round the hall with an expression, timid and forlorn, like a woman who has reached an island in a crowded thoroughfare and who pauses, as if afraid of a new plunge into the dangers of the traffic. For a few seconds she was quite at a loss. Then she remembered, took refuge in the next thing. There was a place under the apple trees in the old orchard where the weeds had got very bad. If she did not clear it, Hawkins would, and he would be sure to dig up all the violets which she had planted there last year. Hawkins was much too drastic with that fork of his. But she would forestall him.

It was only in these empty moments, when she had finished some task and could not remember what came next, that her widowhood overpowered her. For Dick had been dead seven years and she had got used to being alone. There was always a great deal to be done, in the house and the garden and the village. After one thing there was sure to be another.

She went upstairs and presently reappeared with her thick boots on. From the hall drawer she took a pair of leather gloves and from the cloak cupboard a sacking apron and an old black hat. Hope, who was reading by the drawing-room fire, protested:

"Why do you always wear your hats on the very top of your head?"

"Because they make them so small nowadays," complained Ellen. "I haven't had a hat for ages that didn't give me a headache. Which reminds me . . . do you think I ought to have a new one for Rosamund's wedding?"

"Of course you must. You'd better let me choose it for you or you'll be getting ostrich feathers again."

"I thought ostrich feathers were supposed to have come in again."

"Not as you wear them. Standing up like a hedge all the way round a high crown. You mustn't go to Rosamund's wedding looking like a District Councillor."

"But I am one. And I sit on D.C. meetings much oftener than I go to weddings. If I get a new hat . . ."

"I'll choose one that'll be right for both," promised Hope.

Ellen pushed open the long window and disappeared into the foggy November morning. She went up to the potting-shed for a fork and a wheelbarrow. Every twenty minutes or so she went rumbling past the window again, with a load of weeds for the rubbish heap.

And Hope was able to go on reading *The Story of My Life* by Elissa Koebel, which she had brought down with her to enliven the week-end. It was only just published and she had been longing to get hold of it for two reasons: because it was said to be very scandalous and because it revived an episode in her own past.

Some twenty-five years earlier the Napiers had spent a summer holiday in the North-West of Ireland, sharing a house there with a tribe of aunts, uncles and cousins. It had been a memorable and romantic summer, especially for the children, since the house was really a small castle on an island in the middle of a lough. Their nurseries had been in the old Keep and they had gone to bed up winding turret stairs. It had been like living in a fairy tale. And part of the legend had been Elissa Koebel, who was suddenly of their party, and who was, as they all believed, the greatest singer in the world. She lived, like a witch, in a little cottage on the mainland, and nothing that she did was in the least like anything that anyone else ever did.

When they left Ireland this glamorous being vanished from their lives as suddenly as she had come. But Hope continued secretly to worship her. From time to time she heard stories of Elissa which were all fuel to her flame. As she grew older she realised that certain of her childish impressions might have been, perhaps, a little extravagant. There might be greater singers. But she was still sure that there had never existed a more remarkable woman. That brilliant and tragic progress, the colossal misfortunes, the equally colossal success, the string of world famous lovers, could not belong to anybody but a genius.

Even now, when she thought of these things, Hope could not quite escape from an odd little pang of envy and regret. For as a child she had confidently expected to be just like Elissa when she grew up. She too had meant to be a great woman, ravishingly beautiful, to flout the world and to live a free, adventurous life. She had never asked herself how this was to be managed, and she never knew at what moment the fantastic expectation began to crumble. She had been a stout, plain, uncharming child. She grew into a handsome, practical young woman, prudent in money matters and disliking insecurity of any sort. At twenty-six she married. She had three children. Neither before nor after her marriage had she felt inclined to take a lover. Yet there were still occasions when she felt that her life had been mismanaged in some way, that she ought to have been somebody quite different, that she would have been somebody quite different if only she had tried hard enough.

So that she looked forward to the publication of Elissa's autobiography with an eager, half-bitter curiosity, scarcely knowing whether she was going to envy or censure the woman who had lived and written so frankly. Of the frankness there was no doubt; the reviewers in the week-end papers had already made that perfectly clear. They could talk of nothing else, though one or two of them had been dispassionate enough to complain also that the translation was poor, and that Elissa, who spoke seven languages, would have been better advised to make a translation of her own. But their criticisms, as a whole, were meek, slightly dazed, as though they needed a little more time to recover from the shock of Elissa's experiences.

There were no pictures in the book, no portraits of the Diva in her principal rôles. Elissa had always refused to be photographed, just as she had never allowed any records to be taken of her voice. It was possible, as one of the critics hinted, that she had been wise. Neither her features nor her voice had the qualities which survive mechanical reproduction. It was a question of the indwelling soul. Both her beauty and her art were articles of faith, to herself, and to her admirers.

But Hope was disappointed to find no pictures. She had wanted to remember exactly how Elissa looked. After hunting in vain through the volume she turned back to the list of chapters at the beginning. A title caught her eye: *A Summer in Ireland*. She stiffened with excitement.

"It must be about Inishbar," she thought. "It must be about us!"

She found the place and began to read.

2

Extract from *The Story of My Life* by Elissa Koebel, translated by Fanny Bartlett, with a foreword by Johann Heinrich.

SPRING found me again in England, very ill and almost penniless. X thought that I was dying. I had been ill in Paris before we started and when we reached London I could scarcely speak. Terrible spasms of shivering shook me. Nothing could keep me warm. X knelt beside me in the train, chafing my hands and begging me to recover. It was a terrible journey. We thought that it would never be over. But at last we had arrived. We descended from the train.

A strange figure I must have looked, tottering down the platform, my long, white cloak wrapped round me like a shroud!

"Why do all the people stare at me so? What is it that they are staring at?"

"They think you are dying, Elissa. Let us drive immediately to a doctor."

"No. I cannot pay a doctor. I have exactly ten francs. Let us drive to the hotel."

But in the automobile a frightful fact assailed me. I became galvanised, alert. I recovered my powers of utterance.

"To what hotel," I demanded, "are you taking me?"

Always, during my previous visits to England I had stayed with friends or, if at an hotel, at the Ritz. It was to the Ritz that we were now going. Poor Noemi had given the direction as a matter of course. I was furious. I loaded them with reproaches.

"Am I for ever to be surrounded by imbeciles?" I shouted. "Can you not understand that I have exactly ten francs? Take me some place where I can die in peace for ten francs."

"But where, Elissa, where? We have never been in London before."

X lowered the window and addressed the driver. He could not speak English at all, and I was too ill to help him. Those spasms, that dreadful shivering, had come back. I could only lie in Noemi's arms, moaning and sobbing:

"Find me a place where I can die in peace for ten francs."

Need I say that this prayer was not granted? There was no place in London, it seemed, where one could live, much less die, for as little as that.

"Then let us go to the Ritz. . . ."

If one has not enough money to go to a bad hotel one should stay at a good one. I have always found this to be true. We went to the Ritz and we remained there for six weeks, in spite of our poverty; whereas, if we had gone to a cheap *pension* in a poor quarter of the town they would have thrown us out because we could not pay. My old suite, overlooking the park, was ready for me and already there were flowers from friends who knew that I was coming.

But our troubles were not over. My friends would gladly have died for me, but they were not practical. It was always I who had to think and act. I lost no time.

"We must have money, it seems. That is the first thing. I have still some jewels which we must sell, as soon as we have recovered our luggage."

"But your agent, Elissa, could you not ask him for an advance?"

I laughed at them.

"We shall see."

In my despair I was still able to laugh.

That afternoon this same agent, who appeared such a wonderful individual to my poor friends, came to call upon me.

"You will be so good, Mr. Perkins, as to cancel all my London engagements. I cannot sing."

"But, Madame . . ."

"I cannot sing."

"But, Madame . . ."

"I cannot sing. I cannot sing. I cannot sing."

It was quite true. I could not. My beautiful voice had left me as the soul leaves the body when it is dead. It was as if I had actually died on that terrible journey. That glorious fountain of music, which was my very life, had ceased to flow. I was convinced that I should never sing again.

There comes a time, I think it is written in the stars for every artist, there comes a moment of chaos, of nothingness. It is winter in the soul. The flowery promise of spring, the rich fruitfulness of summer, appear to have departed for ever. The earth lies frozen, spell-bound, under a sullen mist. The sap is stagnant in the trees. The warm currents of inspiration have ceased to flow.

For nature, which is without memory and without hope, this time is a season of sleep and forgetfulness. The trees, shorn of their leaves, feel no pain and no regret: they have forgotten all past springs and they know nothing of springs to come. But Man is not as wise as the trees. He is not content to lie fallow. He suffers. He remembers. He is impatient for the revival of his powers. He knows that he has ceased to find beauty and significance in the objects which surround him, and yet he still endeavours to create a false spring in the midst of winter, and, knowing it to be false, he despairs. He cries:

"My God! My God! Why hast Thou forsaken me?"

It was to such a valley of desolation that I had now come. The experience was new to me. Heretofore my life had been all summer. In spite of a thousand misfortunes my inner light had never failed me. I could not account for it. I was in despair. In vain did they tell me that I could not sing because I was ill. I knew better. I was ill because I could not sing. My God had forsaken me. In everything that I did there was the same quality of deadness. My life appeared to have no continuity, and no meaning. Nothing could move me. I visited picture galleries. I gazed upon the most glorious masterpieces of Raphael and Titian, and they were no more to me than senseless daubs. The poetry which had so often inspired me had no message of hope—the volume of Goethe or of Dante would fall from my listless hand. Nor could I fly to music as a refuge. That was the worst of all. The noblest Sonatas of Beethoven, the tenderest nocturne of Chopin, were nothing but a noise, a *bruhaha*, exasperating to my nerves.

And through it all, day after day, I had to endure the mockery of seeing the sunshine, the flowers, the gaiety of early summer: that most beautiful of all the phases of the year. It was the time of the London season and every mail brought us a number of invitations to the most brilliant balls, concerts and receptions. My English friends had been anxious to fête me, and to my other distresses this was now added—that I was obliged to disappoint them. I would see no one. I would go nowhere. I had shut myself up like a nun in her cell.

All my life I have been happy only in giving. Just as I give of my art, so also I give of myself. To go into society, to grimace and to speak politenesses where no genuine current of sympathy is flowing, this is as impossible to me as to sing badly. If, upon the concert platform, I will not offer the cold shell of my voice to the public, so, in the drawing-room, I will not offer the cold shell of my heart to my friends. . . .

London is beautiful in summer, especially, I think, at night. Above the brilliantly-lighted streets there is a sky of a peculiar vivid green which I have not seen in any other city. Sometimes, after a day spent in pacing my little room at the hotel, I would wrap my cloak about me and rush out to mingle with the crowds that move slowly about on the pavements beneath that strange green sky. I drew a sense of comfort from the simple kindness of these people as they made way for me to pass. I felt that they some way shared the trouble of this strange woman, this tall ghost in her white cloak. Their looks followed me, a little awe-struck, as though they had beheld a vision flitting past them. I enjoyed a greater communion of sympathy, here in the streets, than I would have felt among the distinguished and titled people who had begged me to visit them.

I would ride long distances on the street cars, out into the suburban quarters of the town, always with that strange green sky above me, and always saying to myself:

"If I go far enough there will be no more houses, and no more people. I shall come to a place of silence and peace. . . ."

My friend Emmi Waldstein was singing at Covent Garden. Once, having wandered into the vicinity of the Opera House, I determined to pay her a visit. It was the impulse of a moment and yet, as so often, that moment was a turning point in my life. For it was Emmi who suggested that I should go into the country: it was she who made me understand what it was that I needed—the space and silence of nature.

It so happened that she was singing "Isolde." I went to her in her dressing-room during the intermission. She rose, almost in tears, to greet me, distressed at my altered appearance.

"But Elissa! What has happened, then? You have become so thin!"

We stood together before the long mirror in her dressing-room, and a strange contrast we made! Emmi had remained as charming as ever, so plump, so debonair, a little too short, as I always think, for the rôle of Isolde, but very graceful in her white robe, smiling back at me from the mirror with that peculiar expression of hers which is at once so infantile and so shrewd, so naïve yet so alert.

I had indeed grown thin; the mystic quality in my beauty had become accentuated by suffering so that I looked, as X said, more like a tragic muse than a woman.

I smiled, a little sadly.

"I think it is I, and not you, Emmi, who should be singing the "Liebestod" to-night."

But she, as always, was highly practical.

"You will be ruined, my dear, if you continue in this manner. If you are ill you should see a doctor and get well again as quickly as possible."

"My body is not ill. My soul is ill."

"I understand perfectly. I have myself said this upon an occasion . . . Confide in me, my dearest friend. Who has given you the basket?"

It is impossible to become angry with Emmi. I, for one, cannot do it. Her kindness is so entirely sincere, there is so much *naïveté* and good humour in her manner, that I am obliged to capitulate, especially when she uses the *argot* of our girlhood, of the period when we were students together at the *Conservatoire*. There is something about this great singer, something genuine and simple, which has survived all the onslaughts of fame and of public achievement. At heart, she is still a young girl. She has had many lovers, but to her they have all been just a little ridiculous. She transports me back to those days when we hid laughing behind the curtain while certain of our admirers in the street below paced slowly up and down on the sentimental *Fenster Promenade*.

"Unfortunately, no one has given me the basket. It is more than eighteen months since I have loved anyone at all."

"My God! Is that possible?"

"It is quite true. It seems that I have lost the power to respond to such feelings."

"But, my dear, this is terrible! For you it is most unnatural. I do not wonder that you are *ennervée*. I implore you to take a lover immediately."

"Pardon me, Emmi, but I cannot arrange matters quite as easily as that. If I have no lover it is because there is nobody, but I say it, nobody, who can succeed in attracting me. I know it is unnatural, but I cannot help it. I cannot go to a store and purchase a lover as I would purchase a pair of gloves."

"Naturally. One cannot concoct a *grande passion* to order. But one can amuse oneself."

"I cannot. I have never been able to amuse myself, as you say. For me the passion of love must be all-devouring. It must arouse my most sacred, my deepest feelings. I require to be entirely swept away. I have nothing cynical or frivolous in my nature."

It was impossible that she should understand me. She had not the tragic temperament. Her life was like her singing—cool, delicious, perfectly poised. Her art was perfect but it was not sublime. There were no supreme moments for her. Her greatest rôles have been those of comedy, in Mozart and in Strauss.

For none of her lovers had she felt very deeply. Each affair had been, for her, a delightful episode, whereas each, for me, had been a tragedy. I had given all and I demanded everything. That is my nature and I cannot alter it, even if I would.

"But there is your career to be considered, *mein Kind*. I repeat, you cannot continue in this manner. I do not think that you should remain in London if you cannot sing. It is not sensible at all. Believe me, it creates a very bad impression, not only with the public but with more important individuals. There comes an idea that one is *passée* . . . a failure. The effect upon contracts in the future is very bad. If one is ill, if one cannot sing, it is much better to disappear until one is well again. Everyone knows that you are in London and they are saying strange things about you."

"But where do you advise me to go? Is not every

place the same? London . . . Paris . . . Rome . . . New York. . . ."

"In a town it would be the same. But you must not remain in a town. You must go into the country. I have spent many weeks myself at a farm in the Black Forest, two years ago. You must do the same. I will give you the address. I can assure you that it was not at all disagreeable. One becomes very fond of the country."

"Indeed you are mistaken if you suppose that I do not love the country, Emmi. I am never happy anywhere else. The most beautiful period in my life has been spent living quite simply among the peasants in Styria."

"By yourself, my dear?"

"Ah, no," I sighed. "Then I was with Rudolf."

"Precisely. When one is by oneself it is even more peaceful. One goes to bed as soon as it is dark. One sleeps all night. One rises early. One learns to milk the cows . . ."

She continued her exhortations until it was time for her to return to the stage. I accompanied her to the wings, and as I stood there, listening, a terrible nostalgia for the opera overcame me. This was my world and I was cast out from it! Voiceless, despairing, I breathed the air of home.

Great cliffs of scenery towered above me and, in an island of dazzling light, I could see a little section of the stage . . . the form of Emmi in her white robe, kneeling over Tristan. And beyond that lay what I could not see, the great, darkened opera house, silent and intent. The pure clear notes of the "Liebestod" floated away into that unseen world. Why was it not my voice?

A violent rebellion against my lot surged over me. I leant sobbing against the scenery, oblivious of the little crowd of friends who had gathered to welcome me. Drowned in tears I stumbled once more into the street. And of the weeks which followed I can write nothing. They are blackness. They are night. But at some moment the power to save myself returned. I left London. I left my friends. I went alone to Ireland.

Why had I chosen Ireland?

Was it because Isolde was in my mind? Isolde was a princess of Ireland. Or was it because fate had chosen Ireland for me? Unknown to me, the inspiration that I needed was waiting there. It is not chance which governs these things, though at the time it seems so.

My Irish friend, Caroline Nugent, the wife of the British Ambassador in Rome, had once offered to lend me a little cottage that she had built on the banks of a lake, on her estate. The thought of it returned to me.

"It is always ready," she had said, "always waiting for you. Go there whenever you wish. The key lies on a great beam above the door."

I recovered. I remembered her words. I set off.

I travelled alone, consumed by the desire to be by myself. And it was well that I did so, for the little house was too small for a party. One large room it had, and over half the space a loft, like a deep musicians' gallery, to which one ascended by a ladder. Here was to be found a curtained bed. Caroline had built the little cottage for herself as a retreat when she wished to be alone. In the lower room there was a great fire of turf, a dresser with blue plates, many books . . .

When I had lit the fire I was at home. I clambered up the ladder to my great curtained bed in the loft. I slept as

I had not been able to sleep for many months. I could have lain dreaming there for ever, I think, if I had not at last become very hungry. I had eaten nothing for three days except the chocolate which I had brought with me. It was time to go out and purchase some food. Caroline had told me of a village at the end of the lake.

Hastily flinging on a few garments I ran out into the fresh air. A cry of joy and wonder broke from me.

Where had I seen this place before? In my dreams? In some former existence?

I think, only in a dream. It is only in dreams that we see these colours, so soft, so vivid, so unreal—these mountains that we shall never climb, these pale waters. . . . Or has the world appeared to us like this in our childhood?

I do not know. I can only say that I achieved a moment of rapture, beholding a scene that was familiar and yet strange, remembered and yet new.

That scene—how shall I describe it?

A lake, pale as nacre, yet clear, holding in its bosom the crowded shapes of mountains: a bloom, a haze, an infinite softness: two worlds, a world in the water and a world in the air, and in the centre (ah! it was *that* which I remembered so well) a little island floating in its own reflection. Again and again my eyes returned to it. I could discern it now, among the trees, grey walls and a tower. I had always known it. A castle that was waiting for me. It had been waiting all my life. It was for this that I had come.

"To-morrow," I said, "I will take my boat and I will row out to the castle on the island."

And the next day, as I came out of my house, I said the same thing:

"To-morrow I will go."

And yet I did not go. It was many days before I attempted to pierce the mystery of the island and the castle. Why did I linger? Perhaps because I knew that I was not, as yet, ready for it.

I was so happy in my little cottage. Every day I recovered strength. My solitude was precious to me. In those days I only spoke to the peasants in the village where I purchased food. A delightful gipsy freedom possessed me. I went barefoot, like a young girl, my long hair hanging in two plaits. My youth flowed back into me, into my body and soul. It shone in my eyes. When I gazed into my little mirror it was no longer the Tragic Muse that gazed back at me; I saw again the face of a young and beautiful woman, still in the springtide of her life.

I tended my fire, I swept my little house, I cooked my simple meals. I lay for long hours beside the lake gazing towards the island . . . the castle. . . .

"To-morrow I will go. . . ."

I knew now that there were dwellers there. I had seen boats gliding over the water. I had seen smoke drifting across the trees. But these people were not strangers. I knew that they also were waiting for me.

As yet I had not sung. The wish to sing had not returned to me and I was content that it should be so. I waited serenely, understanding at last that some beautiful experience was drawing nearer to me. Until there came naturally a day when my solitude was over, and when my little cottage appeared also to be waiting. I became conscious that the chair upon the other side of my hearth was empty. I no longer slept quite contentedly alone in that great bed in the loft. And then I knew, with a mysterious finality, that it was time for me to go to the island.

It was very early morning, and I had spent a restless night, often groaning and crying out in my sleep. A light haze like a thin, imperceptible curtain hovered between the lake and the full light of the sun, and in that silver radiance, upon those milky waters, the island and its trees looked strangely dark and formidable. As my boat drew nearer that dark shape grew taller until at last it had hidden the sun and the friendly hills behind it. I floated into the shadow and rested for a moment on my oars.

I could see a stretch of very green grass, a little lawn stretching gently up to the grey pile of buildings. Something told me that they were all asleep. And then an old woman came out from under the arched doorway. She crossed the green grass and stood beside the lake, looking at me in my boat. A cold shadow, a premonition, fell across my heart. I thought:

"This woman is not my friend. She is guarding the island against me."

Her white apron, her black dress, her neat grey hair repelled me. Who was she, this old sibyl? A servant . . . an old nurse, perhaps.

But these old women, how terrible they are! What secrets do they not conceal behind the drab and formal neatness of their appearance? What fierce passions, what a deadly hatred of life, of love, of youth and joy, is raging in their shrivelled bosoms? All my life I have been afraid of old women and their crafty wisdom.

I dared not speak to her. I turned my boat and rowed quickly away from the island.

Ah yes, old woman! You and destiny were too strong for me.

Next day, when the silver light had turned to gold and the lake waters were blue, my courage returned to me. I determined once more to make the attempt. But this time I did not approach the northern shores of the island, where the grass sloped down from the castle door: I rowed stealthily round, exploring the little coves and beaches among the trees. On a stretch of fine white sand I drew in my boat, and climbed ashore. I pushed my way in among the trees. My bare feet pressed delicately upon a sumptuous carpet of moss. Presently I paused to listen.

There were voices, close at hand, ringing out across the water, children's voices, happy and laughing. And now there was singing. Another voice, a woman's, had raised an air and soon all were singing, too. I hurried towards the sound. Standing on the crest of a high bank I looked down upon a lovely sight.

Little naked children were bathing on the beach below me. It was their beautiful mother who was singing, as she sat in the sun beside the lake. She sang as the birds sing, with a voice untrained but sweet. I gazed down at her and knew that she was destined to be my friend.

When the song was over I cried out *bravo!* from my hiding place among the bushes. She looked up in astonishment and I showed myself.

"But who are you?"

"I am a dryad . . . an undine . . ."

Afterwards she told me that she had almost believed me. In my ragged green dress, with my little feet bare, I really appeared to be some spirit of the forest or of the lake.

Standing still on my high bank, smiling down at them, I suddenly commenced to sing. I heard my own voice pouring out, with an astonishing power and purity, into the golden air of that summer morning. In a moment it had all come back to me—the strength and the desire to express myself. My body had become once more the vehicle of my art. Without conscious effort I was singing those words which my dumb heart had so often whispered in silence:

> *Du bist der Lenz*
> *Nach dem ich verlangte*
> *Im frostigen Winter's Frist . . . .*

To whom was I singing?

As yet I did not know. I only knew that my winter was over and that my voice had returned to me. It had returned in all its perfection. I have never sung better.

I have experienced all the supreme moments in an artist's life. I have known that tremor of a sacred delirium which flows between the singer and his audience, and I have known that instant of silence, like a great deep sigh, which hangs between the last note and the first sharp crackle of applause, the applause which falls like a single stone, a shower, a vast avalanche into a deep lake of peace which I have created with my art. But I have never—I say it,—I have never sung more perfectly than on this golden summer morning, to this simple audience—a woman and her children, who wept to hear me.

"But you are Elissa Koebel! We have been expecting you."

Did I not know it! I laughed and sprang down the bank. I wished to laugh and I wished that everyone should laugh as well. A mad exhilaration seized upon us. No child among them was as wild and merry as I. I had found my friends. They had been expecting me. I knew it.

These delightful people were highly unconventional. I soon learnt to know them all. The castle on the island became my second home. Often the stars had risen before my boat returned to the cottage, and if I wished to stay all night there was always a bed for me. An irresistible impulse drew me towards them.

My new friend, Louise, remained the dearest. I discovered that she was indeed the mistress of this charming house. Beautiful and gifted, she was not, I think, entirely happy. An artist at soul, she had sacrificed those sacred impulses to husband and children and I see her always like some lovely captive bird, pining for a freedom that is only half realised. I know that she often envied me my fuller and more vital life. And, as is so often the case with these talented and wasted souls, she offered to her friends the gift of a most perfect sympathy.

For her husband, an Oxford professor, I soon cherished a deep and affectionate respect. At first, I was chilled by his grave formality; I felt that our hearts would never speak to one another. But as I came to know him better I learned how delicate and gentle a soul was hidden beneath this cold and precise exterior. It was his ambition to introduce me to a study of the classics, and in my conversations with him I began to comprehend for the first time a little of that severe beauty which inspired the poetry of Homer and of Virgil. I have still a beautiful translation of the *Idylls of Theocritus* which he gave me. . . .

But everyone in that household was delightful.

c

Louise, with characteristic hospitality, had thrown open her doors to her entire family and their friends, all gifted and beautiful people. So that I found myself suddenly transported from solitude to social life of the pleasantest kind.

I was a great favourite with the children and spent many hours of the day playing with them. The naïve adoration of these little creatures was a constant source of pleasure to me. They still called me *Undine* and would never tire of listening to my stories of coral palaces at the bottom of the lake.

Beautiful summer days! By what spell can I evoke your serenity and your delight? Why do I linger, as I record you?

"Come now," I can hear my readers saying, "how tedious this Elissa is being! All that she wishes to tell us may be stated in a single paragraph. In the spring she became melancholy and in bad health. In the summer she went to Ireland, where she recovered. And she made there some new friends."

Forgive me, dear reader, but I cannot agree with you. The truth is never told as easily as that.

During this year I had undergone one of the most important, the most mystical phases which occur in the life of an artist: the sudden and unexplained extinction of my powers, a period of despair, of gradual recovery, and finally of new inspiration. When, eventually, I left Ireland it was to launch upon a magnificent era of new activity and achievement. And all this is a great deal more interesting than if I had only to say that I had sung in London during the Season, that I had been fêted and applauded, that this, or that, distinguished person had done me honour. All *that* you may read in the newspapers, or it may be written by others about me: what I have to say is that story which only the artist himself can tell.

You must be patient.

I was happy, as I have said, yet I was still waiting. I was aware that some new, great emotional climax lay before me. My soul and body were awake and alert; they were already in a tingling ferment of anticipation. I was eagerly desiring this new experience.

Louise had spoken of the expected arrival of another guest, her brother Dick.

I must confess that I anticipated very little pleasure from this new acquaintance that I was about to make. I had already formed for myself a picture of this brilliant, unhappy man. I had learned that he was a doctor and this chilled my sympathies. My experience of men in that profession had already made me impatient. They know too much and too little. Their contact with humanity breeds in them a kind of cynicism which the artist instinctively knows to be false.

Every night, when the evening meal was over, they would entreat me to sing for them. I was delighted to do so. In those days I could scarcely stop singing. I would sing in that great shadowy room, with its windows open to the lake. I would sing until the moon had risen far up into the sky. Upon the piano, standing on a dais at one end of the room, we would place two candles. Louise would permit no other light. To listen in the dark, she said, is an ideal state of things. So I would stand upon the dais, dim and tall in my white dress, and sing song after song, while the glow of the sunset faded, and dusk gathered in the room, and the first rays of the rising moon silvered the edges of the distant mountains. The night was so still that the candle flames burnt steadily upwards, like candles on an altar, upon either side of the pianist.

Scattered among the shadows of the great room this little group of people would sit silent, dreaming. Sometimes, at the termination of a song, a voice would speak and call to me:

"Sing this . . . sing that . . . sing the *Pieta Signore* of Stradella . . . sing the *Dove Sono* . . . sing *Waldege-spracht* . . . *La Procession* of César Franck . . . sing *Du bist die Ruh*. . . ."

A favourite, this last, with the husband of Louise. I must sing it every night for him, and it was usually the end of the concert. The little murmuring accompaniment flows out into the room and there is a sigh of pleasure from my hidden audience. My still, calm voice floats through the night . . .

> Du bist die Ruh,
> Der Friede mild!
> Die Sehnsucht du
> Und was sie stillt!

Thou art the longing and the appeasement! To whom was I singing, then? Who was coming to appease my longing?

On the soft cadence at the end of the verse I lifted my eyes. A stranger was listening by one of the open windows, leaning his arms upon the low sill. I could see a pale face, beautiful and intent . . . my eyes were drawn and held by those other eyes which glittered in the darkness. My voice continued:

Kehr ein bei mir
Und schliesse du
Still hinter dir
Die Pforten zu!

The listeners in the dark room were forgotten. I had now but one listener and already I was linked to him by a secret current of emotion, a knowledge of mutual need. My voice rose triumphant:

Dies' augenzelt
Von deinem Glanz
Allein erhellt!

He for whom I had been waiting had come. My song over, I stood motionless, locked in a gaze that had become an embrace. There was a cry in the room. Louise had risen. She was stumbling towards the window.

"Oh, Dick! Is it you? Have you come?"

The stranger smiled and vanished. Somebody brought lights.

"It is my brother, Elissa! He has come. It is my brother."

But my heart cried to me:

"It is my lover! He has come. It is my lover."

For two weeks we were continually together and yet we said nothing of the passion which consumed us.

What can I write of those weeks? What memory detaches itself from all that fever and anguish?

Only the sense of rapture delayed and a host of little things: a basket of mushrooms that we gathered—a child's laughter in the courtyard—a woman sitting on a low bench in the sunshine by the lake with a piece of white needlework in her hands.

Dick Napier was standing at that time upon the threshold of his great career. Since then honours, distinctions and wealth have been heaped upon him. But when I knew him his brilliance was by no one fully recognised. His beauty, the power and grace of his physique, the fiery intelligence which transfused it, were so remarkable that even now its memory astonishes me. He had a superb body in which was lodged a superb brain, of the scientific type. Louise had already spoken of his amazing promise. As a boy every prize, every scholarship, had been his as if by right.

But there were other aspects of his personality. That cynicism, of which I have spoken, had taken in his case an aspect of profound melancholy. He appeared to be incapable of happiness. Imprisoned within the fortress of his magnificent intellect he remained for ever beyond the reach of human sympathy. I think that only the impulse of creative art could have liberated him; but, despite his keen sense of beauty, he had chosen for himself a life of scientific enquiry which could not satisfy his need for self-expression. Drawn to me, as I to him, by an overpowering desire, he never, even after the fulfilment of his passion, he never once achieved the abandon, the exhilaration, of a happy lover. I, to whom such a moment is all-fulfilling, cannot understand these sufferings of the intellectual temperament. I was impatient of them. The intellect was meant to be the servant and not the master of the passions.

"You will never permit yourself to be carried away," I told him.

"But I have very much permitted myself to be carried away, unfortunately."

"And why, if you please, 'unfortunately'?"

This self-hatred, which some natures have, is a thing that I cannot comprehend. Upon one occasion, when we were living together in my cottage, he called my attention to a passage in a book that he was reading: *What I hate, that I do.*

"But that is ridiculous," I insisted. "To me it is incredible. I never hate what I do. I never do what I hate. All my actions are inspired by emotions which I consider beautiful and sacred. It is only when I have not followed my own impulses that I have felt any regret in my life."

"Then you are a fortunate being."

Up to the end there was always this chasm of incomprehension between us. And in the beginning it kept us apart, as I have said, for many days.

Two scenes.

It is evening and a crimson sky flames in the western end of the lake. I wander beside the water, listening to the sigh of the wind in the reeds, and cooling my fevered body in that soft breeze. In a few minutes it will be supper and we shall all assemble in the great hall where it is already dusk, where the starry candles burn on the table. . . . At the end of the landing-stage a tall man, immobile as a statue, gazes at the water in a posture of profound contemplation. He does not turn his head to look at me when I call to him. But when we are strolling across the grass to the castle he sighs deeply.

"At what were you gazing when you stood by the water?"

"I was watching the fish rise."

"You would have done better to come and talk to me."

"But I don't like talking to you, Elissa. To please me you must either sing or be silent."

"I bore you, then?"

"When you talk you do."

"Why? Do I say foolish things?"

"Yes."

It is morning and I have gone with Louise to bathe in a secret little cove that we have found. We lie naked in the early sun. There is a splash of oars. A boat is coming round the point. Louise springs up in consternation.

"Oh, it is Dick. He has come to fish here. Where is my cloak?"

"But, Louise . . . you have a beautiful body. Why should you wish to cover it up?"

"My husband would not like it."

"Well, I . . . I have no husband. I shall remain where I am."

The little boat comes into view and the fisherman hails us across the water. Louise is confused. She pulls her cloak more closely round her, and cries out:

"Go away!"

She cannot understand that a beautiful woman should not be ashamed of her body. Unable to support the gaze of her brother, she runs away towards the castle. I remain. He draws no nearer to the shore, but, resting on his oars, he contemplates me silently. Between us there is still that chasm and we have no power to cross it.

It is night. The white light of a full moon pours down upon the world with a dazzling radiance. The trees throw inky shadows. The castle and the island stand up, a silhouette cut in black paper against the faint luminance of the grey mountains behind. My oars, dipping into the water, cause a thousand silver ripples, and their gentle splashing, as I glide towards the island, is the only sound to be heard in all the breathless summer night.

I have tied up my boat. I steal across the dim grass. And now the night is full of music. The sound of a violin streams from the open window of the drawing-room. I creep closer. I stand at the window where he stood on the first night that he came, leaning my elbows on the sill. I gaze as if hypnotised at the tall flames of the candles, burning so straight and unflickering in the still air. They are playing the Spring Sonata of Beethoven . . .

He is standing beside me. He too leans his elbows on the sill: he too gazes into the room.

The clear river of music flows on its untroubled course. It fills our souls with an aching sweetness.

It speaks to us, this music, of a time in our lives which will never come again: a time which has never existed, but which might once have been. In our youth the world was never so tender or so gay, but in the deep lake of memory and of regret, where we see our youth reflected, we may perhaps trace these heavenly hues, and know what we have lost. Surely in our youth some lover has passed by us and vanished among the crowded years, some other self in whose arms we could have been thus gay and tender and serene.

But we forget. That tragic lover has no face . . .

His name and form we know not, nor shall know,
Like the lost Pleiad, seen no more below . . .

Was it a passion of regret that spanned, for a moment, the gulf between us?

I cannot tell. But I know that when we stood, locked in a long embrace beneath the shadowy trees, I was murmuring, brokenly, a name that I had forgotten for many, many years. . . .

Beside the landing stage my little boat was waiting. And still the fountain of music played on into the night. I caught his hand. We ran like children across the grass. The splash of our oars broke the water into a thousand silver ripples. The black silhouette of the island receded. The sounds of music grew fainter. . . .

Standing at the door of my cottage a few days later I cried out to Dick:

"Oh, look! The island has gone!"

It had indeed vanished behind an impenetrable curtain of mist and driving rain. Nor did I see it again. During the remainder of my visit to Ireland it concealed itself as though to tell me that the part which it had played in the story of my life was now complete. Destiny had drawn me to its shores, and the same inexorable fate was to drive me from it.

During the first days after we arrived together at the cottage the fine weather came to an end. But we, I must confess, were scarcely aware of this. We were too much occupied with one another. Our passion was not quickly or easily assuaged. We did not hear the howling of the wind or the beating rain.

These hours, these moments of supreme happiness, do they not solve for us the riddle of existence? For what else were we created? And yet, after a few days, I became once more aware of that overpowering melancholy which

overshadowed my lover's mind. It seemed that the chasm
had again opened between us. I felt it, even in his arms.
We had nothing to say to one another.

At heart he was a puritan . . . His continued, brooding
silence began to irritate me. He could not exist merely
in the present, as I did; thoughts of the past and the future
destroyed the harmony of life for him.

"We cannot," he said at last, "remain here for ever."

"Most certainly not. This continued rain is intolerable.
We will go to-morrow. I think I should like to return
at once to Italy. We will take a villa . . ."

"But I cannot go to Italy. My work is in London."

"Your work! Aha! I was expecting this."

Always it has been like this. I have never had a lover
who hesitated to sacrifice me and my art upon the altar
of his career. The egotism of the masculine temperament
is supreme. I could never make them understand that I,
too, must have freedom.

"And what then? How am I to occupy myself while
you are receiving your patients? Am I to be hidden away
in some little nest behind your consulting room?"

"God knows, Elissa!"

"But if you will not come with me to Italy, then I must
go with you to London."

"Both are impossible."

A cold fear, a first premonition of separation, fell across
my heart. I wept aloud, and for two or three days we said
nothing more about the future.

I was to be caught up once again in the eternal conflict
between my love and my art. My power to sing had returned to me and I was eager to exert it. But if I was to
follow that highest call of my soul I must do it at a terrible
price—the sacrifice of my woman's happiness.

Yet it was he and not I who was faithless.

He left me.

It seems that this is a lesson which I shall never learn. To me each love is always eternal until I am made to understand that for a man this is not the case. I would have been faithful to him. It was he, and not I—I repeat it—it was he who broke that sacred bond.

How could I guess that my beautiful island, where I had found strength and happiness, had changed into an enemy? Hidden behind its curtain of rain and mist it was preparing a blow for me. And yet, I might have known. I might have remembered the shadow which fell across my heart on that first day when I could not land because I was afraid—because I knew that the island was guarded against me. An old woman who looked at me across the water . . . a malevolent spirit, defying me. Ah, yes, I might have known!

Wrapped up in my peasant's cloak, I had been absent from the cottage for some hours. I had gone into the village to buy food.

"No, no, it is my turn to go," I had told him. "You do not like the village. You must tend the fire and read your books."

Why did I leave him? He had a morbid fear of going to the village or any place where we might encounter our friends from the island. I did not understand this at the time. He knew, better than I, what a terrible influence they could exert.

We embraced and he remained in the warm shelter of our cottage. When I returned, all was over. They had sent an emissary from the island. He was commanded to return.

It would have been less cruel if he had gone without

a word, while I was away. But he felt obliged to see me once again.

Gradually I came to understand that his egotism, his cowardice, his cold puritanism, were to prevail.

"I must go. It is my duty."

He dared to tell me that!

"Go, then. But do not return."

From my grief and bewilderment he fled as though furies were pursuing him.

And next day the little house, which had witnessed such moments of despair and rapture, stood deserted. The key lay once more upon the beam above the door. In my agony I had flown back to my first and only friend, my work. A beautiful movement in the symphony of my life had come to an end.

I had nothing to regret.

To life I say: Give me what you will! Give me your worst and your best! If I have accepted these gifts I shall have nothing to regret. The puritan, the coward, may fear the future and wish to see the past undone. But I, as long as I have power to suffer and to remember, refuse to regret anything that I have experienced.

I give thanks for the little house where my driven soul was sheltered and renewed its strength.

I give thanks for the island and the friendship that I found, for music and laughter, beautiful days and nights.

I give thanks for the love which crowned this wonderful summer with a supreme glory.

And for the art which drew me back, like a mother to her bosom, and healed my wounds, I give the deepest thanks of all:

> Du holde Kunst, Ich danke dir dafür!
> Du holde Kunst, I danke dir!

3

ELLEN's brother, Kerran Annesley, had bought a small Queen Anne house at Morton, about five miles from Cary's End. He lived there in an atmosphere of such retired distinction that even his family found it difficult to remember that he had never done much to deserve it. His beautiful library was just the setting for an ageing man of letters who might also have been a figure in the world. It was a civilised, rather feminine room, smelling of pot pourri and morocco leather, and, in the afternoons, of well-brewed china tea. There was an Aubusson carpet on the floor. The books, in their grey painted shelves, were cleaned twice a week with a vacuum cleaner.

In this room Kerran sat and read detective novels. He had written nothing since the early days of the *English Review*, to which he had contributed several articles. Nobody could remember what they were about, but they were thought at the time to display great promise. When his nephews and nieces, ignoring the family legend, asked why he had done nothing since, their parents spoke vaguely of ill health and an unfortunate love affair. As a minor official in the House of Lords he had never worked harder than he was obliged, and he retired at fifty on a comfortable independence inherited from his great-aunt Harriet. But he was a man of many friendships, able to win and preserve the esteem of people who were a great deal more energetic and distinguished than himself. They continued to come and stay with him at Morton and their talk was generally of the past, of the period when they also had been promising young men. Their regard for him enabled them to forget that he had never shared with them any period of fruition or achievement—that he had done nothing in particular for thirty years.

If he was alone upon a Sunday it was his habit to walk across the fields and take luncheon with Ellen, who was his favourite sister and who never tried to bully him into writing a book of reminiscences as Louise sometimes did. They would exchange the gossip of their respective villages and sometimes, after luncheon, they would do the crossword puzzle in the *Sunday Times*. Ellen always had a place laid for him, and if he did not turn up by one o'clock she knew that he was not coming. He generally arrived on the stroke of a quarter to one.

But on this Sunday he was earlier, having walked a great deal faster than usual. His leisurely stroll across the fields had been spoilt by an unwonted perturbation of spirits. He had not stopped to look at anything, but pounded along over plough and stubble like a man in a great hurry.

As he climbed the stile into the orchard he heard the sound of a trundled wheelbarrow and knew that Ellen must be gardening. This reassured him greatly, for it meant that life at Cary's End was going on just as usual. He peeped over the quickset hedge into the kitchen garden and saw her up by the rubbish heap. She tipped out her barrow-load and came trundling back towards him along the box-edged path. In another moment, as soon as he could see her face, he would know how matters stood. He knew her look, when anything had happened to upset her. It was exceedingly grim. In trouble or sorrow her features had a way of hardening into a rigidity that was almost wooden.

Timidly he came round the hedge and advanced up the path toward her. The trundling barrow stopped with a bump.

"How early you are!" she exclaimed.

She was not looking grim at all, only rather red and hot, for this was the sixth barrow-load that she had wheeled up to the rubbish heap. A wave of relief went over him. He could have spared himself all this distress. He need not have spoilt his walk. He need not have lain awake last night wondering what on earth he should say to her. It was quite evident that she had heard nothing. On this occasion, at least, they were safe.

He was overwhelmed with admiration. It was so like her to have managed to hear nothing, to remain successfully outside the family cyclone. Now he could feel himself outside it too. Louise might send peremptory telegrams, Maude might pester him with long, indignant letters by every post, but as long as he had Ellen's support he would refuse to put himself out. It was just like them to have made her their excuse for troubling him. *We have Ellen's feelings to consider*, Maude had written. And Louise's last telegram had run: *For Ellen's sake please use influence suppress book immediately*. Even Gordon had seemed to think that Ellen needed protection of some kind; had, indeed, rung up from Oxford on Saturday morning, and had taken the joke very badly when Kerran asked if he was expected to fight a duel with Elissa Koebel.

For it was plain that there was nothing to be done. Any effort to suppress the book now would only mean a great deal of odious publicity. Dick was dead. Only a very small section of readers would be interested in the disinterment of that long-forgotten scandal, which had, in fact, less news-value than any episode in Elissa's career. Amid so much that was startling, where so many famous names were involved, it was likely that the chapter called *A Summer in Ireland* would be overlooked. But the family would never take that view of the matter. They talked about Ellen's feelings and enjoyed themselves, just as they had enjoyed themselves twenty-five years ago, when it all happened. They had put up Ellen's feelings as a kind of stalking horse for their own pleasure and excitement.

And Ellen, meanwhile, had no feelings at all apparently. She was gardening, and her tranquil smile of welcome told him that in her house he would, at least for the present, be safe from these importunities.

Taking the wheelbarrow from her he trundled it back to the place under the apple tree where she was conducting her weeding operations. Hawkins had been ill that autumn and parts of the garden had been sadly neglected. The orchard was overrun not only with innocent groundsel but with all the worst kind of weed, docks, dandelions, couch grass and ground elder. Ellen's cherished violet bed was lost underneath a great mass of sodden and dying vegetation. But she had cleared several square yards and in the newly-dug soil she proudly displayed several disconsolate-looking columbines which Hawkins would never have taken the trouble to save.

"I suppose, as you're so early, you wouldn't like to get a fork and help me?" she said. "I've made a vow to get as far as the path before lunch."

"No, Ellen, I shouldn't. I've got my Sunday trousers on. I think I shall go indoors and read the paper."

"Umph!" said Ellen, grasping the fork again. "You'll

D

find Hope in the drawing-room. She's here for the week-end."

"Oh, is she?"

He spoke without enthusiasm. He liked Hope better than he liked his other nieces, but he would rather have been alone with Ellen. He wanted to tell her about the Vicar of Morton, who had provided a new chapter in the parish drama by reading Benediction in Latin. There had been a very good scene when old Major Trefusis had not only walked out of church himself, but had also obliged his cook to come with him. The presence of Hope at the luncheon table would a little spoil this fruitful topic. She had a way of wanting to talk about things which had nothing to do with Morton or Cary's End, and sometimes, with an irritating suggestion of patronage, she would ask him intelligent questions about Campbell-Bannerman, not as if she really wanted to know, but as if she thought that he could only discuss statesmen who were dead and public affairs which were a trifle out of date.

But he would have been very much more downcast had he known what was going to happen to him in the drawing-room. As soon as he pushed open the window he was aware that he had stepped back into that very cyclone which he thought to have escaped. It had come to Cary's End after all, and only Ellen, wheeling her barrow up and down the garden paths, was outside it. Hope, it appeared, was quite in the middle of it. She sprang towards him with such an expression of indignant horror that he scarcely needed to glance at the book which she brandished before his eyes.

"Oh, Uncle Kerran . . ."

"Good morning, Hope. How is Alan? How are the children?"

"Oh! They're quite well, thank you. Uncle Kerran, have you read . . ."

"No, I have not." He waved the book away. "And I'm not going to. There's nothing to be done, that I can see, and the less we talk about it the better."

"Nothing to be done?"

She stared at him in amazement. She had not got as far as that.

"But is it *true?*"

"True? Why . . ."

"Do you realise that I knew nothing about it? I never had the slightest idea . . ."

"Oh!" said Kerran.

He began to feel very uncomfortable. To face a niece who had heard of the business for the first time was much worse than anything he had expected. Really he could not blame her for displaying emotion.

"But is it true?" She insisted. "Did . . . did they . . . did my father? . . ."

She paused, and began also to look uncomfortable.

Her father had been dead so long that he had lost that blurred outline which softens a living individual in our thoughts. His image had set into a definite mould and she was unable to detach from it certain irrelevant characteristics. For some reason she always pictured him in the top-hat which he had worn at her wedding. And all her memories of him belonged to London, where they had lived until his death. She could stand at an upper window in Devonshire Place and watch him jump into a car from the pavement below. He would come out of the house in a tremendous hurry, putting on his hat. His reddish hair grew very thick all round his head, but there was a little bald spot on the top. And she could see his splendid profile as he sat beside her in a box at the theatre, a profile like a portrait on a coin. And she could feel again that little chill of dismay which his disapproval could evoke—the horror of having said something which he thought childish or stupid. His formidability was the chief feature in the image which remained: she hardly knew which had been the more formidable, the devastating silence with which he listened to most people or the deadly little sentences which he addressed to the very few whom he thought worth answering. Formidability, coldness, immense activity, a bald head and a top-hat—these things made up the man whom she must fit into Elissa's story.

"Is it true," she asked at last, "what she says about my father?"

"My dear Hope," spluttered Kerran nervously, "how can any of us possibly tell? It happened a long time ago and we've all forgotten about it. If only this tiresome woman hadn't . . ."

"But why on earth have I never heard of it before?"

She looked at him accusingly, as though she blamed him. He realised that she was furious at having been kept out of it all, at having missed the excitement all these years. And his heart was hardened against her. If she cared no more than that, there was no great need to consider her feelings.

"In any other family," she stormed, "it simply couldn't have happened—my being kept in the dark like this, I mean. To think that I should hear of it for the first time, merely by chance, out of a library book. A thing which must have been common talk for years!"

"Oh no."

"What?"

"I don't think it's been common talk. Nobody ever knew of it outside the family. There was nobody but the family there, you see, and naturally we all held our tongues."

"But good heavens! Am I not the family? I'm his daughter. Why on earth wasn't I told?"

"Well, you were rather young, weren't you?"

"But, why wasn't I told later on?"

"I couldn't say, my dear Hope. You'll admit that it wasn't my business."

"No. But somebody ought to have. As important a thing as that."

"Important?"

Kerran went over to the fireplace and stood there, warming his hands while he considered the word.

"I don't see that it's so very important," he muttered defensively.

In the course of their conversation his voice had sunk lower and lower, as if in protest against hers, which was over-loud. He would have disliked her egotism far less if it had not been so boisterously displayed and if she had not kept striding up and down the room like a whirlwind. Had she taken things a little more quietly she would have won a larger measure of his sympathy.

"But of course it's important. It must be. It affects us all tremendously. I can't tell you what a shock I got! When I opened the book I hadn't the slightest idea! Even now it seems almost incredible. It simply can't have happened."

"For all that it matters, to anyone now, it didn't happen. If only your aunts would . . ."

"Have they read it?"

"They have indeed read it."

"And what do they think about it?"

"They want me to get the book suppressed."

"Oh, do they? They would! They're fond of suppressing things, aren't they? If there wasn't so much suppression in our family I should have heard of all this before. But what's the use of suppressing the truth? Is it true? That's what I want to know. Did it really happen?"

"It?" parried Kerran.

Hope paused again. Once more her imagination had refused to cope with a picture of her father in a top-hat rowing away across the lough with Elissa Koebel. But, at last, with an effort, she brought it out.

"That he . . . that he . . . committed adultery . . ."

Kerran made a little groaning noise. This was the worst of nieces. They belonged to a generation which said these things. Louise, should she insist upon coming down to tackle him, might give him a very uncomfortable time of it, but she would never talk about adultery in the voice which she used when she talked of cheese. Whatever she might hint, whatever she might imply, his gentlemanly sensibilities would have been left unscathed. He did not believe that she had ever uttered such a word except in church.

"But what else am I to call it?" insisted Hope. "Whatever else . . . do you think that he did?"

Kerran replied in a whisper that he could not say.

"But they went off?"

"Oh, yes. They went off."

"Where?"

"I don't know."

"And then he came back? Just like that! But did everybody know?"

"Oh, yes. I'm afraid everybody knew."

"Were you surprised? Had any of you foreseen it? And why did he come back? It all sounds so incredible. I can't begin to imagine it or to see how it could have happened."

"Nor can I, at this distance away."

"But it's not so awfully long ago. I can remember that summer perfectly well myself. I can remember the castle and the island."

All the things she could remember came crowding back upon her, in a hundred vivid little pictures. She could have described every room in the castle and drawn a map of the island. She could smell the turf fires which burnt continually in the nurseries. She could see the courtyard and the well, and Muffy, her cousins' old nurse, standing beside it, peeling an apple. The long red curl of peel hung down against her white apron, and little Harry Lindsay in a green smock, stood before her, holding up both his hands.

But that was the only picture in which a grown-up person figured distinctly. The others, her parents and the tribe of aunts and uncles, were all blurred, unfocussed presences, a little larger than life, hovering on the outskirts of the scene. Disconnected and fragmentary details came back to her.

Aunt Maude used to wear a motor cap tied with a veil. Uncle Barny had laughed very much when Charles Lindsay upset his money-box on the steps of the dining-hall and a cascade of pennies came jingling down into the courtyard. There had been such yells and peals of laughter that everybody ran out to see, and there was Uncle Barny, choking and holding his sides, while poor Charles lamented: "My money! Oh, my money!"

Aunt Louise had clouds of dark hair tossed up into great waves all over her head, and subsiding into a coil, low on the back of her neck. She used to run about with bare feet. She ran down the slope of grass in front of the castle, her white ankles twinkling under a long skirt of tussore silk, drawn in tightly at the waist to a belt with an enamel buckle. But it was Aunt Maude who had a buckle with angels' heads on it in repoussé silver. Bad taste! A grown-up voice had pronounced that coldly on some forgotten occasion, because Rosamund said it afterwards, when Muffy was brushing their hair, and Muffy had instantly told her not to be affected, and for some days the other children teased Rosamund by talking about bad taste in a squeaky falsetto.

And then there were photographs. Not so very long ago she had come across one that must have been taken at a picnic during that summer. She had made very merry over it. She could believe that her mother and aunts had put on those ridiculous hats and high-collared dresses in order to pay calls or go to church, but that they should ever have sat about in the heather, so bedizened, was incredible. Their ideas and their sentiments must have been as alien to posterity as were their hats. And the children were a depressing sight, especially one of herself and Rosamund, in bunchy holland with straw hats standing up like haloes all round their heads, posed on either side of a bucolic nursery-maid in a black boater.

But of what avail were all these memories? They provided no setting for this extraordinary drama. Of Elissa, whom they had all so extravagantly admired, no clear impression remained. She became a legend almost at once and her memory, for Hope, was crystallised into a legendary figure, a sort of mixture between a Christmas-card angel and a pantomime fairy queen, a creature with flowing draperies and bright, streaming locks, who did not eat or sleep or post letters or read the newspapers, whose existence was scarcely on the human plane at all. And there had been nothing in her own style of writing to disturb this aura of otherworldliness. She wrote of herself very much as the children had seen her.

Only her story would not fit in with those flashes of reality which had survived. It could not be set alongside of Aunt Maude in her motor veil, the photographs or the curl of red peel hanging down against Muffy's apron. It could never have belonged to that past which contained Hope's memories. In proportion and texture it was too outrageously incongruous.

"I was only a child," she said, uncertainly. "I remember it all as a child would. And I knew nothing of what was going on. But you were there too, Uncle Kerran. You must have seen the whole thing! You must remember it as a whole."

"I don't suppose any of us do that. Not even Elissa."

"Oh, she does. I suppose because she has a clearer scale of values than most people. Only the important facts made any impression on her at the time."

"Oh! Doesn't she miss out a good deal?"

"No, I don't think so. Nothing important. She's got a few tiny details wrong. She talks as if Aunt Louise owned the Island and as if we were all her children. And she calls my father her brother, not brother-in-law. But she remembers all the important things as if they happened yesterday."

"I've no doubt she puts in everything that concerned herself. That's what we'd all do. But as for seeing it as a whole . . ."

"Are there no letters or anything? Have you, has anybody, any letters that were written at the time?"

Kerran hesitated.

There were letters. At his mother's death he had found, when going through her papers, a packet labelled *Letters from the Island*. She had been taking a cure at Harrogate during those eventful summer months, and they had all written to her pretty frequently. The episode of Elissa Koebel had been described and discussed from several points of view.

He had re-read these letters occasionally since they came into his possession. And each time that he glanced at them he realised how little reliance can be put on human memory. For they told a story which differed considerably from that which he would have told himself, and from the versions supported by Gordon, Maude, or Louise. Nobody else in the family knew that these documents existed, and he was determined that no one should. His mother had been the recipient of many confidences. To her they had all said the things which were now best forgotten. Maude would not easily forgive Louise for complaining of her vulgarity, even though the complaint had been made twenty-five years ago. Louise would learn with indignation that Maude had suspected Gordon of unfaithfulness and Gordon himself would not relish some of the jokes which had been made at his expense. Even Kerran had suffered some pangs when he discovered how much they all seemed to know about a private trouble of his own which he had been at the greatest pains to keep secret. There had been a moment when he almost blamed his mother for preserving so much inflammatory material. In so discreet a person such carelessness was unexpected, and he could only explain it by supposing that she must have left the letters unburnt through an oversight.

What she had really thought of the business he never knew. The tone of this and of all her correspondence showed that she sympathised unscrupulously with everybody and agreed with all of them. She had not been, he was forced to admit, a very sincere woman, but she had got what she wanted. To the end of her life she retained, not only the love, but the full confidence of both her sons, both her daughters, her sons-in-law, her daughter-in-law, and all her grandchildren.

Now he had been just as indiscreet himself. He had not burnt the letters, though he ought to have done so long ago. They were too fascinating. He would keep them a little longer, read them again, and be sure to destroy them before he died. And he would say nothing about them to Hope.

As luck would have it she did not notice his hesitation, nor was it necessary to give her any answer. Her attention had been distracted. Something had happened which diverted her indignant thoughts into a fresh channel. Even while she was speaking her voice had been drowned by a rumbling noise in the garden.

She turned her head. Ellen went past the window with a wheelbarrow. The rumbling died away and silence fell upon the room.

When Hope turned back to Kerran her face had grown paler. She had become, all at once, subdued and troubled. She said, in a low voice:

"And what about mother?"

Kerran thought:

"Ah! Now, at last, we are getting to it."

4

HE could not understand why she had not asked this question sooner. But then he had not read Elissa's story, so he could not gauge its compelling effect. That Ellen had been suppressed he knew, but he did not grasp how difficult it might be for a reader, in the first moment of stupefaction, to reinsert all the things which Elissa might have overlooked.

Hope had not forgotten the very existence of her mother. But her ideas, in that quarter, had remained static; they had undergone no sudden shock. Because she had been told nothing new about Ellen she did not immediately perceive that here was a person who must be remembered differently. It was hard enough to turn her father into the Byronic hero of Elissa's romance, without realising that her mother also, if this story was true, must emerge from it as a new and unexpected person.

She realised it now. And, seen from this new angle, the episode began at last to take some sort of shape. It was as if the idea of Ellen's betrayal had supplied a key-note which had been missing; there was an emotional quality in it which balanced the passion of Elissa's recollection. The incongruities became less startling. Hope's imagination had boggled at a picture of her father, in a top-hat, rowing off across the lake with a pantomime fairy queen, while Muffy peeled apples and Louise ran barefoot up and down the lawn. Now it focussed itself. From a background of shadowy memories these figures at last stood out, Elissa, Ellen and Dick, free from the trickeries of time. This was Ellen's story, too. It was something that had happened to Ellen.

"What she must have suffered . . ."

Hope's eyes were full of tears. She loved her mother. She had thought that they were so near to one another. And all these years there had been this, *this*, unspoken . . . buried.

"She adored him. She worshipped him. How did she bear it?"

Kerran said nothing. He had asked himself that question hundreds of times. He had thought of several answers, and had rejected them all in turn. Presently, Hope began to think of them, too, and he heard her running through them, just as he would have expected.

"I suppose it was for us. I suppose she wanted to keep her home together for us.

"But she forgave him. She loved him always.

"I suppose she loved him so much, that she had to forgive him. But it must have half killed her."

"I don't know, Hope."

"But it must. Even if she forgave she'd never be able to understand it."

"Why not?" asked Kerran, a little defensively.

Hope explained. Ellen's generation did not understand things like that. She herself could. Elissa had made her see how it all was. But Ellen could never have seen.

"You know what she's like! You know how much she dislikes anything to do with sex. She calls it 'unnecessary.' Why, good heavens, I've even heard her say that *Tess o' the D'Urbervilles* was a book she could never quite like because she thought the seduction of Tess was unnecessary! I simply couldn't make her see that it was the foundation-stone of the story. As for modern novels, they're unnecessary from the first word to the last."

"I know."

"She could never have forgiven him with her mind, though she might have with her heart. Did she ever talk to you about it at all?"

"Never. I don't believe she talked to anyone."

"She wouldn't. She's the soul of loyalty. But how did she behave?"

Kerran considered.

"Quite naturally. Took his going as a matter of course."

"Mother did? *Mother!*"

"You couldn't have been more surprised than we were. Whatever pain she felt she kept it entirely to herself. She never let anyone see it."

"All those weeks!"

"Oh, no! Not weeks. He was only away three days . . ."

"I think you've remembered wrong. By Elissa's account they must have lived together at her cottage for much longer than that."

"I'm positive it was only three days," said Kerran crossly.

Hope smiled.

"On this point I think Elissa's memory is more to be trusted than yours. After all, they were important days for her."

Kerran poked the fire and held his tongue. He realised that he had been upon the point of quoting those letters. He must be more careful.

"Mother knew they'd gone. You're sure she knew?"

"Oh, yes. There's no sort of doubt about that. And

just at first she lost her head. She came and roused me, the morning after they'd gone, in a terrible state of mind. But she very quickly pulled herself together. None of us knew what she really thought or felt. None of us."

Hope drew a long breath and gave judgment. She was nothing if not quick to make up her mind about things.

"Then it must be that she's a sort of case of dual personality. I suppose if he'd committed a murder it would have been just the same. Her love for him was so intense that she saw life, where he was concerned, in special terms. There are women like that. He must have been quite outside that part of her mind which is hampered by not being able to understand things—outside all her prejudices, and the traditions of her education, and all the standards she's grown up by. Her feeling for him must have enlarged her into quite a different person."

"Ah!" said Kerran, sitting up.

"She's too simple, she's too un-selfconscious to realise that she's been two people all her life . . . his wife and the woman we know. She just passed from being one to being the other without noticing it. Because, you know, I'm convinced that she would be very shocked if she were to hear this story about anyone else. She'd say it was all very sad (unnecessary, if it was in a book), and that people ought not to be so uncontrolled, and the wife was probably doing right to forgive him, for the sake of the children, but that of course no woman could ever feel the same. I'm sure that'd be her line. I haven't known her thirty-six years for nothing."

"Are you thirty-six?" asked Kerran in some surprise. "I thought you were younger."

Hope looked pleased, more pleased than she would have looked if she could have realised why it was that he thought her younger.

"But don't you agree with me? Don't you agree that it must almost be a case of a dual personality?"

"My dear Hope, that's the only explanation I've ever been able to accept, myself. But you're the first person who has agreed with me. I say she didn't forgive him because she was never conscious of having anything to forgive."

"But if that's true, if that's true, then Elissa is just nothing beside her."

"I should hope so!" said Kerran with a revival of irritation. "Elissa never did amount to a hill of beans. We all said a good deal about her at the time, but it was your mother who kept us guessing. In some of the letters . . ."

Now the cat was out of the bag. Hope pounced.

"Then there are letters! I thought so. I thought you seemed to be very sure of your facts."

"Oh, well, yes . . . there are one or two . . ."

"Whom to? Whom from?"

"I have some letters that were written to your grandmother at that time. We all wrote, pretty often, when we were on the island. And my mother, rather indiscreetly, kept our letters."

"Did mother write?"

"Yes. There are several of hers."

"Then . . ."

"She makes no reference to the Koebel business at all. If her letters were all that had survived you'd know nothing about it. She ignores Elissa just as Elissa ignores her."

"May I see the letters?"

"We-ell . . ."

He reflected. Five minutes ago he would certainly have refused. But his attitude towards Hope was becoming more friendly. She might turn out, after all, to be an ally, and if this was the case he had better put her into possession of all the facts which he could muster. He wanted support in the present crisis. If Hope could see his point of view she too would be indignant at all this glib reference to Ellen's feelings. Elissa might write what she chose. Gossip might take its course. The woman who had survived the original catastrophe could scarcely be touched by these petty reverberations. She must not be discussed and protected as though she were some querulous victim, concealing her tattered dignity beneath a cloak of denials, falsehoods, and suppressions.

"I'll show you the letters," he promised at last, "if you'll promise to back me up."

"Back you up?"

"In saying that it's much best, now, to leave the whole thing alone. That there's nothing to be done."

"But of course there's nothing to be done," agreed Hope impatiently. "The thing happened and there's an end of it. What I want to know is, what did happen?"

"And you'll hold your tongue? If I show you the letters you won't mention them to anyone else?"

"Not even Alan?"

"Alan's all right. But not to any member of the family?"

"I promise I won't. But why . . ."

"You'll see when you read them. Come back with me this afternoon and have tea, and then you can have a look at them. I'd rather not start posting them about the country."

"But are they very . . ."

E

The boom of the gong interrupted them. And Ellen came in a moment later to ask reproachfully if they were ready for luncheon.

She was pleased with her morning's work, for she had managed to clear the ground as far as the path. She led the way into the dining-room and began expertly to carve the joint while Maggie handed the vegetables.

"I want to come up to London one day quite soon," she said when she had helped them all. "I must buy a new hat. And I want to go and look at some statues."

She thought that would surprise them, and it did. They both sat up with a jerk.

"What kind of statues?" asked Kerran.

"I don't really know. I think any kind of good ones would do. We had such an interesting lecture on sculpture last week at the Women's Institute: such a clever man, he was staying with the Maxwells. It made me feel quite interested in statues, which I never was before, much. He told us so many things that I never knew. He said that sculpture was quite different from modelling."

She paused, a little doubtfully, as though she feared that they might snub her for not knowing all this before.

"He said in sculpture you take everything off and in modelling you put everything on. I mean the way you do it, not clothes: and he said that clay is quite different from marble. He said that modern sculptors try to consider the material they're working in, so one must make excuses for them."

"But didn't ancient sculptors . . ." began Kerran.

"Oh, yes, they did. But then later on they didn't. And that is why Victorian work was so bad. And he showed us a great many slides. They were very funny and made us all laugh."

"Funny?"

"Because they were so bad, I mean. But he showed us some very beautiful slides too. So that really I've begun to get quite interested in statues. I used to get so tired of them when I went to Rome with Dick. I couldn't think why anyone should ever want to make them, and I never knew which were bad and which were good. But now I want to begin all over again. You must tell me some good ones to start with, Kerran."

Kerran suggested the Elgin Marbles, but she looked doubtful.

"I've seen those. I'd rather start with something rather smaller, and something that wasn't broken at all. It bothers me when they have no heads. Hope, is that beef tough? You're not eating anything."

Hope shook her head. The beef was excellent, but she had suddenly felt she was too tired to eat anything. The emotions of the morning had exhausted her. She sat crumbling her bread and listening in a dazed way to this talk of statues and the Women's Institute.

But, gradually, as the meal went on, her shocked nerves began to steady themselves. By the time the steamed pudding came in she had collected her ideas. The nightmare echoes faded. She was able to look at her mother, to hear what she was saying, to know that this was the same woman who had come downstairs that morning with a piece of brown paper in her hand.

"A dual personality!" she thought. "It's not possible. She's herself. She's this. She's never been anyone else."

This woman she knew. This woman she loved. Whatever those letters might reveal, whatever glimpses they might give of an alien, an undiscovered Ellen, she would only be able to repeat to herself, with an absolute certainty:

"That is not so. She isn't like that. I *know* what she is like."

LETTERS FROM THE ISLAND

"Tell me where all past times are . . ."

LETTERS FROM THE ISLAND

I

JANET MURPHY's protest had been like the first shot fired in a battle. She made it and she was silent; but after that there could be no question of peace. In appealing to old Mrs. Annesley before she had been on the island for twenty-four hours she had opened fire.

Her shot was ineffective, perhaps because she failed to say what was in her mind. She composed and wrote down laborious sentences about the stairs, the cold, the damp and the unaired beds, when she was really consumed by another, quite inexpressible anxiety. To Mrs. Annesley it must seem that this was merely old Muffy grumbling again. She wanted to say that she was worried about Miss Ellen, but all that she could do was to give voice to that tumult of protest which had engulfed her when she was first introduced to the castle keep.

"A keep!" she sniffed. "What and ever did they want to keep in it, I wonder?"

For weeks she had suspected that there would be something funny about this old keep of theirs. Louise had been so much too enthusiastic about it.

"I'm going to give up the whole of the old keep to you, Muffy, for your nurseries. Then you'll have it all to yourselves, two big rooms, and two little tower rooms, and your own staircase. You'll like that, won't you?"

She knew that tone. She had not taken Louise from the month without getting to know it. If Louise was extra sweet to you, then she had something to hide. This keep was not all that it sounded.

"It depends," was all that she would say.

And to herself:

"No use making a fuss till I've seen."

Now she saw. And really she was quite disgusted. Never in all her born days had she been asked to live in such a hole. And she had seen some funny nurseries in her time, travelling about the world with Mrs. Annesley. Rats in Malta, she'd had, running about the floor as bold as brass. But that was to be expected in a foreign country, and Mrs. Annesley was a very different person to work for. She always gave you your place. She didn't put you into a stone box, that looked like a prison hospital, and then tell you that you liked it. She didn't insist that a house was dry when it was wringing wet. She didn't go on about the beautiful scenery at the end of a journey that was aggravating enough to make anybody say their prayers backwards. Only Miss Louise would have thought of dragging everybody all the way from Oxford to Ireland when they might just as well have gone to Torquay, like they did last year. Thirty-six hours of it they'd had, and all of them seasick, and then at the end, if you please, a house you had to get to in an open boat, if you called it a house when it was more like Oxford gaol. And nothing ready for them, no fires lighted, the beds all unaired, and not a drop of milk in the house. You'd have thought in the country there'd have been a farm or something. But no; it seemed that everything had to come over from the mainland. . . .

Now the uproar was beginning to subside. She had got great fires burning in both the rooms, she had aired the mattresses, and somehow she and the nursery-maid between them had brought the place into some sort of order. The children were all in bed and she must leave the rest of the unpacking till the morning. For that night she was through.

She took one last look round the great upper room, with its rows of cots and cribs ranged round the gloomy walls. Only three of them were filled, for Rosamund had been given one of the little tower rooms. But when Miss Ellen's children came, she would have seven of them in there, all with pneumonia and rheumatic fever most likely, caught from sleeping in damp sheets.

Her own mattress was now roasting in front of the fire and she turned it before she went downstairs. A little rustle in the nearest cot told her that Jennie was still awake.

"Muffy . . . can I have a biscuit?"

"No, you can't have a biscuit. Not now."

"I'm hungry."

"Then you should have asked before your teeth were cleaned."

Jennie sighed. She had not really expected to get a biscuit, but she wanted to prolong the conversation.

"Can I have a drink?"

"You've just had one."

"Then . . . will you tell me the Three Bears?"

"The idea! You lie down double-quick."

"I've got a pain."

"Then you'd better get rid of it, or there'll be no bathing for somebody."

A faint memory of Torquay sands emerged from the immense vistas of Jennie's past.

"Shall we dig?" she asked hopefully.

"Wait and see."

Muffy took up the candle. Her enormous shadow travelled up the wall and across the ceiling as she stumped away down the long room. Jennie, peeping through the bars of her cot, saw the candle go bobbing away through a low, arched doorway and out of sight. Now there were no moving shadows, only a pink glow in the walls thrown up by the turf fire. It was different from the firelight in the nursery at home. There were no dancing flames and no tall wire guard to throw a criss-cross pattern on the ceiling. For a moment she thought of howling for Muffy to come back, but she went to sleep instead.

Between the upper and lower floors of the keep there was a winding stone staircase, with worn treads and no banisters, dangerous even in daylight. Anyone coming up or down at night would always be obliged to carry a candle. Muffy thought out a dozen unpleasant possibilities as she felt her way along the rough walls. Rosie, bringing up a kettle of boiling water, would trip and scald herself. The children would certainly break their necks. And what about Miss Ellen?

The day nursery was filled with half-open trunks and Rosie was wrestling with a spirit lamp which would not light.

"Now then, not so much dratting," said Muffy sharply. "You can't expect everything in these old-fashioned houses. Have you found the teapot? I put it in the end of the 'old-hall'."

"I thought you wanted to get the big box unpacked first."

"I shan't unpack nothing more to-night, not till I'm told where my cupboards are. We'll make ourselves a nice cup of tea and then we'll go to bed. We've done quite enough work for one day, and that's a fact."

Rosie could hardly believe her ears. It was the first time that she had ever heard Mrs. Murphy admit that anyone had done enough work for one day. But her spirits rose. A nice cup of tea was the one thing which would stop her from using language. She foraged in the hold-all for the tea-pot and some enamel cups, while Muffy got the kettle to boil.

In ten minutes they were both at the table, sipping slowly, their tired bodies relaxed into a pleasant coma. There was something eternal and primitive about their attitudes and the silence in which they sat. They gazed thoughtfully at the flame of the candle between them, but they were not thinking of anything at all. They were reposing.

The day, with its labours, was, after all, only one day in a lifetime of toil. Rosie, at sixteen, was at the beginning of it. Muffy, at sixty, was nearing the end. And their strength came from a secret power which their employers had lost. They knew how to repose. In the littered room, with all its paraphernalia of change and travel, they preserved a note of stability. They sat. It was as if they had been sitting for ever. And when Louise Lindsay came in they managed to make her feel that she had interrupted some ancient and mysterious rite.

"I only came to see if you were settled," she said hurriedly. "Don't . . . don't get up."

But of course they got up. They could repose before each other, but not before Louise. Rose cleared away the cups and saucers and vanished with her candle up the tower stairs.

"You are leaving the unpacking till to-morrow, I see," said Louise, with a conciliating smile. "I'm so glad. You must be tired."

"There don't seem to be any cupboards," observed Muffy.

"Oh, aren't there? There must be. We must explore to-morrow. Did the . . . did the children get off all right?"

"Oh, yes, I think so. If only the beds aren't damp. I put all the mattresses . . ."

"I know. It can't be helped. There is nothing else you want, is there, Muffy?"

Their eyes met for a moment and then they both looked away. Muffy's face became perfectly wooden. She smoothed the corner of her apron. She wanted a dozen things. She had a hundred complaints to make. But what was the use? There they all were. She had been against coming. She had wanted to go to Torquay again, where there were nice sands for the children and a proper nursery with oilcloth on the floor. But she had said her say in the beginning, and she was not going to say it all over again. There was no use crying over spilt milk. She was not going to grumble.

But neither, on the other hand, was she going to be bullied into saying one word of approval. Nothing would ever make her like living in a keep, and nothing would ever make her say that she liked it. And that was to be the next battle. For Louise was never merely content with getting her own way. She insisted that everyone must say that she had been right. She could bear no opposition. She must extort open praise and approval for everything that she did. Now she was in one of her moods. Muffy knew them. When her eldest nursling was like this, quivering, exalted, ready to fall into a passion of despair at the faintest breath of criticism, there was nothing to be done.

Something about this castle had set her off. She had been quite mad about it ever since she saw the advertisement in the newspaper. She had taken it without consulting anyone, and then she had bullied her brothers and her sister into sharing the rent. It had been the castle and the island, and the island and the castle, for weeks and weeks. Nobody else wanted to come. But they must all give in, just as they had given in to her when they were children.

"On her high horse," thought Muffy. "Working herself into a fever because I won't say she's right. I knew how it would be. Waking up my lambs in that dratted boat to make them look at a couple of old swans flying across. And then she was surprised because they made a fuss. As if any child wants to look at scenery at that time of night! But I shan't say anything."

She smoothed her apron.

"Because, if there's nothing more you want, I think I will say good night. I am tired, too."

"Good night 'M."

Louise blenched, in spite of herself. It was only in their most violent moments of antagonism that Muffy called her 'M. This was a declaration of war.

"But I don't care," she thought. "I won't care. I won't let her spoil it. We are here. I have got them all here, and it is going to be perfect. It's only because I am tired that I feel so depressed. That way they were sitting when I came in . . . how mulish servants are . . . just the way they sit in the nursery at home. It's as if I'd brought the Woodstock Road with me *en bloc*. Am I never going to get away from it?"

Her lip quivered. Thirty years ago she would have burst into a fit of screaming. She turned away abruptly and groped among the boxes and bundles towards the door of the keep.

"Take care!" cried Muffy. "There's a step down there."

Louise tripped over her long skirt and just saved herself from falling.

"For heaven's sake give me a candle," she snapped.

Muffy found one for her, and stood listening to her footsteps as they went down the little flight of stairs and out into the courtyard.

"Supposing if it had been Miss Ellen," she thought.

As she felt her own way up to the night nursery again, she thought of Miss Ellen falling about in the dark, being hurt, losing her baby, perhaps. That was something to be resisted. She had resolved to say nothing, but she must speak about that. It was a sin and a shame to bring Miss Ellen to such a place. She would say a word to-morrow. And she would write to Mrs. Annesley. Mrs. Annesley ought to know what a dreadful place it was.

The children were all fast asleep and the firelight on the walls had faded to a pale glimmer. Shivering with cold and fatigue she pulled her mattress back on to its bed and undressed herself. The bed was hard and lumpy. A sharp twinge of rheumatism began to nag at her left shoulder. Her head was full of trains and boats and shifting landscapes and Miss Ellen falling downstairs. She was overwhelmed with foreboding.

She tossed and turned, unable to take refuge in the stoicism wrung from a lifetime of servitude. At the thought of harm to Ellen, her heart's darling, she became vulnerable. She would speak. She would say:

"Mrs. Lindsay, you should study your sister more than you do. You are very selfish. You think only of yourself.

"Louise, you have never been fair to Ellen. Never!

"You are jealous. You're jealous of your own sister.

"You're jealous of my lamb.

"You're jealous because she's got a better man than you have . . ."

No. She would never say those things. She must not even think them. But she could write to Mrs. Annesley, and perhaps they might stop Ellen from coming. There was still a week before she would come. It might be stopped. Mrs. Annesley might understand. At least she always listened. She gave you your place. . . .

2

Louise had expected to be happy at Inishbar. And when she woke up next morning to find that she was not she scarcely knew at whom to hurl the blame. At breakfast, she announced sombrely that they might all just as well have stayed in North Oxford.

Which meant that, in the first place, she blamed Gordon for having married her. It was his fault that she, who loved beauty, was to be condemned to live for ever in an ugly house in the Woodstock Road; that she, cultured and cosmopolitan, should be imprisoned in the trivialities of provincial and academic society. It was his fault that the other dons' wives were so extraordinarily dull, and that the undergraduates who came to call on Sunday afternoon never seemed to know when to go away.

She flung her ruined life at Gordon across the breakfast table, and he promptly absented himself from the conversation. He grew dim and impersonal. He was not there at all. His spirit had retired to some cloudy fortress of its own and only the shell of him was left sitting with Kerran and Louise.

"It will be all right," said Kerran consolingly, "when we have been out to pick mushrooms."

Instantly her face changed. She turned to him with a charming sparkle of excitement and interest.

"Oh, Kerran! That is quite true. I do believe that you understand why I wanted to come here. But why mushrooms? What is it about mushrooms?"

"Of course I understand why you wanted to come

here. It's because you have taken to reading Russian novels."

Kerran stopped to peel himself an apple, and Louise, with earnest pleasure, implored him to go on.

"Why mushrooms?"

"People in Russian novels are always going out to pick mushrooms. And you would like to be a person in a Russian novel. You want to live in a large house in the country with a lot of sensitive, intelligent and talkative relations, who are content to do nothing in particular for weeks on end."

"That is quite true. That is perfectly true. Oh, Kerran! How well you understand me! It's what I have always wanted . . . to do nothing in particular, if I could only find the right place to do it in. I want to get away from all the petty apparatus of living. It's choking me."

"But you have been too faithful to your model, my dear. I know that people in Russian novels generally have a great many relations, but I think you were wrong to bring your family here *en masse*. Maude, for instance . . ."

"We can't have Barny without her."

"Oh, Barny's a Slav all right. He'll fit in perfectly because there must be somebody who strums on the piano all the time, if we are to do the thing in style. And he is always ready to go on with yesterday's conversation."

"Yesterday's conversation! Kerran, you're perfect. How do you know it all so well? Don't you feel that this is a place where one could go on with yesterday's conversation?"

"I know my Turgenev, you see. But what about Maude? Isn't she just a trifle Anglo-Saxon?"

F

"She is going to do the housekeeping," said Louise quickly. "We must have one person like that and she will enjoy it. She loves triumphing over difficulties. And to balance her we'll have Dick. He is tremendously important, because we must have at least one person with overwhelming charm."

She paused expectantly, as if waiting for him to agree. But Kerran said nothing. He had never been overwhelmed himself by Dick's charm, though he had heard so much about it from other people that he supposed it must be there, and he had missed it. Not that he disliked Ellen's husband. They were on very friendly terms. But he was not charmed by a nature which had so much arrogance, and so little simple geniality.

"He must play lead," suggested Louise.

"Play lead? How? All by himself?"

"Why not?"

Louise poured out some more coffee. As she sipped it she looked across at Gordon, who was still in his Olympian cloud.

Twelve years ago, when she was still a girl in her twenties, she had been taken to Oxford for Commemoration Week. She had seen that cultured profile for the first time against a glamorous background of gleaming spires, stately libraries and moonlit college gardens. It had thrown her into one of her moods. In order to be happy (and she always expected to be happy if only she could rearrange a few small details of her life), she must marry a don and live for ever in Oxford. And her chaperone had looked on, smiling fatuous approval, instead of taking her for a warning tour through those regions which lie north of the Parks. She had never envisaged Woodstock Road till afterwards.

Gordon was well off, as dons go. He had private means. The marriage was thought to be a good one and all her friends had told her she was lucky, praising her for choosing a man so much older than herself, who would comprehend and cherish her sensitive nature. For once they had all agreed that she was right.

And then, a few months later, just when the Wood-stock Road and a first baby had begun their dreadful work, there had come the rejoicings over Ellen's marriage. Feeling sick and languid, she had gone home to join in the festivities, to be gracious to this young doctor over whom they all seemed determined to make such a fuss. The cut of her maternity gowns depressed her, but she tried to be glad, for Ellen's sake, and to remember that it was Ellen's turn to take a share of the limelight. She had, in her day, made a beautiful bride. Ellen made a pretty one. But at this wedding the centre of interest had not been Ellen, but the bridegroom. He had an air. There was something about him; they all felt it, though they did not very well know what it was. He was poor. He had his way to make in the world. Gordon's position was infinitely more distinguished. But he cut a better figure than Gordon, both in church and out of it. He seemed able to get whatever he wanted out of life. He was under thirty and on the staff of St. John's Hospital in Bermondsey.

It appeared that he had seen Ellen at a tennis party some years earlier and had made up his mind, then and there, to marry her. Having enquired about her, and learnt that she was not yet sixteen, he made no further attempts to see her until she should have reached marriageable age. Soon after her twentieth birthday he presented himself once more, made his proposals, and was promptly accepted by Ellen. Mrs. Annesley had thought the acquaintance too slender, but Ellen was determined, and there was nothing really to be said against the match.

Louise sat in a front pew, where the smell of lilies made her feel a little faint, and looked at the bride-groom's square shoulders (Gordon did stoop a little), and tried to remember what Ellen had been like at fifteen. Rather brown and sturdy, she thought, and extraordinarily childish. It was amazing. She could not make it out, or believe that Ellen, at any age, could have been capable of arousing so romantic an attachment. Romance did come to the oddest people. It was not quite fair. For Ellen had never wanted to be romantic. This was a feather in her cap which she had neither desired nor deserved. It would have been much less surprising if Gordon had fallen in love with Louise when she was only fifteen. She had been a lovely child, brimful of sen-sibility. She had embroidered a whole tapestry of the Romaunt of the Rose at an age when Ellen could do nothing except climb trees. And yet the owner of these magnificent shoulders had been consumed for four years by a single-hearted passion for the scratched, tanned, tree-climbing Ellen.

It was not Gordon's fault that he had fallen short of this standard. He had never had the opportunity, and as soon as he did see Louise he felt all that he ought. No-body was to blame. And yet she thought it was not fair. The unfairness of it still rankled at the back of her mind, all these years afterwards, as she sipped her coffee and looked at Gordon's cultured profile. Could Dick play the lead all by himself? Indeed he could. He had done it at the wedding, and he had been doing it ever since.

"When we have picked a great many mushrooms,"

persisted Kerran, "and played the piano, and gone on with yesterday's conversation for several weeks, is there to be any sort of . . . sort of climax? I mean, to put it baldly, is anything in particular to happen?"

"Oh no," said Louise directly. "That would be rather vulgar. If anything does happen it must be very, very subtle and Henry James-ish."

In which Dick, with his overwhelming charm, was to play lead all by himself. Kerran grinned. But he did not want to tease her, so he let it pass. It was probably quite true that she did not wish anything to happen in the coarser sense. She liked situations, and these mature best in an atmosphere of contemplative idleness. Having obtained her situation she would never let it grow beyond a certain point. She would keep it well pruned, like a dwarf tree in a Japanese garden, and endless discussion would be the only fruit that she would allow it to bear.

"I feel that we have never had time to discover ourselves, our real selves," she was saying. "Life gets more stupid and vulgar and false every day. We invent a hideous noisy object like a motor or a gramophone and we call that progress. We pay calls on people that we don't like, and catch trains to places we don't want to go to, and buy things we don't need. But here we have got away from all that. We have no neighbours. We shall lead no social life. There are no shops and no trains. We shall be thrown back entirely on ourselves. I am curious to see what we make of it. We are all fairly civilised . . ."

"Is Maude?"

"Don't go on about Maude. Of course I don't mean her, or Ellen either, if it comes to that. I mean you and me, and Dick, and Barny, and Guy Fletcher, if he comes."

"All men except you!"

"I know. But that's not my choosing. If you'll give me the names of a few really civilised women I'll invite them to-morrow. I don't know any. I want to arrive at . . . oh, how shall I put it? . . . at a sort of collective enjoyment and sympathy. A kind of New Republic . . . oh yes, and there's Gordon! Having somebody who really does know a great deal will give us . . . give us . . ."

"Ballast."

"I thought ballast was something which one kept for throwing overboard. But you see what I mean?"

He thought that he did. She wanted to play at a new game. And, as in their nursery days, everybody else had got to come and play it with her. When she wished to blow soap bubbles nobody else might suggest hide-and-seek. Now they were to play at being Turgenev characters, with Dick as hero and a possible situation as a prize. She was so eager and solemn that he felt sorry for her, knowing she would most certainly be disappointed.

This was not the first time that she had set herself, in all good faith, to make a silk purse out of a sow's ear. Poor material had never daunted her. As a child she was always writing plays which the rest of them had to act. Barny would sulk. Kerran would clown his parts, and Ellen, though willing, could never get anything by heart. But none of this discouraged Louise. She continued to believe that they might produce some remarkable and artistic effect if only everyone would do exactly what they were told. Her bribes were as pathetic as her threats. He could remember hiding rebelliously with Barny in some raspberry canes when she had called a rehearsal, and hearing her frantic entreaties as she searched the garden:

"Oh, Kerran! Oh, Barny! Why are you so unkind to

me? I'll give you my camera if only you'll promise not to make it funny in the scene when you're proposing to me!"

Poor Louise! What a pity that she must always be trying to turn people into something they were not! But he would do his best. He would be as Russian as he could. Their holiday would turn out to be no different from any other summer holiday, but he would not leave her unsupported.

"There's only one thing I don't see," he said. "Why was it necessary for us all to come so far?"

"Because it is so beautiful. We must have a beautiful background. And it's isolated. And another thing: we, the Annesleys, have Celtic blood in our veins, I think it is just that side of us that gets stifled in England. Really, we are exiles."

"Aha! I thought we should hear of the Celtic Twilight before we'd done. I suppose the Irish chieftains, who built this place, used to sit round and get on with yesterday's conversation."

At this point Gordon suddenly emerged from his cloud.

"Most unlikely," he told them. "The architecture is pure Norman. Late Norman. So late that I am puzzled. I cannot think who can have built such a castle, just here, and for what purpose. It belongs to a date when English, or rather Norman, influence was little felt outside the pale. I have two theories . . ."

Louise left the dining-hall.

Gordon was to give them ballast. His erudition was to be the most solid dish in that banquet of the soul which she had provided for herself and her family. But she felt that she would savour it better when Dick and Barny and Guy Fletcher had arrived to share it with her.

3

"So you see," she wrote to her mother, "Kerran really does understand. That touch about the mushrooms was exquisite, don't you think?

"And it is all going to be the greatest success. Even Muffy has no criticism to make, except that she has already begun to make a fuss about Ellen, who, if you please, is going to fall downstairs! Really, you know, mother, I sometimes feel that Muffy ought to have gone to Ellen instead of me. She would have, of course, if I had not married and had a baby first. Since she has, and always will have, this passion for Ellen, I wonder that she did not prefer to wait. She has never been fond of me or sympathetic to me. Even when we were children, Ellen was always put first. If it was I, and not Ellen, who had 'a special reason for being careful' (a real Muffyism that!) we should hear nothing about the stairs. Muffy has always been a perfect Spartan to me at those times.

"However! I will not let Muffy spoil my happiness. Nothing will ever make me regret having taken Inishbar, even if Ellen falls downstairs twice a day. The photographs which we saw, lovely as they are, cannot convey one half of its charms. The country all round is bewitching, and the air is so soft and clear. The mountains which roll down to the lough are quite high on the landward side; we can see crags and glens which are sublime enough for anyone except Gordon (who, as you know, will not look at anything smaller than Mont Blanc). To the west, the sea end of the lough, the slopes are gentler.

They melt gradually into a range of sandhills, which are usually the most vivid streak in the whole landscape. Killross, the village where we shall do our shopping, is hidden behind them. We cannot see it from the island.

"The last part of the journey was fascinating. Just before we landed two swans rose up from the reeds and flew away across the water towards the sea and the sunset. The children were enchanted. Rosamund has written a charming little poem about the swans, which I must send to you. At least, I think it charming.

"She appreciates it all, exactly as I knew she would. Children do, I think. It is worth while, taking them to beautiful places, especially when they have the ill fortune to live in a deadly one. They may not know it, but they will store up impressions this summer which will be a joy all their lives, and, one hopes, an antidote to the Woodstock Road. I am so glad I was firm about Torquay. I do not want them to have Torquay minds. It is just possible that Jennie and Harry are too young to 'look at scenery,' but for Rosamund and Charles I am sure it is the right thing. Of course Rosamund is an exceptional child. She is very like me in many ways. I do not expect Hope, for instance, will get so much out of it, though she is only a year younger.

"And, by the way, about Hope! I do want you to back me up in a campaign I am going to have about her *legs*. Really, Ellen ought to take them more seriously. They will be such a handicap to the poor child later on. I am going to drop some pretty broad hints. There must be exercises she could do. Ellen is *much* too vague about *appearances*.

"The island is small and most of it is covered with fine old trees, a great contrast to the bare hillsides you see all round. At the top of a gentle slope of grass you see 'four grey walls and four grey towers.' Three of these towers are round, and one, the keep, is square and rather taller than the others. There are not many rooms. The bedrooms are in the towers, each of which has its own winding staircase, opening on to a central courtyard, a quadrangle, in fact. The great dining-hall (a splendid room with a fireplace at each end) takes up the whole of the southern side. The kitchen and the servants' quarters are to the east, and the drawing-room, a long gallery with windows looking on to the lake, is on the west. On the fourth side of this rectangle, the north, there is not much room because of the great gateway in the middle. But there are two sorts of guard-rooms on either side of the gate, and into one of these the Nugents have put a bath! So you see we are quite modern! I think it should really be quite easy to run, for stone staircases do not need much cleaning, but to silence any possible complaints I am going to get Maude to go over to Killross (when she comes) and see if she cannot hire a couple of local peasant women to help the maids.

"I gather that the Nugents only finished furnishing the place when they decided to let it. They used to come here and picnic, sitting on packing cases, etc. And they have also a one-roomed cottage, over on the mainland, where Mrs. N. comes sometimes, but it, too, is let this year, so the boatmen told us. It is the only house visible from the island, a little white dot on the mountain side, about 2 miles away. I wonder . . ."

Kerran, strolling past the drawing-room window, stopped to look in at his sister.

"The post boat has been," he told her.

"No! Has it gone?"

"About five minutes ago."

"Why couldn't anyone have told me? It's most tiresome. Yesterday they didn't come till past four. How is one ever to know? I never heard of anything so inconvenient."

"The mail car doesn't go out from Killross till tomorrow, I believe. If you've got a letter you want posted, I'll row down and take it for you."

"Oh no, thanks. It doesn't matter." She threw down her pen. "It was only to mother. Did they bring anything?"

"Not much. There was a letter from mother, but it was for Muffy."

"Oh!" said Louise.

"And one or two for you. I put them on the table in the dining-room."

Louise went out across the court. With the tail of her eye she caught sight of Muffy in the doorway of the keep, and her demeanour became at once very stately. She walked more slowly. She swept across the courtyard, letting go the skirt which she had caught up in one hand as she ran down the steps. Her pale face, in its cloudy aureole of hair, became rigid, more aquiline, more set in its displeasure.

This was one of the few things, perhaps the only thing, which she did not like about the castle: the extraordinary publicity of life in the courtyard. Somebody was always standing at a doorway, watching where one went and what one did. In order to pass from one room to another it was always necessary to come out into the open. Each tower had its separate doorway and so had the drawing-room, the dining-room, the bath-house, the kitchens and

the keep. There was no way of escaping from the castle
save through the one great north gate.

She had commented on this enforced publicity to
Kerran, who pointed out that life in the towers, up their
winding staircases, would be, on the other hand, corre-
spondingly private. After a day spent in communal
goings and comings they would each retire into a remote
fortress. Their party would split up completely at night.
They would cease to be dwellers in the same house—
people who go to bed up the same staircase and whose
rooms stand side by side on a single landing.

"But we shan't split into units," objected Louise.
"We shall most of us split into couples. All of us.
Because if Guy Fletcher comes I shall have to put him
in your room."

"Quite so. And these couples will converse the more
freely because the walls are several feet thick."

Louise was not quite sure if she liked this. She foresaw
a number of conversations carried on simultaneously in
each of the tower rooms. This pairing off of married
couples was a nuisance. She had felt it before, even when
they were all assembled in a more centralised house.
Her labours in the daytime were apt to be undone at
night. She would take endless pains to bring Barny, or
Ellen, to her way of thinking, and then Barny would go
to bed with Maude, and Ellen would go to bed with
Dick, and they would talk it over and come down next
morning as obstinate as ever. Kerran was the only one
of them who was not leagued against her in some secret
marital alliance. Kerran was the only one upon whose
loyalty she could rely. Even her mother, so sympathetic
and so uncritical, was carrying on a secret correspondence
with Muffy.

"But I shall take no notice," she thought, as she swept into the hall. "I shan't ask what mother was writing about."

When, five minutes later, she reappeared, the stately displeasure had quite vanished. She no longer swept. Holding up her skirt and waving her letters, she ran right across the court and out at the north gate.

"Oh, Kerran! Gordon! Kerran! Where are you? Do come here."

Kerran emerged from a clump of arbutus bushes.

"Oh, Kerran! Do listen. The most extraordinary thing. Who do you think the Nugents' cottage is let to? Who? You know I wrote and asked if we could use it as a picnic house? And Mrs. Nugent says we can't because Elissa Koebel is there."

"No," said Kerran, definitely and finally.

He had seen the cottage. He had rowed past it several times on his way down the lake to Killross. It was very small. And he had seen Elissa Koebel. It was impossible to imagine that she would be shut up in so very small a house. She would burst through the roof like a jack-in-the-box.

"No. I don't believe it!"

"But she is. Mrs. Nugent says so. She's been ill and she's come here to rest. Read the letter. Read what she says."

He began to read the letter. His incredulity melted into dismay.

"My poor Louise! Just when you've been boasting that you had no neighbours."

Louise took him up with disconcerting eagerness.

"Why? Why? Do you think I ought to call on her?"

"Good heavens, no! But they'll come here, probably. They'll come and want to see over the castle."

"They?"

"She can't be here alone. Whoever heard of a *prima donna* staying anywhere alone? She's probably got her husband there, and several lovers, and some children, and her old mother, and an impresario, and an accompanist, and a maid and a masseuse. I expect that's her motor that we heard on the lake road yesterday evening. You remember? We wondered who on earth it could belong to. I expect it's hers."

"But, my dear Kerran, the cottage only has one room. Mrs. Nugent described it when she first wrote about the castle. One room with a half-loft for a bedroom."

"Good heavens! You don't say so. What an extraordinary thing! They can't all . . ."

"Read her letter. She says Madame Koebel is completely alone."

They had got to the landing stage and they stood there, looking down the lake at the little white speck on the mainland, the little house which had only one room and a half-loft.

"How very, very odd," repeated Kerran.

Louise, for her part, did not think it at all odd. It was exactly what she would have expected. Exactly what she would have liked to do herself, if she had been Elissa Koebel. But only a great artist would have done it.

"It may be so," said Kerran, turning the letter over. "It must be so. By all accounts she's a very unconventional person."

"She wants solitude. I can understand that so well. I want it myself, but I never get it. I'm not a bit surprised. I always thought she must be nice . . ."

"Oh, well . . ." said Kerran. "Nice! . . . Well . . ."

He had unhooked a rowing boat and held out his hand to steady her as she got in. But she needed no helping. She picked up her skirts, leapt in lightly, and took her seat in the stern. He pushed the boat off with one oar, and settled, facing her, on to his bench. The island slid away from them.

"Where are we going?" she asked idly.

"Just for a little row before it rains."

"Is it going to rain? Don't say so."

"Yes, it is. The mountains are much too clear. And the smoke from Elissa's chimney is going straight up in the air."

"Oh! So it is," said Louise, turning round to look. "Do you suppose she cooks her own meals? She must be a wonderful person. 'Nice' is the wrong word, I agree."

"Quite wrong," said Kerran. "Whom was your other letter from?"

"Guy Fletcher. Such a charming letter. He thinks he'll get here some time next week. I'm so glad. He's just the kind of person . . ."

Guy Fletcher was famous for his charming letters. Kerran felt that he must have made a face, for Louise looked up at him sharply. He was afraid that she might be going to bully him into stating his real opinion of Guy, a thing which she had often attempted, and to distract her attention he asked her to read the letter aloud.

As she did so he wondered how long it had taken Guy to write it. For anything so beautiful could not have been produced without considerable effort. There was no flaw in it anywhere. Each sentence had a perfect little rhythm of its own, was placed and set with a care that had been almost too loving and anxious. Kerran found himself growing strained and stiff as he listened. He longed for the relaxation of a clumsy word.

Guy Fletcher was a young don, a colleague of Gordon's and much admired by Louise. In his vacations he wrote essays which were remarkable for their terrific concentration upon beauty. On Kerran, who had to review them, they produced an impression of stasis, but he did not say so, and because he could never quite make up his mind if this was Guy's fault or his own, he praised them. It might be, perhaps, because his own soul was so gross that he should feel that no beauty in the world could be quite worth all this straining. And until he could be sure about it he thought it best to agree with Louise.

When the letter had flowed to its harmonious conclusion he began to row very vigorously indeed, impelled by a desire for some kind of effort that had nothing spiritual about it. Soon they were in the very middle of the lough. They could see the mountains behind the island and the deep blue trough of the haunted glen. They could see things which they had never seen before: the light bloomy haze which covered the hillsides for the last three days had melted and the slopes, with their patches of heather, tumbled boulders and green mossy bogs, stood out in vivid detail. All the mountains had come nearer. They were crowding in on the lake.

Out to sea it was raining. Black clouds piled up behind the yellow sandbanks to the west. In another hour these clouds would have drifted across the sun, and the first breath of wind would have whipped the glassy waters of the lough into ripples and waves. A grey curtain of rain would travel up, hiding the island from the shore and the shore from the island. Storm, wrack and mist would blot out the Haunted Glen. Already the sun had begun to shine a little more wanly, the waters grew paler, and the clear colours of the mountains took on a darker hue.

"I'd better go back," said Kerran. "We shall get wet."

"No, don't," she murmured. "I'm so happy."

She leant over the side of the boat to trail a hand in the water.

"This is perfect," she said, "this is what I came for."

Kerran obligingly rested on his oars and let the boat drift. He did not think it would rain for an hour, and she was sure not to be happy much longer than that.

A tranced, brooding look had come into her eyes. He knew that she must have some tremendous plan ahead. But, after a long pause, all that she said was:

"I do hope Guy will bring his violin."

"Sure to," sighed Kerran.

"And the piano in the drawing-room is quite good. I'm so glad, because if . . ."

Her eyes strayed again towards the shore, where Elissa's chimney sent up a thin column of smoke in the cooling air.

"My dear Louise!"

"Mrs. Nugent says she is resting. I shouldn't ask her to sing, of course. But just think how lovely it would be if . . ."

"Louise, you don't really . . . you aren't really contemplating . . . you don't surely mean to include Madame Koebel in our select little circle?"

"Why not? I shan't intrude myself on her, naturally. But you said yourself that she might want to see over the castle. And you said yourself that we wanted more civilised women."

"If she comes, I think you'd better be out."

"But why?" Louise began to look anxious. "Isn't she respectable?"

Kerran laughed.

"My dear Louise! You've seen her, haven't you?"

"Only on the stage. What nonsense you talk. How like a man, to think that because she's an artist she must be . . . have you heard anything? Anything definite?"

Kerran reluctantly mentioned a few things that he had heard. But she refused to take him seriously.

"People always say that sort of thing about any famous woman. Especially men. Mediocre men like to revenge themselves against a superior woman by declaring that she must be immoral. I suppose you're jealous at the idea of a woman doing anything. Look at Sappho. I'm always coming across that attitude. You say we gossip, but we don't gossip half as much as you do. You're always ready to believe such fantastic things. Especially about a woman. You mayn't know it, but it all comes from a desire to belittle us, to sneer at our achievements."

A fanatical glare had come into her eye and she bounced about so fiercely that the boat rocked.

"That's why we haven't got the vote," she concluded bitterly.

"I know, I know, I know," said Kerran. "You're quite right. One shouldn't repeat hearsay stories. But, as a matter of interest, Louise, tell me this. Supposing you knew for certain that she wasn't . . . er . . . respectable, what would you do?"

Louise immediately told him to begin rowing again. He could see that she had no answer ready, and that she wanted to avoid an argument while she thought it out. She had very strict notions in general about respectability. But she did not wish to admit that these need prevent her from enjoying the friendship of Elissa Koebel. As Kerran rowed back across the lough she sought in her mind for a reconciling formula.

"You can't judge everybody quite by the same standards," she said at last.

"I know. But there's no question of your judging the Koebel. You can refrain from judging a person without making a bosom friend of her."

Louise rallied her forces.

"No. But it's like this. I wouldn't ask an Englishman to dinner if he had two wives. But when the Rajah of Mysond came to Oxford (he has a son at St. Jude's) I asked him to lunch, though he has dozens of wives. In the same way, if some woman of my own . . . of my own class, got divorced, I should drop her. But a woman like Elissa Koebel I shouldn't judge by the same standards that I'd use for myself and my friends."

"But you wouldn't have asked the Rajah to lunch on the island, would you?"

Louise ignored this.

"I know she belongs to another world—the *demi-monde*, if you like. But that's quite different from belonging to our world and becoming *déclassée*. Besides, what harm could she possibly do us? I ask you! Can you see me, or Ellen, or Maude, suddenly deserting the principles of a lifetime because Elissa Koebel has been asked to tea? Can't you realise that women nowadays . . ."

"I'm not thinking of you women. I'm thinking of Gordon, and Barny, and myself, and Guy Fletcher . . . and Dick."

"Dick?"

He had thought that last name would settle her. For the time being she said no more. There was just that element of uncertainty about Dick which could occasionally bring her up short, however confident she might be, however determined that all the others should dance to her piping.

"Do hurry up," she said, shivering. "It's getting cold and we shall be wet through in no time if we're caught."

By now the sun had quite disappeared and a stiff breeze silvered the surface of the water. Kerran rowed briskly and brought them into shelter under the rocky western slope of the island, where thickets of fuchsia and arbutus pressed up against the mouldering castle walls. There was a half-wild garden there and a broad terrace path running under the drawing-room windows. It was on this path that Kerran had stood, earlier in the afternoon, and looked in at his sister writing letters.

Suddenly Louise put up her hand and smilingly bade him listen. Music was in the air. It was Rosamund playing on the drawing-room piano. During the previous term she had learnt two Chopin waltzes and everyone had had a great many opportunities of hearing them since they came to the castle. Kerran bent to his oars and spun round the point towards the landing stage.

"It's what I'd always planned," said Louise dreamily. "Floating about on the lake and hearing music in the castle."

Kerran asked if Hope could play.

"Hope? Hope Napier? Oh no! At least, she may have got as far as the 'Merry Peasant.' I don't know."

"Thank God!" thought Kerran.

He shipped his oars. They were only just in time, for the curtain of rain had already blotted out the sandbanks. Quite big waves were breaking on the beach and the landing stage. He held the boat steady for Louise to get out. But she did not move at once. She was brooding and planning again. Some new piece of generalship had engaged her attention. She climbed thoughtfully out of the boat and walked up to the castle beside him with an unseeing eye. Not Elissa this time, he thought, but something else which needed diplomacy. He could not help asking what it was.

"Do tell me what you're thinking about."

She looked at him vaguely, pushing away the clouds of dark hair from her temples.

"What am I . . . oh . . . only Hope's legs."

4

THE boat, with Maude and Barny in it, struggled out of a solid sheet of rain towards the island. To Kerran and the children, who were watching from a tower, it seemed as though a free fight of some sort was going on. A black object was being thrown, violently thrown, from one end of the boat to the other. The struggle was so fierce that a capsize seemed almost inevitable.

Kerran was the first to guess what was happening.

"Their umbrella!" he exclaimed. "They're fighting which shall have it. I mean which shan't have it. He's in the bows and she's in the stern. They're each determined to be the one who gets wet. It's his umbrella. It's a man's umbrella; she's forgotten hers, and she doesn't want to borrow his. There! Oh, Lord! I thought they were over then."

The children were enchanted. They had had a dull day, cooped up in the keep, and now they blessed the rain which had brought them such a spectacle. It was not every day that uncles and aunts fought one another in boats.

Only Rosamund had the decency to say at once:

"It's very unselfish of Aunt Maude, isn't it, Uncle Kerran?"

"Very," said Kerran; "especially if she upsets the boat."

Rosamund laughed, uncertainly. She was anxious to imitate, if she could, the correct grown-up attitude towards Aunt Maude. But it was not easy and, as often as not, she got snubbed for her pains. A faintly mocking praise appeared to be the safest prescription. They were always saying that Maude was wonderful. They praised her more warmly than they ever praised each other. She was so practical, and so economical: such a wonderful housekeeper, so devoted to Barny, so clever when he was ill, and, above all, so unselfish. The mere mention of her unselfishness could bring a quiver of laughter into their voices. Rosamund had only just found out why.

There was a shrill squeal of joy from Harry and Jennie. Something had actually fallen into the water, a rug, and it was floating away like a little raft. The battle of the umbrella was suspended while Maude clutched at it.

Now the boat had reached safety. It was bumping against the landing stage. Louise, in a sou'-wester and oilskins, was running down the slope, and the loyal Kerran nerved himself for a dash across the courtyard, so that he might join Gordon in the gateway. For Louise's sake they must all keep up an appearance of hilarious welcome.

As soon as he was gone Rosamund drew her brother Charles to another window where they would be out of earshot of the little ones.

"Promise not to tell," she whispered.

Charles wriggled impatiently. He wanted to watch the disembarkation, for there was still a chance that somebody or something might fall into the water.

"You're tickling my ear," he complained.

"Oh, very well then. I shan't tell you. You're too little to know, anyway."

Whereat Charles was obliged to twist her wrists. After a few histrionic shrieks, and cries of *pax*, she began to whisper again.

"Aunt Maude isn't quite a lady."

"Oh, rot!"

"Mother says so."

"When did she say so?"

"Yesterday. She said we don't call a coat and skirt a costume. She said it was bad form. So I said, well, Aunt Maude does. And then she said that. She said I was old enough to know. But you mustn't say anything to the little ones."

Charles looked uncomfortable. He felt that this was a personal affront because Aunt Maude was his godmother and had given him some very nice birthday presents. Honour demanded that he should defend her. But, if his mother had really said such an embarrassing thing, there was very little that he could say. So he carried the war into the other camp. He averred that Professor Grier, who was Rosamund's godfather, smelt.

"You're disgusting," said Rosamund, "disgusting and childish."

She turned away from him with a very good imitation of her mother's sweep.

Drenched and draggled, the new arrivals were being urged up the slope by the welcoming Louise. Aunt Maude's apple cheeks glowed crimson under her dripping veil, and snatches of her laughter floated up, high above the shrieking wind.

"Such fun!" she shouted, as she held the umbrella over Barny.

Even Louise was cowed, became less aggressively cheerful.

"You poor things! You're wet!"

"No, no. We like it. We don't mind getting wet, do we, Barny? So killingly funny . . . in the boat . . .

the umbrella . . . such fun, isn't it, Barny?"

Barny dodged the umbrella which she was still trying to hold over him, caught sight of the group in the window and sent them a rueful grin. He did not particularly mind getting wet, but he did not think it killingly funny either. The three of them disappeared under the gateway. The boatman with the luggage came up after them and disappeared too. It was over and there was nothing more to see. The children turned away from the window. They straggled downstairs to the day nursery. Only Rosamund remained, curled up on the window seat, and staring disconsolately out into the rain. She was bored with the little ones and bored with Charles. She wanted another little girl to play with. For the moment she even wanted her cousin Hope. She thought of Hope with a sudden access of sentimental affection. When Hope came she would have an ally. They would talk secrets. She would swear Hope to secrecy and then reveal the tremendous news about Aunt Maude. Hope might be stolid, plain and fat, a year younger, and imbued with all the depressing familiarity of cousinhood, but she was at least a girl, not a scuffling, insensitive boy.

"Like sisters," explained Rosamund, to some undefined but interested audience. "We're more like sisters than cousins. The two families have seen so much of one another . . ."

Rosamund is lonely without Hope. She sits all day long in the window-seat, wishing that Hope would come. How touching that is! The two little girls run hand in hand away into the woods. Now the grown-ups can see that they are neither boys nor babies. They tell secrets. And the audience comprehends their charm: the interesting appeal of cousins who are really more like sisters.

5

Louise was in despair. The change in the weather had ruined all her plans, for she had meant it to be fine when Maude and Barny came to the island.

"Now they'll be prejudiced against it," she complained to Kerran. "They won't stay. Or if they do it'll be with a grievance."

"Maude seems to admire it all very much."

"Oh, Maude!" Her lip curled. They were indeed in a poor way if they had to depend upon Maude's admiration.

"I wanted it to be fine for Barny. Poor Barny . . ."

She wanted, as he very well knew, to reanimate Barny, to win him back to his own place in their family circle. It was one of the minor miracles which she expected the island to perform. The finger of time was to be moved backwards, and Barny was to be his old bachelor self again, lively, frivolous and enterprising. Ten years of marriage had changed him a great deal. But Louise still hoped to stage-manage a rebellion.

"Poor Barny! One feels one's lost to him so, ever since . . . And this rain gives her such a pull. Did you hear her trying to bully him into saying that he liked it? As if anyone could, on a day like this! I really think that it's her insincerity that annoys me more than anything else. The way she always chooses a wet day, or a fiasco, to show how bright and cheerful she is. 'Isn't it fun?' Did you hear her? I could have slapped her face."

"She is rather a dry blanket," agreed Kerran.

"A what?"

"The opposite of a wet blanket. Instead of damping your enthusiasm she gingers it up when you're depressed. She imparts a desiccating and spurious warmth. But you missed all the best of it, leaving us in the hall like that when you went to see about the luggage. I got her first impressions. She thinks it's 'too too.' "

"She thinks it's what?"

"Er . . . too too. I think that was the expression she used."

Louise almost stamped.

"Where does Maude pick it up? I should like to know. Do you suppose they talked like that in Penge, or wherever it is she comes from? And what does it mean?"

"It is, I believe, a piece of antiquated slang. It expresses approval. I don't know if it was ever used in Penge. But I think she's rather proud of it. You see, she's very anxious to live up to us. She knows that we think she isn't out of the top drawer . . ."

"Kerran! You're as bad as . . ."

"But she tries to show us that she, too, knows how smart women talk."

"But they don't. I never . . ."

"You never read *The Lady's Companion*. She knows a great deal more about smart women than you do."

"It's a wonder she doesn't cultivate the Devonshire House drawl, like a provincial *belle* in the 'sixties."

"Oh!" Kerran settled down to the subject. "I'd never thought of that before. I'd often wondered why pretentious young women in Victorian novels always had to drawl. You suggest that it had percolated . . . that it took forty years for a fashion set by Caro Lamb to reach the solicitor's daughter at Exeter?"

"I can only suppose so. But it must have undergone

modifications. I don't suppose that Georgiana Reade, in *Jane Eyre*, talked like old Aunt Harriet. You remember? She called herself Hoyet!"

"Hoyet!"

"No. Not quite. More Howiett."

"Howiett!" practised Kerran. "Howiett! Howiett!"

"Howiett took out her tarrier in a yaller chawiett."

There was a faint scuffling and fumbling at the far end of the room. Maude, with exaggerated diffidence, was peeping round the door.

"Am I interrupting?" she asked.

Kerran and Louise, surprised in the midst of their Howietts, felt uncomfortable. It was impossible to explain that they were practising the Devonshire House drawl. Louise, who never on principle explained anything to Maude, took absolutely no notice. She turned away and began to throw fresh pieces of turf on the fire. It was left to the kind-hearted Kerran to say sheepishly:

"We were imitating our great-aunt Harriet."

Maude did not believe this for a moment. She repressed an inclination to sniff, as she always did when they dragged their great-aunt Harriet into the conversation. They never seemed able to forget their titled relations.

"No, I won't sit down," she said, retreating from the chair which Kerran was pushing towards her. "I only just ran down to ask"—she cast a doubtful glance at Kerran—"if there's any hope of a hot tub before dinner."

Louise straightened herself angrily and shook the peat ash from her skirts.

"Dressed up to the nines," thought Maude in dismay. "In the country, too! Whatever for? I wish I'd brought my foulard . . ."

And then she made an effort to be more charitable.

"Louise! What a perfectly sweet tea-gown! Liberty, isn't it? I always think their things are so artistic. And just your style."

"Are they?" asked Louise unpromisingly.

"Oh, yes. But I didn't know you were going to dress up so much in the evening. I'm afraid I've only brought . . ."

"Oh, that's all right," interrupted Louise. "Everyone is to wear what they like. I happen to like this, so I wear it. But you can come down in your nightgown if you like, Maude."

"Really!"

Maude shot another arch look at Kerran and giggled faintly.

"Or a dressy blouse," added Louise with vicious sarcasm.

A dressy blouse was just what Maude had been intending to wear. She looked happier. She pursued the subject of baths again, in a slightly hushed voice, as though she did not really like to mention such things in the drawing-room. Louise must be sure to say if it was inconvenient, but a hot tub would be just the thing to keep Barny from catching cold after his wet journey. He had been so naughty about the umbrella in the boat, just like a man . . .

"Why on earth didn't you bring an umbrella apiece?" snapped Louise.

That, alas! had been Maude's fault. Just as the luggage was being put on the cab she had discovered that her own umbrella had gone the way of all things. She must have left it in church. And what Barny's mother would say to her she could not think. For she must write at once and tell Mrs. Annesley that they had arrived quite safely. She had always done that, ever since she married Barny. She felt that his mother appreciated it. It was one of the ways in which a daughter-in-law . . . but she had always felt that Mrs. Annesley was just like her own mother. Only it would be dreadful to have to confess that she had let poor Barny get so wet, all through a stupid mistake.

"Because I implored him to take the umbrella in the boat. It doesn't matter about me, I said, I like getting wet. It never does me any harm. But he was as obstinate as . . ."

"But Barny's very strong. A wetting wouldn't hurt him . . ."

"He's not so strong as you all seem to think. He's not nearly as tough as I am. But about baths . . . if there's a shortage of hot water I could have one later, but I think that Barny . . . and, by the way, where is the bathroom?"

"In the gate-house."

"The . . . ?"

"Just by the front door. I'm afraid you have to go out, across the court, to get to it. Personally, I find it's better not to have baths when it rains."

"Oh!"

Maude was taken aback and showed it.

"But how killing," she said. "I mean, how funny! Fancy! But what do we all do about it? I mean, do we all run about in our dressing-gowns, or what? Through the courtyard . . . I mean, in a large mixed party . . ."

Kerran took flight. He could see that Louise was about to say something inexcusable and he always took care not to be present on occasions when she did this, so as to avoid being called in later as a witness. (*I said nothing at all, did*

I, Kerran?) It was much better not to be there.

This talk of hot baths had put a new idea into his head. He thought he would go and sit in one until dinner time. It was the only thing to do at Inishbar on a wet day, and the bath-house, once reached, was a pleasant haven. It was the warmest corner in the castle. Muffy kept a great furnace blazing under the copper, and there was always plenty of hot water. He had sat there, on the warm stone edge of the copper, for a long time that morning while Gordon took a bath. If this sort of weather continued, he foresaw that the place might become a kind of men's club, where he and Gordon and Barny and Dick might go and wallow for hours, safe from feminine intrusion.

So he dashed through the rain to the gate-house and was soon comforting his chilled body in water as near to boiling point as he could stand. He had hung his watch on a convenient nail in the wall and he did not mean to get out until it was time to dress for dinner.

Louise, he reflected, was a fool, for all her cleverness. She had no respect for Barny's loyalty to his tiresome wife: she did not see it as loyalty, she merely thought him stupid. She loved him dearly and felt bitterly that she had lost him, but she could not understand that continuous brutality to Maude was not the way to win him back. She recognised that the marriage was an inevitable disaster, and yet she could not let it alone.

That it was a disaster, even the tolerant Kerran was obliged to admit. Barny had been caught on the rebound. His first love had refused him and he married Maude in an explosion of chivalrous compassion. He had known her for a long time, for she was the sister of a school friend with whose family he had spent a great many summer vacations. Nursing his broken heart, he went to join them at the seaside and discovered that Maude loved him. She was unhappy. Her health had given way under hospital training and she was obliged to live at home, doing the work of an unpaid housekeeper. Her father bullied her. The younger sisters cut her out. She had no future save that of penury and spinsterhood. Yet it was in Barny's power to make her the happiest woman on earth. He had a lively imagination coupled with a kind heart, and together they were too much for him. He married her.

He did not love her, and she must have known it. But she tried to reward him for all his goodness by an extreme wifely solicitude, by asserting, in the face of all the Annesleys, that he was very delicate, and by refusing to take the umbrella when there was only one. Had he loved her, she would have been content to let him look after her, but, since he did not, it was she who must look after him. They lived in an atmosphere of continual restless fussing, which must have been, at times, an intolerable strain upon his nerves. Unfortunately, they had no children.

Barny bore it all with exemplary patience, but, as time went on, he began to fade. There was no other word for it. He grew dimmer and gentler and more passive. He did what Maude told him, went where she took him, and seemed, every year, to have fewer wishes or opinions of his own to express. Kerran believed that he had grown, in his way, very fond of her: that an enduring affection had sprung up between them which might have its consoling rewards. But Louise would never hear of this. She insisted that Barny's life was one long martyr-dom, and the family ought to interfere. If only Maude could be crushed and snubbed into immobility they might get Barny back, as energetic and lively as he had been before he made his terrible mistake. And in any case, even if this had not been her view, she could never keep her temper with Maude. The sight of Barny's acquiescent blink, as he went off in the morning to put on a thicker vest, because Maude thought the wind was cold, and again, in the afternoon, to put on a thinner one because the sun was hot, was always sufficient to break down Louise's good resolutions.

"If she goes on as she has begun," thought Kerran, as he turned on a fresh spate of hot water, "this is the last time Maude and Barny will *ever* come to stay."

In spite of his comfortable situation, he began to feel depressed and to wonder why they had ever, any of them, given in to Louise over this ridiculous summer holiday. No good would come of it, he felt sure, and when next he wrote to his mother he would take her to task for having allowed them to do such a thing. She was well out of it, herself, at Harrogate.

A rattling at the door-handle restored his satisfaction. He splashed about a little and sang a few bars of the *Messiah* to show that he was in possession. But the rattling went on and he heard Barny's mild voice pleading outside.

"Let me in, can't you? I want a bath."

"You can't have one. I'm having one."

"I know. Let me in. What did you lock the door for?"

It was clear that Barny, too, regarded the bath-house as the men's club. Kerran unselfishly hopped out and unlocked the door.

"We'll leave it unlocked," he said, "in case Gordon cares to join us."

Barny flung off his mackintosh and jumped into the bath before his brother could interpose. He pointed out

H

that there was room for both of them, which indeed there
was, for the Nugents had furnished the room upon a
generous scale. So they sat, very contentedly, facing one
another. The bath water, coming from a peaty soil and
thickened with soap-suds, was of a murky-brown colour,
and their submerged bodies were scarcely visible beneath
it. Above the steaming surface their two necks appeared,
each crowned by a red and perspiring face. They were
not very much alike. Kerran was fair and pink, like
Ellen; Barny was dark and aquiline, like Louise.

"Bloody place this seems to be," observed Barny.

"It is," agreed Kerran. "Bloody. Not so bad here,
though," he added.

"I'll tell you what," said Barny, stretching back
voluptuously. "I should like to have some women to
wash me. I should like to have a harem, you know. A
beautiful slave or two to come in and scrub my back."

"Which reminds me," said Kerran. "Have you heard
about Elissa Koebel?"

"Plenty. Anything new?"

"Quite new. She's our next-door neighbour."

Barny nearly jumped out of the bath. He was a
connoisseur in stories about Elissa and passionately
admired her singing.

"But does Louise know?"

"Oh, yes. Indeed she does. She wants to call."

Their laughter echoed through the steamy room. But
when Kerran gave particulars of his conversation with
Louise in the boat, Barny left off laughing.

"She can't," he said very seriously. "She can't
possibly."

"So I told her. But you know what Louise is."

"She must be told that she can't do it."

"Who's to tell her?"

"Gordon must. The woman's notorious. I couldn't possibly allow Maude to meet her."

Kerran did his best to keep a straight face and agreed that it would not do.

"But for my own part I shouldn't mind meeting her, should you, Barny?"

"Not at all," said Barny with a grin.

Barny could be more fantastically indecent than anyone Kerran knew, but it was a long time now since he had had the spirits for bawdry. A hot bath was propitious. He began to recapitulate some of the major incidents in Elissa's career, breaking away, from time to time, into panegyrics of her singing whither Kerran could not follow him.

"We must tell Gordon."

"Yes, we must certainly tell Gordon."

The door was flung open and Muffy came in with a basket of logs. She ignored the expostulations of the bath club, kicked the door to behind her and began to stoke up the fire underneath the copper.

"Really, Muffy! Really! Really!"

"Women aren't allowed in here. This is the thin end of the wedge."

"Don't you worry. I can't see nothing, not underneath that nasty black water that isn't fit for a Christian to bath in, let alone a gentleman. Besides, haven't I bathed the both of you in days gone by?"

6

THE name of Elissa Koebel came up again after dinner, and Kerran suddenly felt obliged to fling down a challenge. He declared roundly that she could not sing.

"She has a beautiful voice," he said. "There are lovely notes in it. She's a superb actress. But she's not really a very good singer."

There were squeaks of expostulation from Maude and Louise, and a disgusted grunt from Barny. Gordon put down his newspaper and peered over his spectacles at Kerran with a faint surprise.

"She's bamboozled you all."

"And all the critics?" asked Louise.

"Not all the critics. But a surprising number of them, I must admit it. You see, she's the only prima donna who can act."

"That is very likely," observed Gordon. "It has always seemed to me that the level of acting in opera is exceedingly poor. Sometimes it is almost ludicrous. I remember in Bayreuth . . ."

Nobody listened to him. They had all fallen upon Kerran, and Barny was saying:

"Did you ever see her Senta?"

"Exactly," agreed Kerran. "Her Senta! What a piece of acting!"

He was obliged to admit that he had been deeply impressed. From the moment the curtain went up on the second act, long before she began to sing, he had found himself intent upon her. Her stillness and her silence

dominated all the clamour made by her fifty com-
panions, bawling over their spinning wheels. She sat
apart from them, a creature in a trance, caught away into
another world, already doomed. She belonged to her
fate and no power could ever bring her back to the
commonplace safety of these girls. The spinning wheel
was no mere property piece, planted down beside her.
It was her spinning wheel.

"Acting, not singing," repeated Kerran. "She made us
feel . . . all that she wished us to feel, before she'd sung
a note. If you were to put the Waldstein and the Koebel
side by side and tell 'em to sing *Caro Nome* . . ."

"I wouldn't ever tell anyone to sing *Caro Nome*,"
interrupted Barny crossly.

"Or even to sing up a scale . . ."

"I'd rather hear the Koebel sing up a scale than hear
anyone else sing through the whole *Ring*."

"You'd rather see her sing a scale, you mean, Barny.
If you were to shut her and the Waldstein up in a dark
room and tell 'em to sing scales . . ."

"One of them would come out with a black eye."

But Barny was annoyed with Kerran. He would have
been ready enough to argue over the merits of any other
musician, but, like most of Elissa's admirers, he took any
criticism in that quarter as a personal affront. Maude,
perceiving his annoyance, hastened loyally to the rescue.

"I'm bound to say I always think she sings ever so
much better than Emmi Waldstein. I've heard them both
in a lot of the same parts. In *Faust*, for instance, which is
my favourite opera. She was perfectly wonderful in
Faust; didn't you think so, Louise?"

"I don't know," said Louise yawning. "I've never
heard *Faust*."

"Not heard *Faust!* Oh, but, Louise, you must. It's a lovely opera. You'd love it."

"Should I?"

There was a tiny pause. Gordon opened his mouth and shut it again. Perhaps he had better not remind Louise that she had heard *Faust*, at least once, in Paris. She must have forgotten and she would not like to be corrected in public.

Maude looked round, suddenly at a loss. She had felt a little superior, just for one second, when she found that she had heard *Faust* and Louise had not. But now, quite inexplicably, she had been made to understand that Louise, in not having heard *Faust*, could claim to have scored a point. It was all very puzzling. Was there anything wrong with *Faust?* Surely it was *good* music?

Barny hardened and withdrew himself a trifle, as he always did when Louise was unkind to Maude. The conversation wavered upon shipwreck, and it was left to the amiable Kerran to pull it together.

"I heard her in *Faust*," he said hastily. "She was extraordinary. I quite agree with Maude. She made one feel she was the only woman who has ever been seduced."

Maude gave a little start of protest. It was nice of Kerran to agree with her, but he need not have put it quite like that. Unaware of her discomfort, and anxious only to revive the conversation, he went on developing the point at quite unnecessary length.

"That first entrance of hers! It was incarnate innocence crossing the stage for a moment. She was so pure, so untouched, you felt almost frightened. Not that Melba wouldn't have sung those *legato* phrases twice as smoothly. But one did feel that only Margarete, the girl herself, would have uttered precisely those sounds. And then, the horrible, cumulative spectacle of ruin that she managed to build up! The jewel song! A lamentable business, technically. (Yes, Barny, it was! If you weren't so besotted, you'd know it.) But the first suggestion of lost innocence was there all right. The flower was blooming just a little too luxuriantly, as it were. And then there was a revelation of sensuousness in the way she moved . . . before ever Faust came on the scene she'd fallen a prey to her own frailty. She didn't yield to him, but to something in herself which she hardly understood. She brought out the inevitability of seduction . . . the weakness that attracts the exploiter, the weakness which betrayed her in every scene, so that she had no defence against remorse, and despair . . . disintegration . . . she had to go mad and die."

He broke off suddenly, embarrassed at his own volubility, as, indeed, they all were. Again there was a pause which Maude found so significant that she was obliged to exclaim:

"What-ho-she-bumps!"

Louise upset the poker and tongs.

"And yet," snarled Barny, "you say she can't sing!"

"She can't. Her phrasing is bad. Her *legato* is so-so. She can't take her top notes *pianissimo*. She breathes in the wrong places. She hasn't a trill. Her middle register . . ."

"I've heard her seventeen times . . ."

"I know. But in this case you're merely a glorified stage-door Johnnie. Your critical faculty . . ."

"Damn you, Kerran . . ."

"Now, now, now!" carolled Maude. "Birds in their little nests agree."

"Your critical faculty isn't working. Your bowels

yearn but your brain goes to sleep."

"Possibly, my dear Kerran. But an active brain and sluggish bowels produce a condition which we all know very well, and its called . . ."

"Barny! Kerran! Barny! Ladies present! We're shocked! Louise, do tell them to stop."

Louise would do no such thing. She did not quite relish this talk of bowels in the drawing-room, but if Barny had been spurred into shocking his wife, that was all to the good. So she turned her back on them all and sat staring into the fire, her elbows on her knees and her chin in her hands, like some dark and brooding sibyl. Kerran and Barny went over to the piano to settle some dispute about Elissa's *rubato*. Gordon returned to his newspaper. There was nothing left for Maude to do but fidget with her bangles.

A great buffet of wind and rain hurled itself against the castle walls. The carpets rose draughtily along the floor. The candle flames flickered, and a fine dust of peat ash blew up from the hearth. Maude yawned. She was cold and she was dull and she was out of it. Barny, it seemed, was in one of his difficult moods, when all her love and care seemed only to irritate him. It wasn't all roses being married to Barny; he could be very charming if he liked, but she saw the other side of the picture.

Still smiling good-humouredly, she got out her fancy work. It was a square of linen upon which she was embroidering spiders webs in thick crewel cotton. She would finish it in no time if every evening were going to be like this one. She began to push the needle up and down, holding the stuff up close to her eyes, for the candle-light was dim. In imagination she was annihilating Louise:

"Oh, I know you despise me all right. I know you

think I'm not good enough for him. But just you try being married to him! If Gordon treated you as Barny does me, it'd do you a lot of good. Just you try being married to a man who's so soft he'd give every penny he had to the next organ-grinder if I didn't keep a sharp look-out. Oh, yes, he's very generous, I know, and all that; I hate a mean man, but there's such a thing as being too generous when you've got a wife to keep. Of course you've got plenty of money, so you can take a lofty line about it. You think a lot of yourself, don't you? What for? You're not so very much better than other people, all said and done, only you've been spoilt and nobody's ever stood up to you, but you needn't think we don't criticise you. If you could hear some of the things Barny says about you in the bedroom you'd sit up; he sees through you all right, and so does your mother even. It'd do you good to see that last letter of hers: *I'm afraid you'll have to put up with a rather uncongenial holiday, for Barny's sake.*

"But she understands me. She sympathises, she knows how I love him and how worried I get. She quite sees how difficult it all is, him being so silly about money, selling out of Consols like that; I knew he'd lose it all. He's not strong, whatever you say, and they said if he had another attack it'd have to come out. Supposing he had one here! We're miles from anywhere, that's the first thing I thought of when Louise . . . of course we'd have Dick—at least that would be some comfort. Whatever else he is, he's a good surgeon, so they say, and if he can do a Cæsar . . . But I wouldn't trust him an inch.

"Do a Cæsar! Well, anyhow, that's one thing I've escaped, though I'd be more frightened of a clot. There's something about a clot; I don't know, only I won't think about it, because it's no use grieving and if it's not to be it's not to be, though how you can think it's my fault, well, just look at me! I'm perfectly healthy. It's Barny. There ought to be something done about it. I oughtn't to have to be so unhappy, it's not right. And yet you think I'm not good enough for him. But it's no use getting bitter about it.

"Where was I before? About Dick doing a Cæsar. About Dick. No, I wouldn't trust him an inch. A really nice woman knows; she has a feeling. I wouldn't be a bit surprised. I know what men are. I haven't been a nurse for nothing, and I could tell you a thing or two about the seamy side, my dear. I suppose you think all doctors are angels of light? Well, some are and some aren't. Some aren't by a long chalk, and I wouldn't wonder if this Dick of yours wasn't a bit of a Don Juan on the Q.T., for all he's married into the wonderful Annesley family. Haw! Haw!

"Barny doesn't see it, but then he's got no intuition; men haven't, not like women. You've got nothing to go on, he says, and of course I haven't, only intuition, and little things he's said from time to time. But I know he's got a horrid mind. No reverence. Disgusting ideas about women. Fancy being Ellen shut up with him in the bedroom! Thank goodness Barny isn't like that, he respects me. But you can see he's got a disgusting mind just from little things he says. It's his brains, I've seen it before. They get coarse-minded and cynical. You'd have thought if they were very intellectual they would be more refined; but no, they get so cynical they don't seem to care about anything, so that a woman can't influence them. Goodness and brains don't always go together, Louise, and that's what you seem to forget. You think you're very clever and I daresay you are; you take me up so, if I say anything; I can't answer you. And you look at me as if I were something the cat'd brought in. You and your great-aunt Harriet. We laugh at you behind your back. We just laugh! We laugh!"

Backwards and forwards went the needle. Another spider's web was finished. For a moment Maude's smile disappeared as she sucked the end of her cotton. And then it was there again, as courageously good-humoured as ever.

7

HOPE did not want to be told all about the island and the castle. She did not want to be shown anything. She wanted to tell and to show herself. But there was nobody to listen, nobody who was in the least interested.

"First of all we got into the train. The *boat* train!"

"I know," said Rosamund. "So did we."

No adventure of Hope's could astonish her. And yet her train must have been a very ordinary affair, just a receptacle for aunts and cousins, while Hope's train had been a landmark. So was the boat. The little Napiers had never been taken across the sea before. For weeks they had been preparing themselves. Somebody had told them that you ought to lie on your back, in a berth, so as not to be sea-sick, and they had all practised lying on their backs, night after night.

"The crossing's nothing," said the intolerable Rosamund. "You wait till you've been to Norway!"

Cousins are like that. It was no use telling Rosamund about the boat train which was so immensely long that it only had a middle. Its ends, never clearly apprehended, were lost in the echoing caverns of the station. Only a little bit of it was stamped upon Hope's mind for ever, a long row of carriage doors, the names of distant places written above in huge words that came straggling out of the darkness and disappeared into the infinite so that all she could read was . . . STER and HOLYH. . . . Crowds pushed under the glare of the lamps, there was a hiss of steam in the murky roof, and they were all climbing into a compartment that smelt of dust and soot, so narrow and dark that they could not see where to put things up on the luggage rack. The children thought that all trains at night must be dark like this, but it was only because the lamps were off, for somebody pulled a cord and there came a wan glare which revealed their solemn faces.

This was departure by night, a thing in itself so exciting that it made them feel a little sick. Enormous sacks were pushed past the carriage window on trucks and somebody said, "The Irish Mail!" They had seen the Irish Mail! A woman pushed past another truck with pillows on it, and the faces of the people, hurrying under the lamps, were charged with a tremendous importance, for they were all addressing themselves to this unique journey. "The Irish Mail" they were saying to themselves. "We are going by the Irish Mail!" Even the porters were full of it. They must know that this was a moment, that this was drama. Their faces, too, were solemn and urgent. They moved like generals on a battlefield. There was a rhythm in their activities. They were conducting this chaotic scene to its incredible climax, its curtain. A final pause, and the thing was happening. The train had begun to move. The white faces of porters slid past the window, an endless line of porters. The platform slid past. It vanished. What a moment of emptiness must fall upon the silent and deserted station! The drama has been played and the Irish Mail has gone.

It gathers speed, this train. It thunders through the night. Its music changes as it runs into tunnels or over points. Strange people pass up and down the corridors. A handful of rain-drops splash the smoky dullness of the window. "To *Lan*cashire, to *Lan*cashire, to *fetch* a pocket *hand*kercher," sings the train, and something nearer than the wheels, something in the carriage, has a short, sharp rattle of its own: "Con*duc*tor, con*duc*tor, con*DUC*tor, con*duc*tor," and then: "Had a *cap*, had a *CAP*, had a *cap*, had a *cap*." . . . More people file down the corridor. What are they looking for? Why do they seem so anxious? Two men are standing just outside the carriage door. Sometimes the shoulders of the overcoat of one of them comes into view. Sometimes they are hidden. They are talking endlessly. "To *Lan*cashire! To *Lan*cashire!" A guard hurries toward some imagined drama. For this train has a life of its own. It is a planet spinning through space and it is peopled, not by travellers but by inhabitants. From end to end of it they are living their hundreds of mysterious lives, talking and laughing, taking things down from the rack, tying up their heads, trying to sleep. They exist only in its medium.

Outside there is nothing. We are rushing through a void. Even the scattered lights of towns have no substance, and the dark, empty stations, through which we fly, are but the symbols of solid daytime places. At Crewe and Chester we pause and receive into our cosmos a few inferior people, scurrying rabbits who run past the window looking suitably abashed, for they can never join the community of true inhabitants. They are soon disposed of. The station is silent. It is dead. We go on again. "To *Lan*cashire, to *Lan*cashire." . . . The void is now called Wales. But it has no reality until the thunder changes to an endless, earsplitting rattle, and somebody says: "The Menai Bridge." It is happening to all of us. We are all going over Menai Bridge. We must hurry. We must prepare ourselves. The unseen hundreds are all astir. They are getting their things down out of the racks, and rolling up their hold-alls. . . .

"And then we went on the boat. An enormous boat."

It is almost frightening to get out of the train. There is a moment of dismay, of blankness, as we meet the cold night wind that smells of the sea. What shall we do next? What is going to happen to us? We don't belong to the train any more. The crowd has become alien, incoherent. We cling together. We are the Napiers; Hope and Peter and mother and Emily and the babies. We are travellers, with no place of our own, hurrying through the darkness and the night.

And now the drama has taken shape again, for here suddenly is the boat, almost before we remember that we were going on a boat. It seems to be part of the station, but its two funnels and its long line of port-holes leap out at us with their promise of adventure. It too has no ends, only a middle with a gang plank, up which we stumble. A hurried and perfunctory business this, and over too soon, so that nobody seems to be saying: "Now we are on a boat." It is too much like being on land, even when we climb down those unusual stairs, are pushed into a narrow, smelly place and see what we have been picturing for weeks and weeks, our berths, one above the other. This part of it, which we have so vividly imagined, is dull. It is flat. The drama stands still. The boat will not go. It is not a real boat. For hours and hours nothing seems to happen at all, save senseless noises which go on and on: thumps and bumps, footsteps overhead, low voices, shouts, the screaming rattle of a crane, bumps and thumps. What can they be doing all this time?

This is not being on a boat. It is lying shut up in a

horrid little place that is clammy and stuffy The top
berth is too near the ceiling and the trampling footsteps.
It was fun to climb up there, but now it is not fun any
more. Just below, in the dark caverns of the under-berth,
mother is already trying to go to sleep. If you lean over
you can see her head, tied up in a scarf. Emily and the
babies are somewhere else. Peter is poking his head out
of the other top berth, a bright yellow head on the end of a
long, thin neck. His eyes are popping, and he makes a
face. "I say, Hope! This cabin smells of sick!" Oh,
disgusting! It does. But we have been trying not to
think so. We have not even started and already we have
begun. . . . "Mother! Mother! I feel sick." "Try to go
to sleep, darling."

Let me get to sleep! Oh, please, let me get to sleep! But
what . . . oh, what is that! What a glorious noise!
VOOOOOOOOOOOOOOOM! VOOOOOO—OOO-
OOOM—ooooooom! We are on a boat. At last we are
on a boat. It is alive and it has spoken. The echoes of its
tremendous, jarring voice come back, and back, over the
water of a harbour which is really there, outside. There is
space, out there, the gleam of lights in the water, a vista of
wharves and quays, the waiting funnels of other ships,
and somewhere, close at hand, the sea. Now the harbour
knows that the boat is going. She has discovered her
purpose. She is gathering herself together with a faint
vibration of engines. She has become separate from the
land. Now, surely, she is moving, surely that is a sound of
waves rushing past. The pulse of machinery grows
louder.

The footsteps still scurry overhead. The bumps
and the thumps go on. They never go to bed on a
boat. They run up and down, up and down. Everything

in the cabin sways slowly, first one way and then slowly the other. We must be out of the harbour by now. We are on the sea! The tossing, desolate, uneventful waves are all round us.

The sea knows nothing. Its waves fall this way and that, without end or purpose. But our boat knows. She is more wonderful than the train. The train had a path. Here there is no path. But our boat goes on, straight as an arrow, towards Ireland and the morning. She stalks through the night so proudly that she makes even the sea seem unimportant. . . .

If Hope could have told it all . . . but there was nobody to listen. They had all been in the train. They had all been in a boat. Yet she still felt that it must have happened only to herself, even though she had not composed a poem on arrival, like Rosamund. She was shown Rosamund's poem and she thought it affected. What she herself could have told would have been ever so much more exciting. But she could not tell it. She could only say:

"First we got in a train. And then we got in a boat."

Rosamund did the honours of the island patronisingly. She spoilt it all. She always knew about everything first. She allowed no exploring.

"And that's the Haunted Glen. Isn't it beautiful?"

"All right," said Hope, gazing at it stolidly.

"I'm glad you appreciate it. I'm going to write my next poem about it. What shall we do now? I can show you a place up in the woods. . . . Shall we go up there and tell secrets?"

Down by the lake edge Charles and Peter were throwing ducks and drakes. Their little flat stones went skipping over the surface of the water. They were

I

shouting and scuffling about, in cheerful, mindless activity.

"I'll go and throw stones with the boys," said Hope.

Rosamund sighed. It is impossible to love one's cousins.

8

ELLEN was so tired that she took her breakfast in bed.
And when she had finished she did not hurry to get up.
It was so nice to have arrived and to feel that there was
nothing more to do and to settle. She was at the beginning of a real holiday. Muffy would look after the
children and Maude would look after the house. In the
whole day before her there seemed to be no task at all
except that she must write to poor Dick, who had been
left behind in London. She must do that every day until
he came. She hated writing letters, even to Dick, unless
there was something special to say. She could not talk on
paper.

Until he came she could not be quite easy in her mind.
To be separated from him gave her a one-sided feeling, as
if she were walking on the edge of a cliff. On the one hand
there was firm ground, on the other there was nothing,
so that she could not walk quite easily. When first she
woke up that morning it had been to know that Dick's
bed, beside her, was neat and empty—a gap.

Far away, in London, Dick had also wakened beside a
gap—if he wakened at all that morning. It was just as
probable that he had been out all night—more probable.
During the last eighteen months it had seemed to her as if
there must be some law of nature arranging that all
emergency operations and all abnormal confinements
must take place in the middle of the night.

They would call Dick up, out of his bed, and next
morning he would come stumbling home again, too tired

to eat any breakfast, too tired to sleep. Early in the morning, when the milk carts were rattling down the street she would wake up and find him standing just inside her bedroom door.

"Ellen?"

"O-o-o-h . . . Dick? What time is it?"

"Half-past five. Do you think the water's hot? I'd like a bath."

Of course it was hot. She had drilled the household into that, and he could have a bath at any moment of the day or night. But he seldom took it at once. She could hear him moving up and down his dressing-room for hours, loudly yawning, with pauses and periods of complete silence, when he was probably reading for a few minutes out of one of the many books that lay piled about the room. And then at last there would be the sound of bath water. Just when she was getting up he would come in again and lie on the sofa at the foot of her bed and tell her what he had done the day before. Or, he would fall into a half-doze as he stared at the early sunlight winking on the crystal bottles on her dressing-table, and turning her cloud of soft hair into a golden haze as she brushed it and brushed it.

Gradually he would recover from the effort, the concentration of the night, as the sun rose higher over the opposite houses and the noises of London outside grew louder. From upstairs would come the thumping of small feet and an echo of shrill voices. The children were having their breakfast. Day would catch him up. It was his morning at the hospital. He would look suddenly at his watch, kiss Ellen and rush out. The front door slammed behind him.

He was overworking himself. She had known it for

months. He was losing the power to snatch sleep when he could get it; he never relaxed, and his assertion that all his friends were in the same boat did not completely reassure her. She was used to the spectacle of overwork and it was difficult to know when the Rubicon had been crossed, the border-line between the fatigue which must be accepted as a chronic evil and that which had become an active menace. He said, and she always believed what he said, that if one had not got the health to stand it one might as well sweep crossings. But she could not help thinking that other people stood it better.

"I wonder how Mrs. Thring manages," she thought. "I wonder if Dr. Thring's hair ever peeled off like that at the top. . . . Dick says it'll grow again and I do hope it will. It would be dreadful to have a bald husband, like Louise's. Why should Gordon be bald? I'm sure he never did one day's work in his life as hard as Dick does every day. I wonder how much sleep Dr. Thring gets. Perhaps he's just the same, but his hair looks very nice. He must have been quite run down, getting influenza like that on his holiday, bother the man!"

For it was Ensor Thring's fault that Dick was still behind, in London. He should have been back a week ago, but he had gone down with influenza in the South of France, and Dick, who was looking after some cases for him, had thought that he must stay until his colleague returned.

Ellen reproved herself for worrying. It was only a little delay and there was no point in making a fuss. Dr. Thring would be back in another week, and seven days more of it could not possibly make any difference to Dick. She must remember how quickly a healthy man picks up. In next to no time he would be quite himself again, rested, and sleeping properly, if only he would not immediately begin to say that he had a paper to write. She would know that he was all right as soon as he stopped bothering about his old papers, though it might be a day or two before he grew calm enough for that. And, anyway, there was nothing to be done now, and thinking the same thing over and over again was worse than useless. She was worrying, and that was bad for her baby. Dick said . . . .

"Oh, for heaven's sake, let me think of something else."

But even when she thought of something else there was still that queer feeling of tightness, as if some nerve had been stretched taut. Dick gave her that feeling all the time now. He was stretched and taut, and she, being so close to him, must share the tension.

The moment had come when lying in bed ceased to be pleasant. With her mind she leapt out of bed and began briskly to put on her clothes. But her body was still tired. It protested against exertion and lagged behind her eager thoughts, which raced ahead and took her out into the pleasant sunshine and the enjoyment of the summer day. Her body moved slowly through the ritual of washing and dressing, a little sick and heavy, burdened with a task of its own which was independent of her conscious will. She was wearily brushing her hair when Muffy came in to take the breakfast tray.

"You should have waited to let me do that, Miss Ellen."

Muffy took the brush out of Ellen's hand and pushed her into a chair in front of the dressing-table.

"I'm worried about Dick, Muffy."

The cry broke from her, before she could restrain it.

"You didn't ought to. It's bad for you."

"I know. But he's overdoing it. He never stops. He's up all night and he works all day. Besides John's, you know he's got five appointments at other hospitals, now, and he does a terrific amount of teaching, as well as continually being called in to give advice to public committees. And all that on top of consultations every other minute and his private work and the hospitals. And his hair's coming out."

"Bay rum," said Muffy. And then, after a pause: "Yes, I daresay he wants a holiday, and knows it as well as you do. He'll get a good rest here."

The brush moved down Ellen's head in long, gentle sweeps. It was very pleasant, and the morning sun winked on the crystal bottles of the dressing-table, just as it did at home. Ellen was one of those women who take all their household gods with them: her dressing-table was always arranged in the same way, wherever she might be. All that she had was solid, plain and valuable. Dick gave her nice things, which he bought in a hurry at the Army and Navy Stores. When he had more time he meant to look round and find something rare for her. But the giving and receiving of presents had never been much of a ritual between them, though they were too conventional to neglect the proper occasions. At Christmas, on birthdays, they produced their offerings in silver, ivory or leather without any sentimental ponderings.

"If it's hard for him, why it's hard for all of them," continued Muffy. "It's the same for all of them, once they begin to get on."

"Yes . . . I know . . . but . . ."

Ellen looked up at the old face in the glass. If she told

Muffy all that was in her mind, then she might be able to forget about it.

"It isn't just ordinary overwork, Muffy. It's . . . oh, I don't know . . . it's more his mind than his body, somehow. I mean, he's always said himself that it's fatal if a doctor begins to worry. He's always quoting examples of it. He says about somebody: 'Oh, So-and-so lost his nerve: between you and me he simply got so that he daren't operate.' Or else he says: 'So-and-so retired because he thought he'd made a mistake' . . . as if we didn't all make mistakes. He says that worry is a vice. He says you do your best, and if you think anyone else could do better, you hand your patient over to him. You have to make decisions and if you couldn't take the risk of making a mistake a lot more people would die than do, even now. And the most you can hope to know is only a very little. And you may see you've made a mistake, but you did your best at the time and that's an end of it. He always says that. And he says, once a man begins to worry over his cases he's done for. He had a friend, who lost his nerve, and he went on a six months' cruise, but he never . . . he was a gynæcologist too, and Dick gets a lot of his work. He says it's fatal to worry."

"Very sensible," observed Muffy.

"Yes. That's what he *says*. But he's doing it. He's quite different. But it's come on so slowly that I've only noticed it just lately. He talks about his cases in a different way, somehow. The way he talks, shows that he's never done with them, in his mind, even when they're over. Oh, you know."

"Yes, I know. But how does he show it? What way does he talk?"

"Oh, it's so difficult. But he's sort of . . . sort of

uncertain and contradictory . . . and going over what he ought to have done, and wondering if he was right, as if he simply hated having to make up his mind. And yet he has to spend his whole life making up his mind! And then, some weeks ago, Dr. Barlow, from John's too, you know, was dining with us and he was laughing at Dick, half in fun, but seriously too, for always ringing up the intern about cases, to ask how they were getting on, much more than he used to. I mean, quite unnecessarily. I mean, I felt that there was something behind it and they were saying at John's that Dick was getting fussy, and he wanted to hint it in a nice way. And he said to me that Dick really ought to get a holiday, quite gravely. Because I know that state of mind so well, don't you, Muffy? When you're out of sorts and think you can't trust people to do their work properly. I know it's always a bad sign with me when I simply can't sit still and believe that Nannie has carried out some order that I've given her, but have to go fussing after her and reminding her. It's a sign of nerves. But I think women are more able to have nerves than men. I mean, it's worse when men get them.

"And then there's another thing: he seems to mind about other people more, and if they're criticising him behind his back. He says how he simply couldn't make up his mind or something, and then he says: 'Oh, I hope So-and-so didn't spot it; he squinted at me sideways once or twice.' Or if he's called in to a consultation with someone he doesn't know, he always says something afterwards about what impression he thinks he's made with this new man: he says: 'I didn't cut much ice with that fellow' . . . but he never used to worry about this sort of thing. He never used to mind what other people thought of him. And then, once or twice, I'm sure he's sent patients on to other men, cases that he could perfectly well have managed himself, simply to . . . simply to get out of having to . . . to take the responsibility. And he thinks they criticise him at the hospital. Even the students . . ."

Ellen stopped and sighed. It was inconceivable that she should be saying all this, out loud, to anyone else. But it was a great relief. She wanted no comment from Muffy, and Muffy made none.

"Oh, I know it all sounds rather petty. But it's not like him. He gets upset about things that never used to upset him. In March he read a paper to some society and some old stick-in-the-mud, Sir Norman Kevin, criticised him and heckled him rather sharply. And he minded frightfully. It upset him for days. As if it mattered tuppence! Before he got like this he'd have quite enjoyed having to defend himself. He used to like operating with an audience. I know he did. He often said so. But now he simply hates it . . . and as for Mrs. Briggs, I really think if anything goes wrong with her, he'll have a breakdown or something."

"Who is Mrs. Briggs?" ventured Muffy.

"Oh, she's just a patient of Dr. Thring's. She's the chief reason for Dick staying in London, because he thinks she needs constant watching. She's going to have a baby . . . I think it's four or five months on, and she has an appendix that ought to come out. Dick and Dr. Thring are doing it for nothing. Dr. Briggs is an old friend of theirs; he was a student when they were, but he's badly off; a struggling G.P. and all that. So Dick feels he must stay and keep an eye on her till Dr. Thring gets back. But the ups and downs we've had over this appendix! He couldn't make up his mind if he'd take it out or leave it. First of all he says: 'What'll Thring say if I operate, and she aborts?' And then he says: 'What'll Thring say if I don't operate and she gets peritonitis?' Personally, I'd have asked what Mrs. Briggs would say, but I suppose it's more professional to mind what Thring would think about it. If ever he does get a clear night in bed he's sure to wake up and wake me up to tell me that in nine cases out of ten it's best not to risk the operation during pregnancy. I've never known him get a case on his mind so badly, yet it's a very common one. And I have a feeling that he's got so jumpy about it that he'd be terrified, now, if he did have to operate. Luckily it seems to be quiescent. He's made me jumpy, too, so that I get almost to feel that if he did have to operate he might sew up the dressing scissors inside her or something. I never used to feel he could do anything wrong. And then it's awful the way his hair is coming out. But I told you about that."

This seemed really everything, and Ellen felt better already. It did not sound so bad, now that she had said it, and she would not have been surprised if Muffy had told her not to be silly. But Muffy said:

"Well, by all accounts, it's high time he came away. Though I don't call this a place I'd choose for a nerve cure, not by a long chalk."

"Oh, Muffy! Are you still hating it? Don't you like it any better? Mother wrote to me . . ."

Muffy's face, reflected in the glass, became mulish. She said nothing, but it was clear that she never would, never could, never wanted to like it any better.

"I suppose it's rather inconvenient from your point of view."

"Oh, it isn't only the inconvenience. There . . . I don't know. There's a lot I don't like about it. It's so . . . so outlandish, somehow."

"Too lonely, you mean?"

"Not sure that I do. Not lonely enough, in a manner of speaking. There's some very funny sort of people about in these parts."

"Funny people? On the island?"

"Not on the island . . . *yet*. But hanging about." Muffy lowered her voice mysteriously. "I saw one yesterday. Early before breakfast. I went just outside the gate to see what sort of a day it was. And there, as bold as brass, was a person rowing up to the island."

"A person?"

"A lady. Only she was no lady, that I'll swear. A bold-looking woman, she was. One of these actresses, I shouldn't wonder."

"Actresses? What actresses? Muffy, what do you mean?"

Muffy nodded solemnly in the glass.

"There's actresses come here, Miss Ellen, and people of that sort. You see what I mean. It isn't a gentleman's house, such as you'd expect Dr. Lindsay to take for the summer. It's got something queer about it. This person looked for all the world as if she'd the right to come here. Rowed up close to the landing-stage. She'd no paint on her face, that I will say, but she was bold-looking and her hair, you wouldn't believe, hanging down all over the place like yours is now. And her arms all bare and no collar to her bodice, so you could see her neck and her bosom, almost. It was disgusting. Like a slut out of the slums. Supposing if any of the gentlemen had been out and seen her! If she'd got on shore I'd have sent her

about her business. 'And what might you be wanting?'
I'd have asked. But she thought better of it. After a bit
she took herself off."

"How extraordinary! Where could she have come
from?"

"That's not for me to say. But she wouldn't have
dared come up like that to a gentleman's house. You see
what I mean, Miss Ellen. Those sort of people wouldn't
come hanging round a house if it was all as it should be."

9

EVERYBODY was disappointed that Dick had not come, but they, none of them, not even Kerran, understood how bitter a blow it was for Louise. They were all so pleased to see Ellen and the children, this matriarchal tribe which came trooping possessively into the castle. They had exclaimed when they counted the heads in the boats, they had asked one another where Dick could be, but their spirits had not fallen to zero.

Child after child had been lifted out and deposited on the shore. They came stumping up towards the castle, clutching boats and spades and buckets. There were only four of them, yet they were like an army, generalled by Ellen and the nursery maid. They beamed at Louise in the confident belief that they were welcome. They volunteered dull pieces of information. They expected to be kissed.

"Such a wonderful crossing!"

"Oh, Aunt Louise, we've brought our spades and buckets."

"Where is the nursery?"

"We came in the Irish Mail!"

"Are there dungeons in this castle?"

"Why, Louise! You're looking quite sunburnt! Dick? Oh, he couldn't come. He had to stay in London. Listen! I'm afraid we've had to leave some luggage at Killross. Could one of the boats go back for it?"

Louise stood thunderstruck. No Dick? And what was to become of all the fun which she had planned?

Even a Russian novel must have a hero.

The invasion swept past into the castle, where Muffy and Maude were only too ready to swell the prosaic bustle of unpacking and settling in. She felt that their "party" had received a formidable reinforcement. For already she had mentally divided the castle community into two sections. There was her own group, who were to enjoy the pleasures of cultivated idleness, and there was the useful domestic rabble of women, children and servants. It was important that the activities of the latter should not be allowed to impinge upon the tranquillity of the former. The rabble must be kept in its place. But now it seemed to be ubiquitous.

For the first time she began to wonder if it was not a disadvantage to be the only woman in her group. It had been quite easy to dispose of Maude before Ellen came, but the spectacle of the pair of them, so arrogantly commonplace, so determined to turn the abode of romance into a seaside lodging-house, was disconcerting. She did not tell herself outright that a close understanding between these two was undesirable, but it was an impulse, born of some such thought, that lay behind a new cordiality which she suddenly felt for Maude. She compromised. Ellen had Muffy, anyhow: to balance them there had better be Louise and Maude, even though that might mean certain sacrifices. Maude, in spite of her deficiencies, must have a sort of place in the superior group. Ellen was better qualified for such promotion, but she had put herself out of court by leaving Dick behind her.

It was easy to get on terms with Maude. For the sake of a little confidential gossip she was ready to forget all her grudges. And she saw Louise's point at once. Dick ought not to have allowed Ellen to come alone.

"Supposing it had been a rough crossing!"

"Lifting heavy things up on to racks!"

"Gordon would never . . ."

"Barny would never . . ."

"She looked fagged out when she got here."

"I'm so glad I persuaded her to take breakfast in bed. Muffy's looking after her."

"I know."

Ellen had her own allies. Muffy, who would not even allow Barny to have a chill, was now brushing Ellen's hair. Muffy had been making a fuss about Ellen the very first night she was in the castle. She had planted her standard on the keep and sat inside it drinking tea and disapproving of Louise. Louise and Maude were both against Muffy, and that drew them together.

They continued to abuse Dick. It was a conversation which could only have been held between two women, for no man would have understood that they were really blaming Ellen for allowing Dick to allow her to come alone. Everything which they said against Dick was really an arrow aimed at Ellen.

"But this Dr. Thring," repeated Louise, "if this Thring person has asked Dick to look after his cases I suppose Dick could equally well hand them on to somebody else. He's not the only gynæcologist in London. Gordon's just the same. They like to think they're indispensable. You can't ever get them away without manœuvring a bit."

"I know. And considering all this we've heard about how much he overworks, she ought to have played every card in her hand to get him away."

They had been strolling on the grass slope in front of

the castle, and at this point Louise made a gesture which definitely turned these tentative openings into an alliance. She sat down on a stone bench, by the water's edge, and signed to Maude to sit beside her.

They settled to it.

"I don't think she manages him very well, do you?"

"No. I do not. But then, I never . . ."

Maude bit her lip. She had been about to say that no nice woman could hope to manage such a nasty man. But that would have broken up this pleasant atmosphere of sympathy. They were united over Ellen, who had failed to tame her wild hawk, but they were not really agreed over Dick.

"She doesn't understand her job, as his wife, in the very least," said Louise. "She lets him overwork himself. All this unpaid hospital work, and lecturing, surely by now he ought to give up all that. She doesn't seem to realise that people are beginning to talk about him as *the* man. Oh yes, I know they all do a certain amount of it, but she ought to discourage it as much as she can. She shouldn't calmly submit to letting this Thring, or who-ever he is, thrust his patients on to Dick, while he goes for a holiday. It isn't as if they were making this sacrifice in order to get Dick on professionally. If it were anybody very important. . . . But then she's no idea of pushing him. Socially, I mean. A wife can do so much. I'm not a snob . . . I hope . . ."

"Of course not," said Maude, genuinely forgetting great-aunt Harriet.

"No, I don't think I'm a snob. But one does realise, one has to realise, that there's a snobbish element in all worldly success. One regrets it, but it's so. It isn't always the most brilliant men who get to the top of the

K

tree, it's the men who know how to climb, unfortunately. One doesn't want Dick to push himself. One's glad he isn't that kind, it's all part of his charm. But one wants him to be pushed. Ellen doesn't realise . . . but she'll have to realise."

Louise jerked her head in an angry way that she had when people would not realise and would have to be made to realise.

"Or if they weren't so comfortably off," suggested Maude cautiously. "But then, they don't have to worry about money."

This was a delicate subject, for the money was mostly Ellen's. Dick was making a good income for himself, now, but he would never have been able to marry when he did if his bride had not been well dowered. And some of the Annesleys thought that he took it very coolly, that he had too many children, enjoyed his comfortable home too much and treated Ellen's money as if it had fallen, like manna, from the skies. His arrogance annoyed them, and, though they all knew that no man could work harder, they would have preferred to see him show a little embarrassment at his position. Maude, especially, thought this, because she and Barny were poorer than the rest owing to Barny's unfortunate habit of speculating. She was the only one of them who really believed that Dick had married for money.

"Oh, I wasn't thinking of that," said Louise, in the tone of one who can afford to be above such things. "But she doesn't understand him. She's neither the one thing nor the other. She takes a narrow view of his career. She has no ambitions for him, and she takes no trouble from the worldly point of view. And on the other hand she isn't the right companion for him . . . as a man. They've no interests in common, except their children. He's intellectual and she isn't. He is imaginative and sensitive and she is about as romantic as a leg of mutton."

"Then you think he's not happy with her?"

Louise pondered. This was a point which should not have been pressed in such a hurry. They were feeling their way towards it, but she was a little disconcerted at being asked such a question so soon.

"He's very loyal to her. No . . . I don't think one can go as far as that. I think he's been quite happy with her, up till now. I don't think one can call it an unhappy marriage . . . quite . . ."

But neither would she call it a happy marriage. How could it be when Ellen had not learnt to manage Dick, and did not even understand him? Louise and Maude were happily married. They lived on a nicely-balanced see-saw. They sacrificed themselves, consciously, and the security which they had achieved was worth the trouble. Maude held umbrellas over Barny's head and Louise was obliged to live in North Oxford. Sometimes they complained of the demands which had been made on them, but more often they boasted of the rewards they had reaped. Their husbands were faithful and domesticated.

But there was no see-saw in the Napier household, no sacrificial compromise. Dick gave Ellen children, spent her money, told her what to think, and made her, to all appearances, a happy woman. She was satisfied, not with herself, but in him. And to Louise, who had never known an instant's satisfaction in the whole of her life, this primitive serenity was galling.

"No," agreed Maude, "they get on all right. But it's a fluke."

"That's just what I was thinking."

"If anything should happen . . ."

"I know."

"Well, after all, supposing Dick were to be very much attracted by someone else? Has she ever thought of that?"

"My dear Maude, Ellen doesn't think. That's the one thing one has to remember about Ellen. She doesn't *think*."

"I suppose I've got a horrid mind."

"Not at all. It's a possibility that no woman should ever forget. She's a fool if she does."

Maude drew a long breath and risked it.

"I mean . . . well, this stopping behind in London, for instance. It may be all quite true, I'm not saying it isn't. But if I were Ellen I don't think I should awfully much like the idea of leaving him to his own devices in London."

Louise sat up with a jerk. Her face grew very red.

"What on earth are you suggesting?"

"Oh dear! Oh dear! I said I'd got a horrid mind."

"You have, Maude. He isn't that kind of man at all. I know him better than you do. He's not the kind who's kept late at the office on business. It wasn't that sort of thing that I was thinking of."

"Then what . . ."

"Not vulgar little infidelities. She needn't ever be afraid of that. But how would she manage if he ever fell really in love? Because I don't think, though I'd only say this to you, mind you, I don't think he's ever been what I call romantically in love with Ellen. It began when they were too young. He told me once that he first made up his mind to marry her when she was fourteen, when she was only a child. Well, he couldn't have felt about her then what a man feels about . . . about a mature woman. He must have idealised her in a transcendental sort of way . . . the way young men do. And then he married her and she turned into a nice prosaic wife. I don't think he knows what it is to be passionately in love."

Maude shook her head solemnly.

"I see what you mean. But for all that, and in spite of you saying that I've got a horrid mind, if I'd been Ellen I shouldn't have left him behind in London. I'd have brought him with me or stayed to keep an eye on him."

This was really too much. The dinginess of Maude's mind was more that Louise could bear. It was impossible to sustain any prolonged communication with it, even for the sake of mutual support.

Louise got up abruptly, and said that she was going to take all the children for a bathe on the other side of the island.

10

ELLEN had gone with the three men over to the mainland to explore. She steered them to a place where a little stream ran down a narrow glen, its course marked by thickets of birch and mountain ash. It was the sort of stream which the wanderer is bound to track up to its source, simply for the sake of its many adventures, its hidden pools, waterfalls and mossy boulders, and the smaller streams which tinkle down the hill to join it.

Once on land they all separated. Barny, with the light of the explorer in his eye set off up the glen at a great rate, followed more slowly by Gordon, who kept stopping and poking about in search of rare ferns. Ellen walked slowest of all, for the path was steep and slippery. She picked bog myrtle, and rubbed it between her fingers, and sniffed at it with a sigh of pleasure. When she got up about a hundred feet she sat down in a patch of heather to rest. High up above her she could see Barny, leaping like a wild goat over the mountain side. Gordon had disappeared round the turn of the glen, and Kerran, down below, was wandering along a rough cart track which ran beside the lake. He was anxious to see what lay hidden round the next little point.

They had separated because each wished to enjoy the peace and leisure of the summer morning in his own way, and at his own pace. They were all half conscious of a sense of release and freedom. They had got away from the narrow confines of the island, and the even narrower constriction of the boat. They had got away from

Louise. They were in a place where they could stretch their legs and think their own thoughts.

Ellen thought:

"This is nicer than the island. I like it better. I shall bring the children. We will have a lot of picnics here."

Barny had got right up on to the skyline. He could look down over the whole of the lake and he could see the blue ocean horizon beyond the sandhills and the rocky crags to the west of the Ardfillan mountains. His thoughts turned to rock-climbing, which he had long ago given up, because it made Maude anxious. He had been a very good climber once. He played with the idea of an expedition with Dick. They might go and climb those crags. And he saw himself climbing as an onlooker might see it, enjoying the ripple of muscles and limbs and the secret rhythm of balance, that was like music. Dick was a good climber too, intrepid, sensible and agile, but he had none of Barny's instinctive poise. And at the top there would be pipes to smoke, and the knowledge of achievement, a moment complete in itself away from Maude. He would like very much to go. "Perhaps Maude will let me go," he thought hopefully. But if the proposition upset her he would give it up, for he was always very careful not to flout her wishes when they were staying with Louise.

Gordon had found a rare variety of sundew, which he wanted to take home, only he could not think where to put it. If he used his hat the sun would blister the bald crown of his head. He could not put a lump of wet moss in his pocket. Eventually he carried it in his handkerchief and started cautiously down the steep path again. It was rather tiresome, having to carry the sundew so carefully, and after a few stumbles, he wondered if it were worth while. But he wished very much to show it to someone and explain its carnivorous properties. He would take it, anyhow, as far as Ellen, who would certainly be interested.

From time to time he stopped, in order to take in the view. It was remarkably fine. Very fine indeed, he thought. But not equal to the Lake District. The colouring did not please him so well. It was all too illusory, and there was something enervating in its softness. These were not Wordsworth's "lonely hills," and that lake could never have found a place in the prelude. There was something wanting, some element of grandeur. No noble thoughts occurred to Gordon.

Kerran had got round the next little point and found there another glen and a stream exactly like the last. He looked about him aimlessly, for a little while, and then retraced his steps. For when he was quite alone he could think of nothing but his unhappy love, the sorrow which had become so constant a companion to him that he had grown quite used to it. Solitude could do nothing for him. It was a mistake to come to the mainland and walk about alone; he would have done better to remain at Inishbar, absorbed in the close little dramas of the castle.

He quickened his pace and got back round the point again to Ellen, where she sat in the sun upon her boulder. She knew all about his affairs and he could say just a word or two now and then, to her, without feeling that he had been betrayed into a confidential scene. He could not trust himself to speak of his trouble save in the most commonplace way, and Ellen was comfortably incurious.

He began now:

"When you're writing to mother next, you might just let her know that it's all off, absolutely off, between Nathalie and me."

"Yes," said Ellen, "I will."

"I saw her, a week before I came away, and she's quite firm, so there's nothing to be done."

"She won't marry a Protestant?"

"And I can't become a Catholic. So it does seem quite hopeless. We've decided not to see one another again."

He picked a stalk of heath and began pulling off its pink bells and pouring them from one hand to the other.

"She's going abroad. I rather think . . . I'm pretty sure . . . that she'll end by becoming a nun. I believe it's that, more than my being a Protestant. But as mother knows of my . . . my . . . attachment . . . you'd better let her know it's all over."

"I'll tell her," said Ellen again.

She knew that Mrs. Annesley had probably been told already, for poor Kerran's plight was fairly common property. Nathalie Power's sister had confided in a friend who had passed it all on to Louise. Nothing of the last interview had been kept a secret. But Louise had fortunately made up her mind that the affair was unimportant, a mere sentimental aberration on Kerran's part. She had never liked Nathalie, and she discouraged comment or discussion. Ellen's baby and Kerran's romance were forbidden topics at Inishbar.

"I'm glad I didn't have to change my religion to marry Dick," said Ellen. "I don't think I ever could have believed in the Virgin Mary."

"Believed in . . ." Kerran sat up with a jerk. "My dear girl, what do you mean? Do you doubt that such a person ever existed? Or don't you accept the Virgin Birth? Or are you talking about the Immaculate Conception?"

"Oh, don't flurry me," said Ellen. "You're as bad as Dick. Isn't the Immaculate Conception the same as the Virgin Birth?"

"Indeed it's not," said Kerran.

He began to explain at some length, for he had a purely academic interest in theology and was an authority upon the career of Pius IX. Ellen saw that she was in for a history lecture, and very soon she left off listening.

"All this has nothing to do with religion," she thought. "Religion is about God."

But even as she thought it she was aware of an oppression, a menace hovering somewhere in her thoughts. For she was a religious woman, a communicant, and she believed in four Gods, or rather, four Persons who bore the same name. She believed in the God of the Old Testament, and had a very distinct idea of His character. He was definitely anthropomorphic, grossly unfair, a materialist in the matter of rewards and punishments, callous of suffering, but noble, uncompromising and full of majesty. He had nothing to do with the Presence lurking in the background of the Gospel story, an impersonal and unsatisfying divinity, who was said to be loving and merciful but who had sat safely up in Heaven while His Son died on the Cross. Ellen did not know it, but she had never liked that second God. "He gave his only Son . . ." There was a kind of sentimental unfairness about the idea of which the God of Israel would never have been capable. Nor could she identify either of Them with Jesus, the Man of Sorrows, a pitiful, defeated figure of goodness and pain—a victim. And fourthly, there was the Holy Ghost, a mere name, without personality or shape at all.

She had been taught that all these four people were

really one and it was only lately, since she had come to
be so much worried about Dick, that she had found this
difficult to believe. In her trouble she had prayed more
fervently and more intimately than ever before, and she
could not escape from the feeling that her prayers were
being heard by a committee, by four people who would,
so she had been assured, take a kindly interest in herself
and her affairs. But did they? Or rather, since she must
remember that there was only One, did He? Somewhere
at the back of her mind she had a feeling that she would
think more of Him if He did not, and that He would think
more of her if she held her tongue. Only that was not
what she had been taught, and what she had placidly
accepted through the tranquil years of her girlhood and
her marriage. She could pray to four Gods in whom
she did not really believe, or she could believe in one to
whom she could not pray. It was all very wrong, in a
religious woman, and a communicant. It was doubt.
She had heard of people losing their faith, but she had
never thought that such a thing would happen to herself
and it frightened her.

Kerran had got to Lourdes and the vision of Bernadette
and she began to listen again, until it was time to make
them all go home to lunch. The little expedition had just
filled in the morning, which was satisfactory. In these
days, while she was waiting for Dick, she needed some
kind of definite routine.

"You must row quickly," she said, when she had
collected her three men, "or we shall be late."

"Give us twenty," said Barny earnestly.

Smiling, she counted twenty, while Barny, Kerran and
Gordon tugged at their oars. The boat flew across the
water and the island bore down on them. A tolling bell

from the castle told them that lunch was ready just as they shipped oars smartly beside the landing stage.

Louise was running down the grass slope, all ready to tell them the news. For there was continual drama on the island; under her sway that was inevitable. If people went away for a morning, they would be sure to miss something.

Louise was transported with excitement. And she had taken off her shoes and stockings. Her white ankles twinkled under her linen skirt as she came bounding over the grass. They all stared first at her feet and then at her glowing face. Ellen rose up in the boat, crying:

"Dick? Has Dick come?"

"No, no! Not Dick. No. It's Elissa Koebel. I've asked her to lunch."

The three men had begun to smile at the prospect of Dick arriving, but at this announcement they left off smiling abruptly. Ellen, who had heard nothing about Elissa Koebel, looked bewildered.

"I've never seen anyone like her," cried Louise, as she hurried them out of the boat. "Like somebody out of a fairy tale. She came suddenly out of the woods when we were bathing. Really like somebody out of a fairy tale. Ow!"

There were little thistles in the short grass and Louise sometimes walked on these, but after the first betraying exclamation she managed to ignore the pain they gave her.

"I felt as if I'd known her all my life. I can't tell you . . . there we were, bathing on a little beach, and all at once this absolutely beautiful person just . . . occurred. There's no other word for it. She was suddenly with us. And she sang! She sang to us (Ow!) just sitting on the beach. I thought she would vanish at any moment. But she didn't. She's in the dining-hall at this minute. Isn't it fun?"

Ellen was so deeply disappointed that she said nothing at all for a moment, and then she asked what had happened to Louise's shoes and stockings.

"I threw them into the lake," said Louise, laughing.

"Oh, did you? Why?"

Louise was hobbling painfully over the gravel path in front of the north gate and did not reply. Once on the grateful smoothness of the flagstones, she recovered poise and asked "Why not?"

"Er . . ." said Gordon. "Er . . . er . . . er . . ."

In private he had agreed with Barny and Kerran that such a person as Madame Koebel could not possibly be received in the castle. When he heard what they had to tell of her, he had assured them that there was no danger. Louise would be the last woman to make such a friendship. So now he could only flush and gobble.

"Er . . . er . . . er . . ."

He had never seen the woman, or heard her sing. He knew nothing about her save what Kerran and Barny had told him. But he pictured he knew not what of disreputability installed in his dining-room. His acquaintance with the half world had been slight. He associated easy virtue with paint, powder, strong perfume and *Gals Gossip*, which friends of his youth had all thought very funny but which was full of jokes which he could never understand. He rather expected that Elissa would wear a very large hat and a veil with black dots on it, like a dreadful person in the *Bal Boulier*, to which he had been taken while in Paris, who came up and pinched his behind. To find that Louise had accepted all this, Louise, to whom any sort of vulgarity was torture, left him without powers of speech. He could only clutch his sundew and make helpless little noises, as he followed her across the courtyard.

Kerran and Barny were already looking self-conscious, like cows turned into a field with a bull. All their sex had come to the surface, so that they had left off wanting to laugh, and were quite grave, as they clattered into the hall after Louise.

Elissa and Maude were sitting in silence at the long table that stood on the dais. Maude's silence was that of a charged thunder-cloud. At any moment it might have dissolved into a peal of laughter or a series of shrieks. She did not speak because her feelings were too much for her. But Elissa was silent because she had nothing to say. It was evident that she had forgotten the existence of Maude. Leaning her bare white elbows on the table, she had fallen into a profound reverie, while the food on her plate grew cold.

Nor did she immediately look up at the little party advancing across the hall. She remained as unaware of them as though footlights had lain between. Her attitude was that of Sieglinde, sitting at Hunding's board and listening to Siegmund's story. Her loose draperies flowed about her limbs and fell carelessly into folds that were classic, traditional. Her hair, of that miraculous gold which is seldom seen outside legend, hung down on either side of her head in two thick braids. The face between was pale, severe almost to harshness. She had taken on the stern beauty of the great bare hall, so that she seemed to belong to it, as it had belonged once to the barbarous chieftains who had made their home in the castle. She sat at the table, as if by right, and Maude, beside her, was such an anachronism as to be scarcely there at all.

"My husband . . ." Louise was saying. "My brothers
. . . my sister, Mrs. Napier."

Slowly the stern pose was changed for one of grave
recognition and attention. Elissa came out of her
trance and acknowledged these introductions, looking
from one to another as if she would ask what they
wanted of her. It was difficult to remember that this
was their house and that she was the stranger. She
said nothing until she caught sight of the handkerchief
which Gordon still clutched. Then there was a definite
movement of interest. A faint smile quivered on her
lovely mouth as she asked:

"What haf you got there? Show me."

Her voice was deep and beautiful. It was the
loveliest speaking voice that any of them had ever
heard, and its foreign accent lent it an unexpected
charm. It obliged them all to feel that she was a great
woman, a rare and gifted creature, condescending to their
hospitality.

"S—s—s—sundew," stammered Gordon, putting his
handkerchief on the table and revealing its contents. "A
rare specimen . . ."

"It is not beautiful," observed Elissa, looking at the
handful of crushed moss.

"No. But it eats flies."

"Ach, so! Tell me, please?"

He stammered a confused explanation, to which she
listened attentively.

"But this is wonderful!" she exclaimed. "I also love
flowers, but of sundew I have never heard. It is *macabre*,
this! Could we not catch a fly for it?"

"Try it with a crumb," ventured Kerran.

She looked at him for a second, and he blushed. He had

never seen such eyes, so wild and strange and unabashed, in any woman's head before. They gave him a sensation as if one of his vertebræ, low down near the base of the spine, was missing. And they made him feel queerly ashamed of himself. He was aware that in all his thoughts, all his conversation, about this woman, he had been guilty of gross vulgarity. She might be abominable, but the scandal which he and Barny had been talking was too small for her. He looked over at Barny, who had taken his place by Maude. And he saw that Barny was very cross.

Gordon's soup got cold while he tried to catch a fly for the sundew, and explained just exactly how rare this species was. Never before had he had such a success with his botanical discoveries. Their guest displayed the most flattering attention. She plied him with questions for twenty minutes. And then, half-way through the pudding course, she rose abruptly.

"Forgive me," she said. "I am going back into the sunshine. I have eaten sufficient, and I find it a little cold in here."

Without further apology she left them, walking slowly down the hall as though she was making a stage exit. They all stared after her until she had vanished into the sunshine of the courtyard.

Maude spoke first. She said:

"How very rude!"

To which Louise replied:

"Do you think so?"

"But who is she? Who is she?" asked Ellen.

"What is going to happen next?" asked Kerran.

Barny and Gordon said nothing. Barny was too angry to speak. He considered that Maude had been insulted.

As for Gordon, he was head over ears in love.

11

Letter from Ellen

MY DEAREST MOTHER,—

Thank you for sending me the wool. It is just what I wanted, so beautifully soft. I shall have enough to make six little vests, and I don't think I shall need any more; they grow out of the first size so quickly. So if you have any time for knitting, would you concentrate on another shawl, as I find that one or two that I thought would do are so washed up they have gone all felty?

We go on very well here, the weather is beautiful; I only hope it will not break before Dick comes. No news of him, at least I get a letter every day with nothing in it. It is tiresome that he should be kept hanging about all this time in London.

I am very well. It is nice to have nothing to do. The bathing is very nice. The children seem to be very well, though I do not think it is a very bracing place. I would have liked a more bracing place for Dick. No other news. We have a great deal of music, which is nice, and will have more, I suppose, when Mr. Fletcher comes, as he is bringing his violin. Madame Koebel sings every evening. She is a strange person, but she certainly sings beautifully, and one cannot help admiring her. But I would have to know her much better before I could be quite sure if she is always sincere. It is so difficult to know what foreigners are really like.

I go over every day that I can to the mainland. It is a nice change from the island, where we seem to be rather cut off, somehow. I think this is because we never see anything of the country people as one does generally in the country. There is a nice woman in a cottage some way up on the north shore, a Mrs. Gallagher. She keeps bees and sells very good honey. I will send you a comb. She has seven children "at foot" and an eight months' old baby. I see them running about the bogs, six little boys and a girl. The boys all wear frocks, even the ten-year-old, I think because their mother cannot make trousers. They wear one long homespun garment, rather like a cassock. The little girl, Nellie, wears quite a short frock with half a dozen petticoats under it, like the peasant women. She has red corkscrew curls and is very self-possessed. It would make you laugh to see them all come stringing over the bog, these great boys with their cassocks flapping round their legs and the very feminine Nellie clambering after them.

The post is going, so I must stop.

Your loving daughter,
ELLEN.

Letter from Gordon

DEAR MRS. ANNESLEY,—

Louise has commissioned me to write and tell you that she has remembered about the spirit lamp and is writing to the stores. I transcribe this message verbatim and trust that you will understand it.

We are so glad to hear that Harrogate is doing you good, but we miss you sadly here, for this is certainly the most delightful holiday that we have ever spent. In fact, we have become so enamoured of the place that we plan to spend every Long Vacation here.

Louise will have written to you an account of our new

acquaintance: I may say friend, for she is with us so much that we have come to regard her as practically one of our party. I expect the intimacy will surprise you a little. That she should "fit in" so well must be almost incomprehensible to anyone who knows her only by repute. Indeed, I could not have imagined it myself ten days ago.

But you will have gathered that she is a most remarkable woman. Her unconventionality, which is at first a trifle disconcerting, springs from a sincerity which rapidly wins respect. There is an element of greatness, of nobility, not only in her art but in her character; she moves, speaks and thinks with a direct simplicity which is only possible to genius, and in her company one has a glimpse of a freer and grander world. The most abiding impression which she gives is one of beauty, a beauty which neither begins nor ends with her art but which inspires all her approaches to life. It is difficult to imagine how this child of the gods can have survived all the insincerities and the petty vulgarities of the stage. One can only imagine that Apollo himself has protected her.

She has a mind which constantly outruns the narrow scope of her profession. It is not a trained mind, nor always a very well-informed mind, but it has the liveliest and the most delicate perceptions. One instance I will mention: I happened in the course of a conversation to quote a few lines of Vergil, in English of course (my own translation). She looked at me as though she had just received some specific revelation. The words, the whole meaning of the passage, so fixed her attention that she returned to it again and again. Who had written these lines? To whom did they refer? I must describe for her the whole narrative, the purpose and intention of the Æneid. She must read my translation. She must do more. She must read the original. You will scarcely believe me when I tell you that for three days she has been learning Latin in order that she may not, as she says, die before she has read Vergil.

She has infected Louise with her enthusiasm and a strange business we make of it, for they are both determined to read the Æneid at once and when they have conjugated a few verbs we sit, all three of us, upon the banks of the lake construing Dido's lament. And then, in payment, she sings for me. I little thought that I should ever have two such pupils, and these golden hours are an idyll which I shall remember when I am old.

Louise had some message about a spirit lamp . . . but I see that I have given it. We all send our fondest love.

Yours very sincerely,

GORDON LINDSAY.

Letter from Kerran

DEAR MOTHER,—

The Koebel epoch is in full swing, though how long it will last I do not know, or what harm could really come of it. Louise, of course, is infatuated, and so is Gordon. Barny and I scarcely dare open our mouths. He entirely refuses to credit any of the stories about her; says it is all club gossip and so on. I had never realised before quite how unworldly the poor man is. He believes her to be all that is respectable, simply because she does not answer to his idea of a *demi-mondaine*.

But a word from herself may at any time shatter these delusions. I will say for her that she is a creature of no concealments. You couldn't possibly call her a *shady* character. It is the sheerest accident that she has not yet told Gordon her life history. She will one day, and then we shall see wigs on the green, all sorts of wigs, because Louise is much further gone in *Koebelismus* than he is. She threw her shoes and stockings into the lake on the first day and heaven knows what she has not discarded since. She now holds a brief for all sorts of things which used to be very *mal vues* in the Woodstock Road, and I heard her this morning talking (a little nervously, I admit) about Sacred Impulses. Not that she makes any claim to such things, as yet, herself. It is the enviable Koebel who must, at all costs, be allowed to have them.

I thought at first that Barny was going to kick. He admires her tremendously, as an artist, but is very much shocked at Louise for bringing her here. But I imagine that Maude has talked him into a kind of surly acquiescence, though what Maude's game is, I do not know. I think she likes to feel that it is upon her tact and forbearance that the peace of the household depends. She makes him play the Koebel's accompaniments, with a bright firmness, which must be galling to Louise. He always begins very sulkily, but wakes up in spite of himself, to a real enthusiasm when the Koebel has sung for a little while.

Still no Dick. Ellen is looking a trifle haggard, and I think she is worried about him. She goes about looking as if she has lost something, and Maude says that he has not written to her for three days. But I may be quite wrong. It may be her condition.

Love,
KERRAN.

Letter from Rosamund

CARA NONNA,—

That is the Italian for grandmother and I am going to call you it because it sounds nice. Thank you for the

Yellow Fairy Book. I love Fairy Stories best. Elissa *believes* in Fairies. She says she sees them. She says she has second sight, and she thinks I have it too. She says it is a great gift, but I will have to pay for it when I grow up because people who are not so sensitive, like Hope, are really happiest. I had a lovely birthday. Mother gave me a book to write my poetry in, and the children gave me a No. 1 Brownie. I have taken a snap of Elissa; she says it is the only photo that has ever been taken of her, and she just did it for *me*. Father gave me a purse and Hope gave me a pin-cushion she made herself, and Aunt Maude gave me *The Imitation of Christ*, by Thomas Akempis. Uncle Barny gave me 2s. 6d., but Uncle Kerran did not give me anything. I had fifteen presents.

Your loving little granddaughter,
ROSAMUND LINDSAY.

Letter from Hope

DEAR GRANDMOTHER,—

Do you like this writing paper? I got it at Xmas, but I save it up for special letters. It has different flowers, but I chose the forget-me-nots because you like blue. We had a very exciting journey; first we went in a train and then in a boat. The island is very exciting. I can swim 100 strokes. I have written some poetry! It is about Madam Kerble, because she would not let me take a snap of her. It is this:

STANZAS WRITTEN IN DEJECTION AT INISHBAR
By Hope Napier

Long have I been a maiden glad.
Long have I lived in this world so sad.
From time to time I have had a grief,
But youth always came to my relief.

But now, alas, my dear one,
Now, alas, my fair one
Has refused my only boon.
I little thought that I so soon
Should know despair!

I wish I had a silent tomb
In a lonely situation.
Where the rustic population
Would come with sighs and gloom
And lay the willow wreath above
And say This Maiden died of love,
She knew despair!

Will you honestly and truly tell me if you think this is
as good as Rosamund's poetry? I will now close as I have
not got any more forget-me-not paper.

With kindest regards,

Yours affectionately,

HOPE.

Letter from Maude

DEAREST MAMMA,—

You will be glad to hear that Barny seems to be
standing the climate here very well. But, oh! How I wish
you were here to help me with him! He wants to go rock-
climbing!!!

Of course I pretend to agree, and say how lovely!
But I have persuaded him to wait till Dick comes, IF
Dick ever does come. (He has stopped writing to Ellen!
But we suppose he is still in London.) Don't you agree
with me that it would be VERY risky? Or am I merely

being fussy? Do write and tell me what line I ought
to take.

Of course I cannot blame him for getting a little bored
here, for there are really *no* interests for him, except of
course the music, which we get almost *more* of than even
he wants. He said to me yesterday—only jokingly of
course—that he never expected to entirely spend his
summer holiday in a conservatoire!

Louise of course is quite taken up with her new *friend*.
You know what I think, Mamma, and I have not changed
my mind about the good lady. I do think somebody
ought to say something. Barny agrees with me absolutely,
and, as he says, we pay part of the rent and we ought to
have some say in who comes here. I find it very difficult
to get him to be polite to her even, but I do want to keep
the peace if I can. Luckily he does not have to see much
of her. I take him off for whole day expeditions. He
thinks that Dick will make a fuss about it, but I am
not so sure.

Kerran and Ellen just laugh at me. They say the whole
thing is platonic because they spend all their time learning
Vurgil. But a woman like that simply couldn't *be* platonic.
You have only to look at her. Barny says she has eyes like
a basilisk, or an odelisk, I forget which, and I am sure that
all the servants are talking. What I mean is there are times
when the very best of men act very strangely. They
cannot help it. Don't you agree with me, Mamma? Even
a man like Gordon is a *man*, I suppose, like everybody else.
I wonder if Louise will find that out to her cost one of
these days. Could you drop her a little hint, perhaps?
Anything *you* say she would listen to. If you said something, sort of joking, that might make her think. It would
be such a dreadful thing, with all the children in the

house, it is too horrible to think of! But when one has had some experience of the seamy side of life, one knows what *can* happen. It would ruin his position, a divorce, I mean. And even if they shared custody of the children, it would never be the same thing.

I can see you smiling at me, ever so wisely, and telling me not to cry "wolf! wolf!" Am I an alarmist? Of course I am! But I do WISH you were here to tell me so! Do send me just one line about what I ought to do. At a word from me Barny would put his foot down. But I do *not* want to wilfully make trouble if I can help it.

Ellen seems to be keeping very well, but I think Dick ought to write to her. But I suppose that is sentimental. You do not say how your rheumatism is. A bulletin in your next letter, please!

Your very loving

MAUDE.

P.S.—I have tried to stir up Barny to write, but you know what he is! I shall not say anything against the climbing idea till Dick comes, as if Dick *doesn't* come, then it will all fall through. Do you think that is wise?

M. A.

Letter from Louise

. . . I have discovered that letter writing is a futile occupation. A letter reflects the mood of the moment and moods change. I feel exquisitely happy to-day, but on Friday, when you read what I have written, I may be feeling wretched and all that I have said will be false.

But I must write, for I feel that some of the others are against me, and I do not know what they are telling you. I want you to understand how inspiring and how beautiful a thing is this influence which has come into my life.

You know I have never been a very happy woman. I live in a prison—a prison where everyone is very kind to me but where I never have room to stretch my wings. I have been cut off from the friendship of people who would have been really sympathetic to me. All that I am asking is that I may take a little holiday from my prison, and from the conventions and insincerities that are stifling me. Here, in this beautiful place, I am able to do so, and to live naturally: not to say this and do that because I *ought*, but because I *wish:* to enjoy the freedom of an intercourse which expresses the "genial current of the soul." Is this too much to ask?

In Elissa Koebel I have found much more than a friend. She is all that I was meant to be, and that I can never be. If I had been brought up in different surroundings, and if I had not been married so young! I do not blame you, Mother. You wanted to see me a happy woman. And I daresay that I am happier than I would have been if I had followed my stars. Some people are destined for tragedy, and if they deny their destiny they must remain, in doing so, unfulfilled.

What has Maude been saying about Elissa? I can well imagine how that narrow, provincial mind must see her. But, Mother, I want you to understand this. Elissa never denies that her life has been unconventional. She has told me a great deal of her experiences and I must say that I find in them much beauty and much tragedy, but nothing which I can dare to blame. Her friendship with Gordon gives me no uneasiness. It is purely intellectual, so much so that we have laughed about it, Elissa and I. And even if there were, as Maude would say, "something in it," what harm would that do? A thing is only wrong if it makes people sad or angry. I do not know that it would make me either sad or angry to know that Gordon was enjoying some beautiful emotional experience. His life has been too parched and academic.

But I know who *will* fall in love with her, and that is Guy Fletcher. They are made for one another, those two, and it will be wonderful to bring them together. I have talked about him a great deal and she is already anxious to see him. She said to me to-day: "I feel that happiness is coming near to me." And I feel so, too. There is a wonderful sense of anticipation in these beautiful days which we all enjoy so much. I am glad that he did not come before, when we were not properly settled into the rhythm of life here. Ellen is perturbed because she has had no letter from him. But I can understand that. He may not be in the mood to write. Dick, I mean.

Your

LOUISE.

Letter from Ellen

DEAREST MOTHER,—

Just a note to tell you that it is all right about Dick. We have had a wire to say that he comes this evening, and I am just off down in the boat to Killross to meet him. I am so relieved.

Your loving

ELLEN.

12

It was not until they got out of the train at Dunclough that Guy Fletcher could be certain. In London he had seen a tall, sandy-haired man hurrying down the platform, a man who might be Dick Napier, but he could not be sure, even when they encountered one another again on the boat. This person was not quite up to the standard of his memories.

They had only met once, at a dinner party in the Woodstock Road. It had been one of those undonnish parties which Louise sometimes succeeded in giving, in spite of her environment. Guy had enjoyed himself and had always looked back upon the occasion as having been a good evening. The conversation had struck him as having something of that range and ease which comes more easily to people who are in touch with the larger world of affairs than to those who live in a narrow and cultured circle. Nothing very brilliant or memorable had been said, but he had felt at the time that Louise was right when she complained that the academic mind is often so unbearably "poky."

It was obvious that she thought the world of her brother-in-law, and Guy, who was something of a hero-worshipper, was inclined to agree with her. Dick Napier was impressive, not only by reason of his formidable good looks, but also because of the amazing self-confidence which expressed itself in everything that he said or did. It was the confidence of a man who knows his own abilities to be so first-rate that he has no need to display them, who can afford to be commonplace and yet hold his own in the pack. Guy was not absolutely sure whether he liked this or not. There was something a little depressing about so much superiority, and he could never imagine himself growing fond of Napier in the way that he was fond of Gordon Lindsay. But he was impressed. Their conversation had given him a sense of value and expansion and he hoped that they might meet again.

But there was nothing of this glamour about the problematic stranger on the journey to Dunclough. Guy took a good look at him on the boat and decided that he must have been mistaken. The two men could not be the same. There was a similarity of build and colouring, but this was altogether a slighter, a less important individual. Also he seemed to be drinking a good deal, and that did not fit in. When he was not morosely prowling round the deck, he was morosely gulping down whisky-and-soda in the bar.

Yet, when they landed, they came on in the same train together.

"If he gets out at Dunclough I shall know," thought Guy.

He did get out at Dunclough. They alighted at that lonely little station together, late in the afternoon, and discovered that no vehicle had been sent to meet them. They would have to walk seven miles into Killross.

Guy ventured to make himself known.

"We met, do you remember, at the Lindsays'?"

Dick nodded. It was possible that he remembered nothing about it, and that he was displeased at the prospect of company on the walk. He explained that he had telegraphed to Inishbar, but that they might not have heard in time, at the island, to send a conveyance up from

Killross. And then it seemed as though he was pulling himself together in an effort to be more civil. He suggested, with a kind of dim geniality, that they might get a drink somewhere before they started.

Guy's heart sank. But it turned out that no drinks could be had in the neighbourhood. Outside the tiny station a desolate road led away across a brown bog. They set off resignedly upon their seven miles' trudge.

It was an uneasy walk. Guy made a few nervous remarks, and he got short, inattentive replies which were not exactly surly but which damped his spirits. Covertly, from time to time, he examined his companion, trying to make out what was wrong and in what way his memory had played him false. He found that he had always thought of Dick Napier as one thinks of an admirable, high-powered machine, and now it was as if the machine was not working. The dynamic quality had left it: the whole personality seemed to have come to a standstill, obscured in a queer kind of frigidity and inertia. The frigidity had been there before, he thought, even at the Lindsay dinner party. It was an unsympathetic nature. But its coldness had been tempered with brilliance, energy and pace. No trace of that agreeable combination was now to be found. The man was "not himself." He was plodding along the road as if he had been walking in his sleep, staring always in front of him into the middle distance as if he expected to see there some obstacle which might force him to turn back. How little he knew of his surroundings was made plain when, after a couple of miles, they came to a bend in the road where a rough cart track ran off in a straight line across the moor. He went straight on over this track, not noticing the turn of the road, and had got some yards away before Guy's shout recalled him.

"Isn't this the road?"

"What?"

He started, stared and came back. Guy realised suddenly and uncomfortably that he was drunk. That was the solution of the whole thing, and a very unpleasant one it was.

He resented it the more because their walk, in other circumstances, would have been so immensely enjoyable. It was exasperating that the central figure in such a scene should be a drunken man. He tried to put Dick out of his mind and to see only the line of hills, indigo against a primrose sunset, and the pale horizons of the sea, of which they caught a glimpse whenever they climbed a hill. The air was soft and melancholy, full of aromatic memories, whiffs of peat smoke and bog myrtle. It was a moment to remember for ever, if only it had not been for this piece of human discord at his side. Discord of any kind was anathema to Guy. It worked in his mind like yeast, fermenting and leavening his whole being until he felt himself almost coming out in a rash with irritation. Things like this were always happening to him. He worshipped beauty, and pursued it, but he was seldom allowed to enjoy it in peace.

"It is not," he reflected, "the world's slow stain that I am afraid of, but the bits of orange peel left on the top of Snowdon."

He had long ago given up all efforts at conversation, but during the last mile or two his companion began to talk. He said suddenly:

"I'm not drunk."

"Of course not," agreed Guy, who feared that he might have reached the truculent stage.

"Merely sleepy. Had a very difficult case. Been out of bed three nights running, counting last night on the boat. Forty-seven hours it lasted. They called me up—let me see, when was it?—in the small hours of Tuesday morning, and as I was anxious I went round at once. I'd been anxious about the case all along, you see. Do you know a man called Ensor Thring? . . . No. I suppose not. He's got influenza."

For a few moments Guy imagined that Ensor Thring must have been the patient, but when Dick began to talk about pregnancy he realised his mistake.

"I'd been worried all the time, you see, weighing the risk of abortion against the risk of this thing flaring up again."

"Oh, yes," said Guy, quickening his pace.

The word abortion was so ugly that he wanted to get away from it, but Dick's long legs were more than a match for his and he had to listen.

"It was an appendix abscess . . . quite a small one . . . and it had ruptured. She was in a bad way when I got there, very thirsty and restless, and speaking in a whisper. I operated at once. She took the anæsthetic well enough, but she had peritonitis. There were a lot of adhesions, and I had to decide how to get proper drainage . . ."

The story, the inexpressibly horrible story, proceeded in a mist of details that were mostly incomprehensible but none the less revolting for that. It went on and it went on. Guy almost began to believe that the operation itself must have lasted for forty-seven hours. He had always felt a morbid aversion for such topics: the sight of blood made him feel sick, and the thought of a human body (perhaps, some day, under an evil star, his own body) being cut up, the inhuman knife ripping through flesh and muscle, was quite intolerable. When obliged to think of it, he had imagined that surgery must be something quick, daring and miraculous, a terrible kind of conjuring trick. It was not a man who did such things, but a pair of hands backed by an unerring brain. But this sounded like a most ghastly muddle. The brain behind the hands had been harassed and frightened, trying this, and seeing that had failed, not infallible at all. And the woman had been pregnant, a thought which could only have beauty, for Guy, when divorced from its physical significance.

Nausea clutched him. He strove to shut his mind, not to listen, but in vain.

"I ought to have risked an operation in the quiescent stage. It would have been possible to drain the abscess without letting the infection get into the abdomen . . ."

This was the worst thing that had ever happened to anybody, this enforced listening, this progress through hell upon hell of uncertainty and defeat. Some time, at some point, this nameless being, "the patient," would die and be out of it. But that was not all. The end was still going on. The end was panic.

Over the last steep hill they struggled. A clear twilight had fallen and they could see below them the quiet lake and the little white town. A few lights had begun to twinkle and thin threads of smoke rose up in the calm air.

"I shall be sick," Guy kept saying to himself. "I shall be sick."

Thring had come back into the story, and he thought now that Thring must be the husband.

"I shall give him the facts, just as I've given them to you. He can make what he likes of them. It doesn't matter what he thinks or what anyone thinks, because

M

they won't get another chance to say I've made a mess of it. I'm not going to make any more. The strain's too much, and I can't stand it. I've known I couldn't, for months. I've been expecting something like this, and I've been saying to myself: 'When it happens, then I'm done for.' I can't stand failure, in the state I've got into. Just lately I haven't been able to tackle the simplest jobs without sweating like a pig. It's been a perfect nightmare. Take Monday. I had a hysterectomy. Ninety-nine times out of a hundred that's one of the easiest . . ."

"Look! There's Killross."

"But this is the end. I shall go into the country and start a chicken farm."

They stumbled in the twilight down the rough road towards the roofs and the scattered lights. A few minutes brought them out on to a little quay where all the male inhabitants of Killross seemed to be standing about in small, murmuring groups. A couple of public-houses did a roaring trade, and towards one of these Dick began to drag his unwilling companion.

"We can get a drink here."

"Hadn't we better see if they've sent the boat?"

Down on the water, a little way off, they could see that a boat was waiting. Two fishermen were resting on their oars and in the stern there sat a woman in a hat, not a country woman. Dick, as he caught sight of it, fairly took to his heels and bolted into a doorway.

"That's my wife," he muttered. "She's come to meet us. Look here, Fletcher . . . " he clutched Guy's arm. . . . "I'll get a drink and come on later. I'll get one of these chaps to row me up. But you go, and you tell her what I've told you. I can't do it. Tell her everything."

He fled into the inn and left the protesting Guy outside.

Guy thought that the people in the waiting boat had seen them. It drew nearer and a call came from the woman in the stern.

"Dick!" her voice came over the water. "Is that you?"

"It's Guy Fletcher, Mrs. Napier."

"Oh, how do you do? Is my husband there?"

"Yes. But he's coming later. We've to go on without him."

"But . . ."

The boat bumped against a little flight of steps and he clambered down beside her. The population of Killross all gathered at the edge of the quay to watch them push off.

"But I thought I saw him. Where is he? Why . . ."

"He asked me to tell you that he's coming later. To explain. He doesn't want us to wait for him."

The oars splashed and they drew away from the quay and its lights, and the murmuring knots of men.

"He has bad news," explained Guy in a low voice. "And he told me to tell you. A patient has died . . ."

"Mrs. Briggs!"

"He never told me her name. I thought it was Thring."

Ellen seemed puzzled by this, but she said at last:

"No, no! It must be Mrs. Briggs. Thring was the doctor in charge of the case, and he asked Dick . . . was it a woman with appendicitis?"

"Oh, then you knew all about it!"

"Only that Dick was very . . . and she's dead! What happened?"

"He operated too late."

"I see. Does he . . . does he think it was his fault?"

"I think so. Yes."

"Is he very much upset?"

"Horribly."

"O-o-oh . . ."

It was a long sigh that she gave. She said no more.
There was silence save for the splashing and creak of oars.

He felt that she knew, had grasped the whole story,
which Dick had told him. And in her silence, as she sat
beside him in the boat, she communicated to him that
mood of overwhelming sadness, that resignation which
comes immediately after some terrible disaster, before the
mind has had time to recover from its shock and to
resist.

He knew her better than he knew Dick, for he had met
her several times at the Lindsays'. He admired her
extravagantly, even more that he admired Louise. There
was something in her gentle voice and blonde dignity
which very nearly raised her to his ideal of what a
woman should be. She filled a niche in his mind which
had been empty until they met. At the end of the avenues
of his thought he would often see her strolling, as she
had once strolled over the grass in New College Garden
on an afternoon in May; a gentle, gracious creature in a
white dress, living for ever in a garden. And he had
always known that, in the face of disaster, her stillness
would prevail. No discord could ever touch her, and no
discord could touch him when he was with her. He left
off feeling sick. The painful story, which he had been
obliged to hear, was over at last, and the drunken panic
was over. He had left it behind him with Dick in Killross.

The world was very terrible: it was full of sad things,
ill done. A dead woman, a fine career cut short, how
many times before had this not happened? He thought of
it remotely, philosophically, like some book that he had
read.

There was nothing to disturb or exasperate him in Ellen's silence, her long sigh. Only he felt that he would never again be able to think of sorrow without re-living this moment of twilight and peace, as they crossed the lake, towards a clear star trembling above the trough of the haunted glen.

It was too dark to see more of the island than a vague mass of shadows, travelling nearer. Lights began to shine among the trees, and there was an imperceptible current of sound in the air. It quickened into music.

"But what is that?" asked Guy. "Isn't it someone singing?"

Ellen roused herself and said that it was probably Madame Koebel, and indeed he had recognised that voice himself almost before the words were out of her mouth.

"Koebel? Elissa Koebel?"

"Yes. This is the landing stage. Can you see? There's a path goes here up the slope."

She led him up to the north gate, and the singing grew fainter, for it came from the windows on the west side of the castle. He could hear, instead, the soft whisper of the wind among the trees, a new sound after his long walk across the bare mountains. Ellen was fumbling at the gate, which had been shut and barred.

"How tiresome!" she exclaimed. "They can't have told the servants to leave it open for us. And there's no bell. We must go round and shout through the drawing-room window."

He followed her, under the dark walls and round a tower, to the little terrace which ran along beneath the three great windows on the western side, overlooking the lake. They were all open to the warm night and they were set low in the wall, so that he could see through them into the great caverns of the room. He caught sight of the back of Gordon's head, glimmering like a white egg. An unseen piano was playing a soft prelude.

"We'll wait till she's finished," whispered Ellen.

The sweet voice rose up again and Guy lent against the wall to listen.

Du bist die Ruh
Der Friede Mild!

It was unbelievable! For this was the air which had always drifted through his mind when he thought of Ellen. It was the image of Ellen made into music, of that stillness and calm which could heal the wounds of the spirit. To that image, to that tranquillity, he could for ever return and be safe. Completely happy he stood at the window and listened, thinking of the shadowy lake and the star hanging low in the east, and Ellen's sigh. He wished that this moment would last for ever.

At the end of the first verse he went on a little way down the terrace and saw through the next window the clear profile of Louise bent eagerly forward. It was too eager, too uncalm. Still he could not see the singer or the piano, so he went on to the third window and blinked a little as the glare of the candles fell upon his eyes. At the tall white column that must be Elissa Koebel he blinked still more. For here again was orange peel on the top of Snowdon, and by his own restlessness he had put an end to the moment which he had desired to preserve. He should have stayed still by the first window, contemplating only the top of Gordon's head.

Upon her face there was an expression of sensuous rapture. He hated expressions of rapture. There was too much of her. She was too tall and too white, her hair was too long and her eyes too large. Yet he could not look away, any more than he could shut his ears to Dick's story. She had ruined the beauty of his mood and he was quite helpless.

Good heavens! What a woman!

He could scarcely have told why it was that he detested her so immediately, and why she seemed so evil to him. Of her beauty he was scarcely aware, for he had come from beauty of another sort. Snatched from an excess of spiritual rapture, he could only see in that face and form the incarnation of unrestrained sensuality, the symbol of that discord between the body and the soul which had always been his greatest torment. And the song, which had so entranced him, took on a new meaning now that he could see her. It became unholy as the song of Circe, luring her victims to a brutish end. Yet he must stare and listen, until the dreadful moment came when she saw him there, returned his gaze with a wanton leer, and sang, he was convinced, directly at him. That was too much. He fled and rejoined Ellen, who was standing at the end of the terrace, looking out intently over the water.

"Isn't that a boat coming?" she asked.

It was. The splash of oars drew nearer.

"It's Dick," she said quickly. "Mr. Fletcher, will you please say nothing to the others about this . . . about what has happened. It will be worse if they know."

And she called, low and clear:

"Dick!"

"Hullo-o-o-o!"

The answer came back across the hidden water, from all the mountain sides. In the castle the music had stopped. There was a clamour of voices and Louise, carrying a candle, appeared at one of the windows.

"Is that Dick? Has Dick come?"

"Yes. We've come. But, Louise, the gate is shut."

From far, far away, perhaps from the Haunted Glen itself, came the last ghostly echo:

"Hullo-o-o-o!"

13

THE noise and bustle, the coming and going in the castle yard, the hasty preparation of a meal, all this gave Ellen time. Dick had been clever. Or perhaps merely fortunate. Nobody knew that he had not arrived with Guy Fletcher and herself. It was not likely that anyone to-night would take her aside and ask what was the matter with him. The two men, eating cold meat in the hall, were mere belated travellers, and the household were too busy beholding them as such to perceive that something was very wrong with one of them. She would have time, before to-morrow, to stave off questions by supplying facts in advance.

She must tell them that poor Mrs. Briggs was dead, and that Dick was very sad about it, because they had been his friends. Coming from a heartrending scene, his spirits were not, perhaps, quite as good as usual. Doctors have to live through very sad things sometimes, but it is much worse for them when the people are personal friends. Dick had been so fond of Dr. Briggs.

She was very much frightened, and fear had quickened her imaginative powers to an unusually vivid degree. She saw that the real trouble must never be known. Dick must not be shut up in this narrow place with a lot of people who knew what was on his mind. The island was so small, the castle so constricted, that an idea, a suggestion, could grow and flourish there like a plant in a hothouse. It would receive strength from every mind which harboured it, and from every comment made upon it. It would grow in the daytime, in the enforced publicity of their life, and it would grow secretly at night when they all retired to their several turrets and talked things over. The suggestion would come back and back at Dick, who had first made it, like the echoes of his shout on the lake. This was the worst place for him to be in, at such a crisis. They must not say or think that he had lost his nerve, that he blamed himself, and that he was playing with the idea of retirement. If they said it, or thought it, the thing was much more likely to happen.

The danger piled up before her, rising and curving like the crest of a huge wave. But it had not yet broken. It was still merely a thought in Dick's mind. She might still, by some heroic effort of will, defy it and make it turn backward. She must cling to her faith in Dick; the immovable belief that this calamity was not his fault and that only overstrain could have brought about that wavering of moral courage which attacks all sensitive people in positions of responsibility. She must imbue him with her faith; she must be for him an extra source of strength. And she must keep the others at bay.

Convinced of the need to act quickly, she left the hall, where Gordon and Barny were watching the travellers eat, and went out into the courtyard. A good deal was happening there. Maids were running about with blankets for a bed that was to be made up for Guy Fletcher in Kerran's room. Lights twinkled from windows on all sides of the little quadrangle and people hurried from one door to another.

Louise was sitting on the edge of the well in the middle, quite obviously remote from all this humdrum bustle. Ellen went up to her at once.

"Oh, Louise . . ."

"Elissa has gone. She wouldn't stay to be introduced to-night, but she's coming early to-morrow."

"Louise, poor Dick has had such a sad time. One of his patients, one of Dr. Thring's patients, has died. He's so much distressed . . ."

"Good gracious! Is this the first time he's ever had a patient die?"

"No, but these people were personal friends."

"Oh, who?"

When Ellen explained the status of Dr. Briggs, Louise jerked her head impatiently.

"I thought you meant somebody I know. I'm sure it's very good of Dick . . ."

"But I wanted to explain why he's in such low spirits. Will you just not talk about it. And tell Gordon and the others not to either."

"My dear Ellen! Do I ever encourage 'shop'?"

"No. I know. But the sooner he forgets about it the sooner he'll be able to enjoy it all here."

"I have some tact. Is that Muffy? Oh, Muffy! Don't shut the big gate because Madame Koebel is coming early to-morrow, early before breakfast . . ."

And that was the best that could be done with Louise. But it would be safer to speak to Maude as well, so as to make sure that the authorised version had been published in both towers. Ellen hurried into the keep. She was afraid of Maude and of Maude's intuitions. She pulled herself together for a battle when she heard Maude say:

"Oh! Poor Dick!"

(Not poor Mrs. Briggs, but poor Dick!)

"They were such great friends, he and Dr. Briggs. Dr. Briggs was Dick's best man . . ."

"I know. And they do so hate losing baby cases, don't they? It's the responsibility. They hate it like poison if anything goes wrong. I suppose they feel that a woman having a baby isn't just like some idiot who's gone and got ill. At least, a doctor friend of mine once put it that way to me. He said that's why so many of them won't take baby cases. It isn't the work, it's the worry."

There were so many things to annoy Ellen in this comment that she lost count of them. For one thing, why must all the family, even Maude, who had some medical experience, believe that Dick spent his time doing what they called "baby cases"? Could they really not grasp the difference between gynæcology and obstetrics? But since Dick was always complaining that he had the same difficulty with the lay committee of the hospital she must perhaps make allowances.

"This wasn't a confinement," she explained. "It was appendicitis. But it's so terrible for poor Dr. Briggs . . ."

Maude nodded understandingly, and then exploded another mine.

"Such a pity! Especially just now."

"Just now?"

"You're the last person he'll want to unburden himself to about it, I should think. I do hope to goodness it won't start him off worrying about you. It does sometimes."

"About me? What nonsense. I'm perfectly well."

"Oh, yes. But I mean he'd much better forget about babies and baby cases for a bit, so it's a pity . . . I beg your pardon, Muffy? What did you say?"

Muffy, who was stooping over a chest of blankets, had said something which sounded like *fiddle*. But at Maude's question she had an attack of deafness, and made no reply at all. Maude's smile grew wider and wider.

"I wish you wouldn't go on about *baby cases*," said Ellen irritably. "Obstetrics is only a very small part—I think he says about five per cent—of all Dick's important work. He . . ."

"I know. But this woman was going to have a baby, wasn't she?"

"Yes. But she . . ."

"And you're going to have a baby. That's all I meant. It'll be more difficult for him to forget . . ."

Ellen fled into the courtyard.

What nonsense Maude talked! Dick never worried about her. Her condition could not possibly come between them in this matter. It was absurd. She was with child, and another woman, also with child, had died. But it was not possible that these two ideas could have any sort of connection in Dick's troubled mind.

The mere suggestion was a shock and made her feel suddenly self-conscious. To face any other people that night was more than she could manage. She went quickly across the quadrangle to her own tower, took a candle from the shelf at the bottom of the staircase, and went up to the quietness and order of her cold bedroom.

Here, reassuringly, she had all her own things about her. Her brushes and combs were disposed neatly on the dressing-table. The two beds, side by side, were turned down and ready. Across one of them lay her night-dress, with its freshly-laundered frills of Swiss embroidery. Across the other lay an ornamental pair of pyjamas, borrowed from Kerran until Dick's luggage could be brought from Dunclough. She felt a moment of happiness and hope at the sight. At least, she had got him near her again. Whatever he had suffered during their separation he would at least have some solace and companionship now.

Bed, she thought, was a very good invention. Being married would be much more difficult if one did not go to bed every night. For twelve years now she had been going to bed with Dick, and she could not remember what it had felt like to sleep contentedly alone. They liked being near to one another. They liked falling asleep and waking up in one another's company. Reason and argument might fail them sometimes, but the marriage bed remained, a symbol of the unexpressed affection and loyalty which bound them together, of the delight which they took in one another, a passion which would live on, after they were dead, in the bodies of their children. "That side of marriage," her mother had called it, when, shamefacedly, and with difficulty, she had broached the subject to her growing daughters. But her mother had been wrong. Going to bed was not at the side at all; it was plumb in the middle of everything.

Quickly, and shivering a little because the room was cold, she undressed herself and put on the long, frilly night-dress, with its collar that buttoned up closely round her neck. When Dick came up and knocked, she was brushing her hair in front of the glass.

Almost before he had shut the door behind him he began asking her about the children, plying her with questions so fast that she scarcely got time to answer. But he did not look at her, and the quiet of the room was shattered by a desolate uneasiness. While he talked he rapidly undressed, splashed his head in the wash-basin, put on Kerran's pyjamas and climbed into bed. She plaited back her hair neatly and went round to sit beside him.

"You can't think," she began, almost shyly, "how horrid it's been here without you."

He did look at her then, for a moment, long enough to let her see the fear in his eyes. And then he looked away, saying something quite meaningless about being glad, himself, to have got away from London.

Ellen felt quite giddy, as if she had been in a lift that was going down too fast. For it seemed to her almost as if there had been dislike as well as fear in the look he had given her. She thought:

"He doesn't love me any more."

But then she knew that this was not true. He was only determined not to speak of his trouble and he was afraid that she would force him to do so. Perhaps it was because she already knew too much. Or perhaps it was that thing that Maude had said:

"You're the last person . . ."

Could that be true? She groped dimly for the sequence, understanding and yet not able to state it.

"He doesn't want to think about me . . . to be near me . . . because of the child . . ."

Not because another woman was dead, but because he had lost courage. He would not take upon himself, any more, the responsibility of seeing that other women did not die. Other women, and Ellen among them, must depend upon the wit and courage of men who were not afraid of such a burden. Stupid men, perhaps; inferior to Dick in skill. But able to carry their part in the heavy burden of the world's work, able to give their best, while Dick's so much finer best must rot unused. These were better men than Dick, and he knew it. A world peopled with Dicks would be a sorry place: it was the Clarkes and the Things who really mattered.

And he was afraid that she knew this. He was afraid she would despise him because he had failed, not merely to save Mrs. Briggs, but to survive a defeat to his own vanity. And how large a part had that vanity played in this power which he had of impressing himself upon the world?

Well . . . they were going to find out.

There was nothing that she could say. He would have to settle this for himself. It was his fence. If he could take it, then everything would be quite all right between them. If he could not, then nothing would ever make it right again. She loved him and she would always love him, but she would have to learn to be ashamed of him.

Without another word she rose and went over to wedge the window which was rattling a little. Then she knelt down beside her own bed to say her prayers. She repeated to herself the Lord's Prayer, the Collect for the week, and the formula which she had used every night since her confirmation. And then, incoherently, she began to implore for help, burying her face in the quilt which had grown wet with her tears. She asked that strength might be given to Dick, that she might be made able to think of something sensible to say, that something might happen to take all this off his mind; that Louise might not find out, that Dr. Thring should write and say that he would have done just the same, and that Dick might consent to go and see a neurologist in the autumn.

"But Lord, Thou knowest how much he would hate explaining it all to another doctor . . ."

Corbett would be the best man to go to. Dick liked him and believed in him as much as he believed in any of them. If only . . . but she was supposed to be praying.

She tried to collect her thoughts, and found that the worst thing had happened, for she was quite sure that nobody had listened. It had been a vague fear for some time, and now it had become a conviction. She was an atheist. She believed neither in the Committee of Four nor in that other, remoter, Deity, to whom she had never tried to pray.

She rose from her knees, blew out the candle and got into bed.

"Good night, Dick."

Her voice was flat and weary. Dick's answer came out of the darkness:

"Good night, dear."

As she lay there a certain comfort returned to her. She became once more aware of the passage of time. Soon they would go to sleep and to-morrow they would wake up, and new things, all sorts of things, might come into their lives, so that nothing would turn out as they had expected. And, anyhow, this moment would not go on for ever. It would be over sometime; it would be in the past. She must fortify herself against it as if it had been physical pain, like childbirth or toothache. It must be lived through.

"I must just get along as best I can," she thought, as she curled up her cold toes in her night-gown. "It's no use worrying. Anything may happen, not just the things one is afraid of. I must do the best I can and not worry. Keep them off him if I can. Not speak about it till he wants to. Let him see he's quite safe about that. If he isn't any better by the end of the summer, remember there's always Corbett. And not bother any more about God. This is no moment to worry about that. I'll think all that out later on sometime. If I'm an atheist, and it

N

looks like it, well, I must just be one. Much better if only I can manage not to think. If I start thinking I shall make mistakes. I've thought enough. I've made up my mind what to do, and now I must stop thinking and do it. Now I ought to go to sleep. That's the next thing. I'll count sheep through a gap . . ."

She fell asleep very soon after.

Dick, in the darkness, turned and tossed and wondered if she was still awake, and if he had hurt her, and if he was now as low a thing in her eyes as he was in his own.

14

ELISSA KOEBEL was as good as her word, for she came very early next morning. The life of the courtyard had scarcely begun and most of the party were still up in their towers. From the kitchen quarters came faint sounds of activity, but an early morning stillness lay upon the little paved square, with its well in the middle, and the empty doorways, and the pigeons fluttering about the grey battlements.

This stillness was very soon broken by Elissa. She perched herself upon the edge of the well and began to warble folk-songs in the clear mountain voice of the Sennerin:

> *Ich grüsse dich*
> *Zehn tausend mal!*
> *Du himmelschöne Ziller Thal!*

The rousing echoes were flung from wall to wall, and the pigeons rose up in a startled flock. Nor were the castle towers quite impervious to sound. The slit windows on the stairs let in a great deal of Elissa's yodelling.

In the keep all the children were just getting up. They began joyfully to yodel, too, until Muffy had to say:

"For goodness' sake . . . if you must sing, sing properly."

Louise and Gordon turned to one another with infatuated smiles, as they leapt out of bed and began to dress.

"Another golden day," murmured Gordon.

"It's too good to be true," said Louise. "And to-day they are really going to meet at last."

A faint chill descended upon Gordon's rapture. He was not so very anxious to see Elissa falling in love with Guy Fletcher. To his mind they all did very well as they were.

Maude and Barny were having a scene in the bedroom and spared very little attention to the yodelling outside.

"You might have let me know how you felt about it before," Barny was saying. "I thought you quite approved."

"I didn't want to annoy you. I thought if I really let you know how nervous I should be, and then Dick didn't come, and the whole plan fell through, I should just have annoyed you for nothing."

"I've written for my boots and climbing tackle. You seemed quite enthusiastic . . . I can't understand . . ."

"I know, darling. Of course you must go. I've no business to be nervous. I must learn to get over it. Only will you just not tell me when you do go? If I don't know you're doing it, then I can't be frightened. You just slip off and climb if you want to, and I shan't know till it's over, so I shall be spared all those awful visions of you lying with your back broken at the bottom of a precipice."

"Of course I shan't go if you feel like that about it," said Barny coldly. "Only I do think you might have. . . . Good God! Is that damned woman here already?"

"Barny!"

"I beg your pardon, Maude. But I do wish you'd say what you mean or mean what you say. It's impossible ever to know where one is with you. I quite thought . . ."

"Oh, now you're cross! How dreadful!"

"No, I am *not* cross. I only . . ."

> "*O Hojo! Ho-jo! Ho-jo!*
> *Mein Heimatland, Tirol!*
> *Tirol!*
> *Mein Heimatland, Tirol!*"

"Oh, Tirol my backside!"

"Barny, you're disgusting! How can you say you're not cross?"

Over in the other tower, Guy Fletcher and Kerran both woke up with a jerk. Their first emotion was one of discomfort upon beholding one another, for they disliked having to share a room. Kerran's prosperous pink face peered cautiously over the blanket at Guy's pale square one. And then they realised what it was that had roused them.

"Does she come every day?" asked Guy appalled.

"She does."

"Good heavens!"

They said no more, but for the first time in their lives a small spark of sympathy began to flicker between them.

Dick, in the room below, was the only person to be taken by surprise. He was already up and had begun to shave. When Elissa gave tongue he started violently and asked:

"What the devil is that?"

Ellen, who was only half awake, said drowsily that it must be Madame Koebel.

"You know! I told you about her. I wrote about her."

She sat up in bed and rubbed her eyes. And then, as their unhappy plight came back to her, she gave him a quick, anxious look. He turned away at once. In the shaving glass he saw that he had scratched his chin, and as he dabbed at the cut with a towel he swore under his breath. This propinquity, and these loving anxious looks, were more than he could bear.

"Did you write about her? I forget."

Ellen's letters were undramatic, and he had had no accounts of Elissa save from her. He now learnt for the first time of her friendship with Louise, and he was greatly surprised.

"What is she like?" he wanted to know.

Ellen reflected.

"She's queer. She's quite interesting. I mean, she seems to have travelled about a good deal and seen a lot. And I must say she does sing beautifully."

"But all this about her being such a rake, I mean? Is that all moonshine? I suppose it must be, or Louise wouldn't have her here. Or Gordon either."

"Oh!" said Ellen, opening her eyes very wide. "I don't know. Maude thinks it isn't. Not moonshine, I mean. She thinks Louise is making a terrible mistake. And she thinks that Madame Koebel is . . . is drawing off Gordon."

"Drawing off!"

Dick began to laugh, both at the idea and at Ellen's idiom. It was with a briskened sense of anticipation that he finished dressing and went down into the courtyard. His attention had been diverted by this unexpected little drama, and he felt that the presence of Elissa in the castle might make everything a great deal easier than he had expected.

He wanted to get out of the room and away from Ellen. All night he had kept on repeating to himself that it was impossible to remain shut up with her like this. He ought never to have come to Inishbar. He ought to go away. But his will to do anything seemed to have vanished. If he could make the effort to go he might equally make the greater effort, pull himself together, and put this dark interlude behind him. Both courses required a moral struggle.

"Thank heaven for Madame Koebel," he thought.

Louise and Gordon were both in the courtyard already, and they too were sitting on the edge of the well. They were examining the peasant dress which Elissa had put on that morning. She, it seemed, was in an earthy mood. She had assumed the full, homespun petticoat and the shawl worn by the barefoot women of Killross, and her golden braids were wound neatly round her head. She would sing nothing but *Volksliede*. Even her face seemed to have broadened, to have become rosier and more bucolic. She radiated good humour and physical well-being, laughed loudly, swung her slender bare feet to and fro, and stared about her with the unabashed, animal liveliness of the comely savage. Gordon and Louise, who knew how she loved to dramatise every rôle, admired and applauded. When they presented Dick they both looked at him anxiously, as if to demand his instant appreciation. But it was impossible ever to know what Dick thought of anybody. His long, cold face had about as much expression as a block of granite. He returned Elissa's bold survey with one short, but observant glance, and sat down without a word upon the wall beside her.

She said smiling:

"But we have met before."

He could not remember that they had, but he did not trouble to deny it. In one way it was perfectly true. He had met her before. There had been something of her in every woman who had ever roused his sensuality. And he had no doubt but that she had met him before, frequently, in other men. Their understanding, on that point, was complete. It had been instantaneous.

Her strange, wild eyes, that unabashed regard which had given Kerran such a turn, held a message which could not be mistaken. He looked at the rest of her, swiftly, and flashed his own message back.

Now he sat beside her on the wall, and marvelled, with mingled relief and dismay, at his own amazing insensibility. She had turned away from him and was talking in German to Louise, but he knew that she was aware of him with every nerve in her body. She was his for the taking: he was perfectly certain of that. And he did not want her. The inertia which had brought him to Inishbar, which was going to keep him there, had put a bridgeless gulf between them. He was too sick at heart to want anything or anybody. He was as safe from all carnal desires as St. Simon on the top of his pillar.

And he thought, sardonically amused, of her fury when she should find this out. For his message, flashed in that instant of greeting, had been an impudent deception. He would not have sent it if he had not known that he was safe. If he had not been safe he would not have been there at all. He was not likely to betray his poor Ellen in this particular way because he was betraying her in every other way. He was allowing his life, and hers, to go to pieces. If the spectacle of her misery last night could not reclaim him, then his case was surely hopeless.

"No, no, my dear," he mentally informed the lady at his side. "I'm a good husband. You just wait and see what a good husband I am!"

But the imagined diversion of this dialogue was not to last for long. The commonplace features of his colleague,

Ensor Thring, peered sideways round a corner at him. He heard Thring's neat little voice saying something, just not audible. It was Thring's face and Thring's voice which would haunt him for ever. He could forget a woman's face, rigid in death. He could forget the sobs of a desolate husband. But there would still be Thring, squinting at him sideways, whispering inaudible things: and in the white glare, the suffocating heat of the theatre (he felt a wrench of nausea when he thought of that light and the heat) there would be myriads of Thrings: Thring on the table, Thring giving the anæsthetic, Thring's face squinting under a nurse's cap, Thring whispering and pushing in the students' gallery. . . .

He sought, with shaking hands, in his pocket for a pipe and a tobacco pouch. Elissa, aware of the movement, turned round to look at him.

"You are very sad this morning," she said. "Why is that?"

Already she was aware of something amiss. She had discovered the gulf across which their messages had flown and now she was running up and down, in search of a bridge. Poor Elissa!

Louise interposed, exclaiming:

"Here is Guy Fletcher."

She jumped up and went to meet the reluctant Guy, who had just appeared at the door of his tower staircase. Gordon followed her more slowly, wishing in secret that Guy Fletcher were somewhere else. For a few seconds Dick and Elissa were left to wage their silent battle by the well.

Elissa's eyes said:

"But how is this? How is this?"

"Find out."

"Am I not desirable?"

"You are."

"Then you must take me or run away from me."

"Not at all. I don't want you."

"You do."

"I do not."

"I am stronger than you."

"Are you? We shall see."

"Quite right, my friend. We shall see. In the end you will either take me or run away from me."

Thring's voice filled up the silence with an inaudible comment, and Louise brought up Guy Fletcher to be introduced. Those eyes which Barny had said were like a basilisk or an odalisk—Maude could not remember which —were turned for a moment in Guy's direction. Dick watched, as he filled his pipe, and saw how Guy shied like a nervous horse. He thought:

"That's what I ought to have done. There, but for a touch of *accidie*, goes Dick Napier."

15

ELLEN might have spared herself a great deal of anxiety, for nobody asked what had happened to Dick. Nobody, indeed, saw anything amiss with him. On the very first day he took his place among the Vergil reading group, and he perversely insisted upon tackling that passage in Book X of the Æneid, which gives particulars of the Lydian fleet. Louise and Elissa, assured by him that Professor Grier had said this was one of the finest passages in the whole poem, waded obediently through the long list of ships and men, noted that Ilva is an island, rich in the Chalybes unexhausted mines, and that not all the sons of Mantua were of the same blood. They would rather have stuck to Dido, but they were afraid of admitting this, and thought well of themselves for being able to appreciate so virile a theme.

The Elissa epoch was at its zenith and even the powers of Nature herself seemed to smile upon the idyll. Day after day the sun travelled slowly across a cloudless sky. It was shining when they woke up in the mornings, and they lived in its benign radiance from dawn to dusk. The island echoed with happy voices, the laughter of children, song and music, and the splash of oars. Louise could feel that her ideal existence had come into being. At last she had escaped from the Woodstock Road. She was living in a world of elfin beauty, she had friends and laughter and song, days of endless sunshine, long, tender twilights, a whole procession of enchanted moments. The barometer in the gate house was set at fair. Maude saw to the housekeeping. There seemed to be no reason why this pleasant dream should ever stop. For more than a week she was able to forget that it could not go on for ever.

And even when she did remember that time passes, it was to experience an emotion of poetic sadness. She did not envisage the return to Oxford in the autumn. She could imagine no middle distance, only a far, romantic future when, in a passionless reverie, she might look back at these days of her vitality and youth. That future had a sentimental link with the present, and she could face it without rebellion—even yield herself to its mood when Elissa, who had discovered a copy of *Moore's Melodies* in the drawing-room music cabinet, warbled such airs as *Oft in the Stilly Night* and *The Harp That Once*, full of a plangent regret for the past. Louise, listening, knew that she too might some day "*feel as one who treads alone some banquet hall deserted.*" When Elissa was singing she could never see the future in less noble terms.

Gordon, to some extent, shared these feelings. He said to her one night as they were dressing for dinner:

"The poetry of Thomas Moore, though inferior in many respects, is singularly expressive of certain moods, don't you think? Or is that merely another tribute to the genius of our friend? I should never have believed it possible to find myself in tears at such a song as *The Last Rose of Summer*."

"I cried too," agreed Louise. "I thought how we shall all grow old and how we shall look back on these days."

"Yet it is little more than a sentimental drawing-room ballad. As an air it would not have been worthy of Schubert, as poetry how vastly inferior, even in crystallisation of a single mood, to Heine! But I was more

deeply moved by it than by anything that Elissa has sung.
And I ask myself if this moving quality, the touch of an
emotion which has something universal in it, is all hers, or
if some of the credit should not be given to the poet.
Was Moore a better poet than I have always supposed?
That last verse:

> And so may I follow,
> When friendships decay!
> And from love's shining circle
> The gems drop away! . . ."

He broke off, shaking his head. This was certainly not
good poetry, he thought. The words were commonplace, but they had moved him. Was it because the man
who wrote them had been sincere, or had it merely been
some accent in Elissa's voice? Or was it because these
lines were so appropriate, because it seemed to him
nowadays as though he formed part of "love's circle"
himself?

He saw the future more clearly than did Louise. He
knew that after this summer there would be the Michael-
mas term, the falling leaves, the lecture room and the
smell of dust on books. The thought made him feel old
and tired and regretful. It plunged him into melancholy.
He nodded sadly when Louise said:

"Oh, if only it could last for ever!"

"We have been very lucky," he said. "At least I
consider myself to have been so. And I owe it to you, my
dear. You brought us here. You brought our little circle
together. I shall be grateful to you for this summer as
long as I have power to remember anything."

"Dear Gordon . . ."

"I don't know how to tell you . . . this happiness . . ."

He found himself unable to speak, and there were tears in his eyes. He took her hand and kissed her.

"We have never understood one another so well," he said. "This happiness has brought us together."

"I know."

"And for our . . . our friend, too, I think it has been a happy chance. We have been able to give something to her in return for all that she has given to us."

Louise sighed.

"If only she would fall in love with Guy!"

"No, Louise! Don't say that! We are very well as we are. Friendship is such a beautiful thing. Why should you want to break the circle . . . love's shining circle?"

"It wouldn't break it. It would draw us all closer together."

"We couldn't," said Gordon anxiously, "be closer than we are. Don't, Louise! Don't want to change things."

But Louise was not convinced, and as the days went on she began to grow impatient. At last she tackled Elissa.

"Don't you think Guy Fletcher is very attractive?" she asked.

Elissa shook her head.

"But brilliant, certainly. Attractive? No! For attraction there must be some magnetism, some electric current of sympathy. I find that there is no current. Not any current at all. I cannot say that he attracts me."

"I am so fond of him," pleaded Louise.

"My dearest friend," said Elissa, softly caressing her arm, "you are fond of everybody. It is a wonderful gift. But in this case I think it means that you pity him.

He is so cold, so timid, so . . . how shall I say it . . . so afraid of life. One feels that he is saying *No!* all the time to life. Just like that. 'No, no, no! Do not touch me!' He will not live. He will not feel. He is afraid. It is *Il Gran Rifuto.*"

"I know what you mean."

"He is like . . ." Elissa searched among her stock of English idioms and continued triumphantly, " . . . he is like a cat on hot bricks! I can only admire asceticism if it springs from passion. If it springs from timidity I despise it. I could never find that type attractive. No, no! It is not Guy Fletcher whom I would choose from among your delightful friends."

She said this with so much emphasis that Louise was startled. For a second their eyes met, questioningly, and then Elissa continued:

"Aha! Let us speak candidly, you and I! You say that you are fond of him, but you do not yourself feel any attraction. It is nothing to you if he is in the room or if he is not in the room. You do not always hear him when he speaks. Your pulses do not run more quickly if he has touched you."

"I should hope they don't," said Louise rather sharply.

"That is what I call attraction. You must feel it yourself. Oh, yes. But we are alike, you and I. We are alike in many ways, in our love for what is beautiful and in our admiration for what is passionate, what is virile. I think, among our friends here, there is only one man who has called to the woman in us."

"Elissa! What . . . what do you mean?"

"Is it possible that . . . but that is hypocritical! It is not like you. When he first came here, that night when you were rushing to the window, what did I see? I saw a changed woman. My little captive bird was transformed. She was free. She was trembling with emotion. 'Oh, it is Dick! He is come!' Could I mistake those accents? It is Sieglinde, I said to myself.

"Elissa, how can you? How dare you? You don't know what you're saying. You are joking and I don't like it."

"Do not deceive yourself. You never speak of him in the voice that you use for other people. Your eyes, your whole manner, betray you. Even before he came I knew that you loved him. But I can understand you so well. It is an emotion that I can share. You ask me if I find Guy Fletcher attractive and I tell you, no. You ask me if I find your brother attractive and I tell you, yes. A thousand times, yes! I would gladly . . ."

"Elissa, stop! You must stop. You're wrong. You're quite, quite wrong. To begin with he isn't my brother. He isn't my brother at all. He's my brother-in-law. Don't you understand? He's no relation at all. He's my sister's husband. Ellen's husband. He's married to Ellen. Ellen is my sister."

Elissa brushed this aside. She had never mastered the exact relationships of the Annesley tribe.

"But that is not to say that you do not love him. We both love him. Is not that so?"

"No. It isn't so. I don't. How could I love my sister's husband? And you mustn't, mustn't say such things. You can't be serious . . ."

Now it was Elissa's turn to look offended.

"Upon this subject I am always serious. To me it is sacred."

"I don't see anything sacred about proposing to fall in love with a married man!"

"*Liebchen*, do not be so heated! I do not propose to fall in love with him. I have already done so. You ask me which among our party I love and I say your brother. I did not ask that it should be so. In these things, as in art, we are inspired. And I think that, if you were frank, you also would admit . . ."

"No, I shouldn't. No, I shouldn't."

"You say that because you are shut up in your prison. You dare not live face to face with the truth, as I do."

Louise was so flurried and beset by so many emotions, all of them disagreeable, that she hardly knew what she was doing or saying. She could not make up her mind which idea revolted her most: that she should be in love with Dick or that Elissa should.

"You must think I have no decency at all," she cried.

Elissa put a gentle hand on her arm.

"Dearest Louise, do not be so angry. I have spoken too frankly. You must forgive me."

"It's so shocking . . . so horrible of you to suggest . . ."

"Let us then forget this conversation. I admit that I should not have spoken at all. Even between friends there are some things which should only be admitted by silence."

"But I don't admit . . ."

"I know, I know. For me it is possible to speak of these things, but not for you. I respect your silence. My dearest friend, forgive me. You are looking so beautiful this morning. I don't wish to quarrel with anyone who looks so beautiful. I will unsay everything. And now let us go and find the children. I have promised to tell them fairy stories."

o

Elissa embraced her flurried friend, but Louise, for the first time in their acquaintance, did not respond.

"It's very kind of you to bother about the children," she said coldly, "and I really do think that they appreciate it. That fidgeting is just a bad habit the little Napiers have got into. I know Rosamund enjoys it, anyhow."

16

"My dear Mother," wrote Kerran,

"I never expected to find that I have so much in common with Guy Fletcher. Our tastes may be widely dissimilar, but it appears that we share one great distaste so completely that we are quite drawn together. To escape from the sight of Elissa Koebel, to be where she is not, has become the ruling passion of our lives. And the island is so small that we do not find it easy. We spend a great deal of time in our common bedroom. We are there now. Fletcher is reading Comus, and I am waiting for an opportunity to slip out and snatch a bathe. I have just asked Fletcher if he doesn't think it would be a wise precaution to keep our door locked, but he is not amused.

"Dick has quite gone over to the enemy, and we cannot forgive him. He prowls round in the wake of the Vergil readers, looking like a werewolf, and nobody can imagine what he is up to. He seems to be out of sorts and out of spirits. Fletcher thinks it is because he is annoyed over the death of that unfortunate lady. He says that wounded prestige is at the bottom of it. He says that Dick is a worldly man; that he estimates the whole of life in terms of material success and that he has, therefore, very little defence against failure.

"I don't know how he knows all this. He says that Dick has no spiritual values. This may be true. I don't know what spiritual values are, do you? And it is evident, from the tone of his voice, that he thinks a materialist on a level with a card-sharper. A queer fellow!

He seems to be so desperately concerned about evil. He worries over it just as Maude worries over germs, and is always having to remove himself, hastily, from its proximity. I wish you could see his face, reading Comus: it has the fixed glare of an inexpert bicyclist who daren't, for a second, take his eyes off his front wheel. He is pursuing goodness and beauty, but it is very hard because evil is always getting in the way and he has to make nervous little dashes like a timid child pulling hot chestnuts out of the fire.

"He objects to Elissa because she is evil, and, much as I dislike the woman, I'm bound to say that I think he maligns her. I merely find her a bore. But then I don't believe in these Powers of Darkness prowling about and trying to distract our attention from the good. 'Matter in the wrong place,' I say. And the Koebel is certainly matter in the wrong place.

"I think the moment is propitious for a swim, as they must have settled down for their morning's Love Feast by now. So I will close. Take care of yourself.

"Your affectionate son,

"KERRAN."

The quadrangle, for once, seemed to be clear. Kerran got safely across to the north gate, and stopped to look at the barometer, just inside the gate house. It was still set at fair, but when he tapped it, it went back a little. The long spell of fine weather was beginning to break up. For two or three days more the sun would shine, perhaps, but then it would rain with the persistence of a long foretold change.

"God help us when we are all shut up," thought Kerran.

Just outside he ran straight into the arms of the enemy. Elissa was picking mushrooms on the greensward going down to the lake. She was alone, a thing which seldom happened. He remembered that Gordon and Dick had gone into Killross to bring out some groceries for Maude, but he could not imagine what Louise had done with herself. It was at the back of his mind that Louise, for the last day or two, had not been quite so cordial to Elissa as before, but he felt that the wish might have been father to the thought.

"For supper to-night," she called to him gaily, "I shall make a mushroom omelette *à l'hongroise*. You will see. I have learnt how to do it, but the *recept* is a secret. It shall be a little treat for all you good people. Now I am picking the mushrooms. There are so many, because the moon is getting larger. Soon it will be full moon, and we shall have many mushrooms. Then afterwards not so many. When there is no moon, no mushrooms at all. That is what I have heard the country people say. Give me your hat. I can't hold them all. Now stand beside me and we will use the hat for a basket. And we will talk."

" 'We' is good," thought Kerran, as he stood submissively beside her, holding the hat.

But he was mistaken.

"I have a question to ask. You do not like me very much, I know."

"Oh . . . really, madame . . ."

"But it is natural. I understand. Louise has told me."

"Why . . . what . . ."

"There is so much sadness in the world, *nicht?* And you, my poor friend, are just now very sad. The gaiety and merriment of our little group is unsympathetic to you. You prefer to be alone. Louise has told me about your most unhappy love."

Kerran nearly dropped the hat.

"I, too, have had such an experience, very long ago, when I was scarcely more than a child. I loved a priest. But his vows were an obstacle. They prevented our happiness. He was obliged to confine himself in a convent in order not to see me any more. I tell you, it was terrible how I suffered. Ah yes, it was terrible. But see . . . here are Louise and Ellen. Now we shall soon pick enough mushrooms to make a beautiful omelette."

Louise and Ellen had just come out of the north gate, and Ellen went down to sit on the little stone bench by the lake. She often sat there, with her needlework, in the morning, unless she could find somebody to row her over to the mainland, which she preferred. Louise, after one glance at Elissa and Kerran, turned round and went back into the castle. Elissa called after her:

"Louise! Louise! Will you not come to pick mushrooms? I am going to make an omelette this evening."

"No, thank you," cried Louise impatiently over her shoulder. "Don't bother, Elissa. We've eaten enough mushrooms. I can't face the prospect of any more. They're an overrated vegetable."

She disappeared into the castle again. Elissa stood silent for a moment, a little puzzled, a trifle crestfallen at so novel a rebuff. She still held a large mushroom in her hand, stretched out towards the castle like a rejected offering.

An extraordinary thing happened to Kerran. He found that he was feeling sorry for the woman. Though he had been longing for Louise to grow tired of her, yet, now that it seemed to be happening, he was not satisfied. Louise was not a faithful friend. She formed extravagant intimacies and then cooled down abruptly. It was not the first time that he had seen her drop somebody in a way that was almost brutal. He had always known it would happen. He ought to have been pleased.

But he was not. He wished that it could have happened in some other way. He did not like Elissa, but he felt that she was what she was. She had never pretended to be anything else and, in her own way, she was perfectly genuine and sincere—far more so than Louise. She had a real affection for the Lindsays and she would suffer if they cast her off. She had done nothing to deserve the shock and the humiliation. Louise was entirely to blame throughout. Kerran, who had a good deal of indolent kindliness, could not endure it. He was sorry for her, and he felt, once more, a little ashamed of himself, as he had felt when she first came to the castle.

"It's easy to laugh at her," he thought, "she is larger than we are."

He had been on the point of flinging his hat at her and taking flight without any excuse whatever. He had felt that he could not put up with any more of her conversation. But now he stayed, in order to give her a certain amount of confidence after her rebuff, because to leave her quite alone would not have been kind. He told himself that he would stay until Gordon and Dick came back, just to teach Louise a lesson.

After a short, puzzled pause, his companion seemed to forget the incident. She resumed:

"I, myself, am a deeply religious woman. But I believe that God has meant us to be happy. These chains which we make for ourselves, they have been forged by the devil. Happily the world is becoming more free. If we are courageous, and if we refuse to let ourselves be bound by puritanical conventions, then we are helping to make it more free. It is so easy to be happy. But I have a question to ask you. Perhaps you can tell me. Why is it that your brother also suffers from this terrible depression?"

"Barny?" exclaimed Kerran in amazement.

"Oh no! I do not interest myself in the amiable Barny. I speak of De-eck."

"Oh, Dick! He's been overworking."

"*Ach so!* I feel so sorry for him. But he has not talked to you? There is not anything . . . perhaps some special trouble . . ."

She looked at him archly, questioningly.

"He's been especially worried about a case," admitted Kerran.

"A case? I understand. I think it is a pity that he should have taken the medical profession. He is too sensitive. He is too much of an artist. It is not enough for a sensitive man to cure sick people. For me, I think that sick people had better die. They are ugly and the world does not want them. I am ashamed to be ill. To be concerned always with sickness and sick people, that is sordid. It is not worthy of him. There is no room in his life for what is spiritual, and what is beautiful. I can see it very well. He says to himself: *this man suffers. I will give him a pill.* That is all. But the artist says to himself: *this man suffers* and he makes of it some great poem. Your brother suffers because he must deny his own soul. He is obliged to become a materialist. *Aber nur* . . . why do you laugh?"

"I beg your pardon," said Kerran, controlling himself

and wondering if he dared quote this to Guy. "But all doctors aren't materialists."

"Not all," she admitted reminiscently. "I once . . . but that is not a mushroom that you have picked, my friend. It is *Sistschwamm*, poison. Throw it down! Don't you know the difference? Look, I will show you. If it peels so, then it is a mushroom. That is the way to know. But what was I saying? I have always so greatly admired your sister."

He thought at first that she was talking of Louise, but a glance which she threw at the stone bench by the lake told him that she had now got round to Ellen.

"She is a true *Hausfrau*, so good and so tranquil. It is charming to see her sitting there in her blue dress, with her needlework. But I find that, for so young a woman, she is strangely inactive. She sits still too much. When we are in the boat she will never row. For myself I would think it nothing to row from here to the sea. Do you not think it strange?"

Kerran stared. Quite obviously she did not know. He would have thought that she would have learnt of it among the women. But then Ellen herself was reticent upon such topics, and Louise had always taken the line that too much fuss was being made by Muffy. However that might be, Elissa had not been told. Or, perhaps, she had been told and the information had made no impression on her. She had a mind like a large meshed net: small items were apt to slip through it.

Although it was no business of his, a certain anxiety assailed him. Elissa was so domineering. She was quite capable of taking Ellen out on the lake and making her row. He said rather stiffly:

"She's expecting another child, you know."

"Impossible!" cried Elissa, in tones of lively astonishment. "But when?"

"Oh, I don't know. Not till after Christmas."

Elissa scrutinised Ellen with new interest.

"But impossible," she said again. "She is so thin! One would say of this child, where will it come from? Her silhouette is still perfect!"

And then, all at once, a cloud seemed to fall upon her. She grew exceedingly sombre.

"I understand," she added, in a low voice.

Kerran thought:

"Well, I'm glad you do."

They picked a good many more mushrooms before she spoke again, and then it was to launch out into a bitter attack upon Puritanism, which she seemed to confuse with hypocrisy. She repeated that God had made people in order that they should be happy.

"But it is when they are unhappy that they are most inclined to think about Him," argued Kerran.

"When I am unhappy," she retorted, "I do not believe in Him. My mood then becomes stoical."

"Oh, does it?" said Kerran.

Suddenly she began to declaim, very effectively, *Mort du Loup*, walking as she did so towards the banks of the lake, for the boat, with Dick and Gordon and the groceries, had come into sight. Her accent was pure. She recited well. Each word floated out with its own classic beauty and distinction so that Kerran, strive as he would, could not escape from an impulse of admiration, or from the knowledge that something noble was being built up before him. The poem was fine, and her interpretation was fine. She could not have grasped the sense of what she was saying, he thought, but she was indubitably inspired, the vehicle of some inexplicable afflatus. She had the gift of prophecy. And he wondered if the priestesses of Delphi, when they had descended from the tripod, might not, in their own characters, have talked as much nonsense as she did.

They had got quite near to the stone bench, and he saw Ellen's startled face peering round at them. There was an anxious, awakened look upon it, as though she had just been informed for the first time of some disturbing truth. When Elissa broke off and went over to the landing-stage to greet the boat, he joined his sister on the stone bench. She asked him at once if that had been poetry.

"What was it she said? *Seul le silence est grand* . . ."

Kerran repeated the passage with some embarrassment at his own accent, which was so very different from Elissa's.

"It's awfully *true*," said Ellen, after profound ponderings.

Kerran thought so too, but he was very much surprised to hear such a comment from Ellen.

On the heels of this surprise he received another. He saw that, instead of her needlework, a book lay in her lap. It was months since he had last seen her so engaged. She was not much of a reader.

"Oh . . . are you reading?"

"Yes," she said, with some satisfaction. "I'm reading a book."

All this was new. It was disturbing. He did not know that he wanted her to read books. She was the only one in the family who did not, though she was conscientious about reading aloud to the children. That she should take to doing so for her own pleasure was bad. It was a sign of upheaval. He asked what book it was and she showed him. It was *Anna Karenina*. Guy Fletcher had lent it to her.

"Do you like it?"

"Oh, yes," she said with animation. "I like it very much. It's very fine. The characterisation is very fine."

She paused for a moment, as if a little proud of this word, and then added:

"The people seem so real, somehow. It makes you quite sorry for Anna. I mean, it makes one see how uncomfortable it must be for anyone in that sort of position. It gives one a lot to think about."

A lot to think about! This was the worst of all. Since when had Ellen begun to ask for a lot to think about? Content with being the stupid member of the family, she had always accepted the general verdict that she could not think.

She had begun to read again, applying herself to the lines of print before her with the solemnity of unpractised effort, almost like a cottage woman spelling out the Bible. Kerran observed her with curiosity and misgiving. An explanation for all this was beginning to dawn upon him. She was absorbing these ideas and impressions from the written word in order, perhaps, to keep other ideas at bay. She was not happy and she preferred to ponder upon Anna Karenina's awkward position rather than upon her own.

17

EVERYBODY had seen Louise and Elissa go down to bathe. And everybody saw how Louise came back alone, hugging her long cloak round her. As she crossed the courtyard and disappeared into her tower, her progress was marked by Muffy, who sat on the edge of the well, by Maude, who happened to be coming out of the kitchen, and by Kerran, from a tower window. And each of them thought immediately:

"It has come."

Meaning that the end of the Elissa epoch had arrived. For the past forty-eight hours it had been imminent, and there was something about this solitary return which told of a climax.

When she had dressed herself Louise went to find Gordon, who was writing in the drawing-room. She said:

"Just one minute, Gordon, if you can spare the time," in the kind of voice which he had not heard for many weeks.

He looked up in alarm and saw that she was almost beside herself. Her eyes flashed, her colour was high, and she breathed quickly.

"Something must be done. I simply cannot have Elissa here again."

Gordon gasped. He had not read the signs of change as the others had.

"She's too disgusting. She's too revolting. I can't think how I ever liked her."

"Disgusting? Revolting?"

"I really don't know how to tell you . . . but I never want to see her here again."

"Louise, what can you mean? What has she done?"

"She . . . she took off all her clothes in front of Dick."

"*What?*"

"She did. We were bathing. We were lying on the grass, sunning ourselves before we dressed. Elissa took off her bathing-dress. She always does. I have had to tell her not to do it in front of the children. We were on the little beach by the boulders, where it's quite private. And Dick came round the point in his boat."

"She can't have known . . ."

"Oh, yes, she did. She waved to him, and laughed at me because I was horrified."

"Good heavens!"

Gordon's head grew pink.

"And . . . and what happened then?"

"I don't know. I just left her there. I couldn't bear it. She was so vulgar . . . so . . ."

Gordon jerked his head in decided disagreement.

"Oh, no," he asserted, "not vulgar."

"But, Gordon!"

"She is simpler than we are. She has other conventions. I have heard that it is the custom in the Caucasus . . ."

"This isn't the Caucasus . . ."

"I have no doubt but that it was quite innocently done."

"Innocent! Good heavens! If you'd seen her!"

Gordon blushed again.

"She was shameless," persisted Louise. "Don't you

understand? She had nothing on. Nothing on at all."

"Elissa is not vulgar. You don't understand her. It is you, I think, who are vulgar."

"I? I, vulgar?"

"You put interpretations which . . . oh, I daresay it was a shock to you. She often says things, the sort of thing which we would leave unsaid. You must tell her that it is not our custom in England."

"What interpretations?" asked Louise, taking up the first part of his sentence. "What do you mean?"

"You put a false interpretation upon what she did. I don't suppose for a minute that it was meant to be provocative."

"Yes, it was. Ever since Dick came she has been throwing herself at his head. I can't think how you haven't seen it."

"Louise, that is a very grave, a very terrible thing to say about our friend."

"Please, don't call her *my* friend. I've done with her."

"And since when," asked Gordon bitterly, "have you so changed your opinion of her?"

"Since . . . since I've noticed what I have told you."

"You have a lively imagination. You have deceived yourself."

"And other things that I've noticed. She doesn't speak the truth. She told us all how she had sung Brunnhilde in Dresden and then next day she said that Waltraute was the only part she had ever sung there. And she said that she could row down to Killross in half an hour when she knows quite well that it takes her forty-five minutes."

"You can't seriously expect me to believe that you think these are good arguments."

"No, but I do feel that perhaps we have been mistaken in her character, and that it was a pity to rush into this friendship."

Gordon took a turn or two down the room before he could trust himself to speak. He was growing very angry and he knew that he would put himself at a disadvantage if he showed it. So much was at stake. The most precious thing in the whole of his life was being threatened. At last he mastered himself sufficiently to say:

"I'm not going to accept these petty accusations as sufficient. Do you know anything definite? Have you anything serious to go upon?"

This checked Louise. She had thought that the bathing incident would be sufficient, and that Gordon would be shocked into immediate agreement. His cross-examination was unexpected.

Of course she knew a great deal, which would have been, even in the besotted Gordon's eyes, definitely against Elissa. There were stories told by Kerran and Barny, at which she had once scoffed and which she now accepted in all their enormity. But she could not cite these because she had already agreed with Gordon that they were the merest scandal. And there were other incidents which she had heard from Elissa's own lips when their intimacy had been at its height. She had not passed them on to Gordon at the time, and she had manœuvred Elissa into a measure of reticence where he was concerned, because she felt that, in spite of his admiration, he might not accept them as tolerantly as she did. After all, it was not three weeks since she had written a letter to her mother in defence of Elissa's sacred impulses. To admit that her information came from that source would have been to involve herself in too many dangerous explanations. It was a difficult position.

She took the offensive.

"You mayn't see it all quite as I do. I know men see these things differently. But that doesn't alter it, Gordon. After . . . what happened this morning . . . I'm not prepared to have her here again."

"You mean that she is not to come to us here any more?"

"I do. I have the children to think of. And there is this that I've told you about Dick. I assure you that I'm not mistaken. She's dropped several hints . . . For his sake, and for Ellen's sake, for everybody's sake . . . Nobody likes her, you know."

"You mean to tell her that she is not to come here any more? Simply because, unwittingly, she misunderstood."

"It wasn't unwittingly . . ."

"I couldn't have believed it of you. Think what our friendship has been! To drop her like this . . . without any cause. It's so heartless, so cruel! So unwarranted. If you think that I am going to lend you my support, you are very much mistaken."

Gordon seldom opposed Louise. It was not often that the issue struck him as possessing sufficient importance. He had never before interfered in her stormy friendships. But in this case his personal feelings were concerned. He loved Elissa. This attack on her roused him to a passion of chivalrous indignation.

"I shall do all in my power to prevent such an insult being offered to any guest in my house."

"But, Gordon, you aren't going to persist in asking the woman here when I've said I won't have her!"

P

"I shall do what I think fit. If you insult her, against my wishes, I don't suppose she will wish to come. But the friendship will not be broken off as regards those of us who are still loyal to her."

"But a husband and a wife can't openly disagree about such a thing."

She lowered her voice a little, as Maude, not for the first time, appeared upon the terrace outside the window.

"There are times," declared Gordon, "when the opinion of one must prevail."

"But it's the wife who ought to prevail when it's a question of who shall be invited to the house. That is the wife's sphere."

"You brought her here yourself, in the first instance."

"I didn't. Nobody asked her here in the first instance. She foisted herself on us."

"Louise, every word you say adds to your own discredit. You know that this was not so: that you have invited her here again and again. When you resort to making statements which we both know to be false, your case must be very weak indeed."

"However it may have begun, it must end now. You can't force me to know a woman whose morals I disapprove of. I have been mistaken in her character."

"I can't force you to do anything. But I shall take my own line: I shall welcome her here, if she comes, and if she will receive me at her house, I shall go there."

"Gordon! You can't."

But Gordon seemed to think that he could. He was losing control of himself. His hands were trembling, he stuttered and tugged nervously at his moustache. And though the physical indications of his rage were ineffectual, even slightly ridiculous, there was so much warmth behind them that Louise was dismayed. She felt that very little more could be done with him, at the moment, and went out to find Maude on the terrace. It was a moment when all good women should confide in one another. Although she suspected that Maude had managed to overhear a good deal of what had passed, she told her tale from the beginning for decency's sake and because it made a very good story.

Maude took the sensible view at once. And it seemed that she also had begun, of late, to change her mind about Elissa. She reinforced Louise's suspicions with several most damaging observations of her own.

"But isn't it extraordinary of Gordon? You'd have thought he'd have been horrified."

"Men!" said Maude with a shrug.

"He's so innocent. Anybody would take him in."

Louise, though she was seeking Maude's alliance, was not going to have it suggested that Gordon made a habit of asking improper women to the house. Angry though she was, she felt that would have been unfair.

"But Maude . . . what am I to do? How is one to get rid of her?"

"If you don't do something she'll go on coming here till the end of the summer."

"I know. And she's so thick-skinned. I don't believe she'd take a hint."

"You can freeze people up pretty well if you like," ventured Maude, with a reminiscent shiver.

"And let Gordon thaw her again under my nose. No, thank you."

"Then write to her."

"I'd thought of that. But if I sent it by post she wouldn't read it. She boasted to me that she burns any letters that come, unread."

"I expect that's a tarrididdle."

"So do I. But she might pretend she hadn't got it. If I could send it by hand . . . but whom could I send?"

"What would you say, anyhow?"

"Oh, I should say that her behaviour this morning convinced me that our friendship couldn't go on. That the way we look at things is too different. It would be much easier to do it in a letter, if only . . ."

"I'll tell you. Didn't she say she was going to Killross to-morrow, and wouldn't be here till the afternoon? Couldn't we manage it this way? If it's a fine day let's suddenly decide on all going a picnic to the Haunted Glen. Tell Gordon that you're leaving a note behind for Elissa, implying that it's to tell her where we are, when she comes to the island, so that she can join us if she likes. Write your note and leave it behind for Muffy to give her. Of course she may refuse to accept it without seeing you again. But if you write very firmly she may crumple up and go away. Then you're rid of her."

"Gordon will find out."

"Only gradually. He'll wonder why she doesn't come, and at last you'll have to tell him. But by then the deed will be done and he won't find it so easy to make a stand. Besides, he'll have had time to think things over and we can get Barny and Kerran, perhaps, to reason with him."

"Ye-es. You're rather clever, Maude."

"I don't see any other way. And I do think it's time something was done."

"But there's all the rest of to-day to be got through. I don't want ever to see her again."

"Then don't. Go to bed now with a headache. I'll tell them. I'll manage it."

"Do you think you can?"

Maude nodded importantly. She was enjoying herself for the first time since she came to the island.

"After all," said Louise, a trifle uneasily, "she'll have no right to call it a bolt from the blue, or anything like that. I did protest. I did show her that I was shocked."

"My dear, everybody will be grateful to you. Nobody likes her except Gordon and Dick."

"Dick sees through her," said Louise immediately. "There's no sort of attraction on his side. I'm convinced of that. I've been watching them, ever since. . . . Whatever she may feel about him, he laughs at her. He ignores all the openings she gives him."

"Oh, does he?"

18

THE keep was full of children standing about and waiting for the picnic to begin. Each child had been equipped with a mackintosh, in case it should rain, and a thick woolly coat in case it should turn chilly on the way home. These garments were continually being taken on and off. A nurse or an aunt would rush into the keep and exclaim:

"Good gracious! Aren't you children ready? We shall be starting in a minute!"

Jenny or Michael would then be seized and muffled up and left until somebody else would come and cry:

"Good gracious! We aren't going to the North Pole!'

And all the woolly coats would be peeled off again.

There was an especial atmosphere of excitement and expectancy about this picnic. They were going to the Haunted Glen. Aunt Maude had come rushing in at breakfast time with the news:

"Children! We're all going to the Haunted Glen! Isn't that fun?"

The name was enough. Even the grown-ups seemed to feel it and they bustled about in a very special way. There was a tremendous amount to be done before they could all get off. The maids cut sandwiches and Aunt Maude ran up and down the courtyard with a list:

"Eighteen cups . . . eighteen plates . . . where's the bottle of methylated spirits?"

This sort of thing went on for hours and hours, and the joys of anticipation began to pall. It seemed that the picnic would never start. A wave of naughtiness swept across the nursery. All the babies began to cry and Charles pulled Hope's hair.

"Unless you stop this very minute you shan't go to the picnic," was a threat dealt out to each in turn.

Rosamund had a little haversack in which she had packed everything she would need for the day. Besides her mackintosh and her jersey, she had sketching things, *The Old Oak Staircase*, her knitting and an exercise book and a pencil, in case she wished to write poetry. Perhaps it might be as well to take another book, as she had read *The Old Oak Staircase* rather often. She had *Countess Kate* upstairs in her bedroom, and she would take that.

As she climbed the stairs, loud yelps of laughter from the night nursery told her that the boys were up there, enjoying some unseemly jest. She pulled her face into a scowl of disapproval which became entirely genuine when she saw that Hope was there too. Peter was regaling them with the choicer anecdotes current last term at his preparatory school. These were mostly on the cloacal theme.

"So the people at the lodgings couldn't think what she meant. They'd never heard of one, you see. And at last they thought it must mean a Wesleyan chapel. So they wrote back and said there's a lovely one three miles away . . ."

Charles laughed in short, sharp yelps, Hope quivered and shook. They thought that nobody had ever been so funny as Peter.

" . . . but at present they are all occupied . . ."

"Oh! Oh!"

Triumphant moral indignation upheld Rosamund.

"I shall tell!"

"What?"

"It's very naughty. You know it is. What would mother say? She'd be frightfully shocked. And so would Aunt Ellen. I'm the eldest and it's my duty to stop you being naughty. If you don't stop I shall tell. I shall tell mother."

She was interrupted by a chorus:

"Tell tale tit!
      Your tongue shall be slit!
      And all the puppy dogs in the town
      Shall have a little bit!"

"Very bad taste!" added Charles, in a ridiculous falsetto.

Rosamund flushed and her eyes filled with tears. They had given her no peace since she had unwisely repeated that comment which her mother had made about Aunt Maude's silver buckle with the angels' heads.

"Cry baby! Cry baby!"

She burst into loud sobs while her tormentors jumped up and down and shouted. More wails were heard from the floor below where the little ones, exasperated by their woollen mufflers, had all come to the conclusion that they did not want to go for a picnic.

Into the middle of this confusion came Ellen, all ready to start, in a long tussore dust-coat and a motor veil which tied up her head. She quelled the racket downstairs and sent the babies off to be stacked into a boat with the two nursery-maids. And then she came up to investigate the trouble there, arriving at the top of the stairs a little breathless and impatient.

"Children! Children! What is the matter with you?

We're starting. Have you got all your . . . why, Rosamund! Was it you making that noise? What's the matter?"

"They're being very naughty," gulped Rosamund. "I said I'd tell if they went on. They would keep committing adultery."

Ellen's face stiffened suddenly. It grew wooden with displeasure, and there was a look in her grey eyes which terrified them all. The unthinkable thing had happened. Rosamund had broken the greatest of all unwritten laws.

"What do you mean?" asked Ellen icily.

"Peter committed adultery."

"No, I didn't," said Peter, recovering himself a little.

"Yes, you did."

"I did *not*."

"He was, Aunt Ellen. He was talking about . . . about . . ."

"That isn't committing adultery, is it, mother? Committing adultery is taking somebody else's wife. You said so."

"Yes," said Hope. "And you said it was a commandment we needn't bother about, because we simply couldn't take other people's wives yet awhile."

"So I couldn't have been . . ."

"My mother doesn't think so," persisted Rosamund. "She said it was telling dirty stories . . ."

"No, it isn't. Is it, mother?"

"Be quiet, all of you. Peter! What exactly have you been saying?"

"I began it," said Charles, hastily, feeling that Peter should not be singled out for blame. "We were only . . ."

"Be quiet. I'll have Peter's answer first."

There was a horrible pause. Peter looked at his

mother. And then suddenly his eyes began to dance. He, too, had grey eyes, but the flash in them had come from Dick. He was a very long, thin child, and his childish face, at the end of this long, thin body, was disarming. When he laughed, and when he wished to make other people laugh, he stretched his neck up like a young cockerel trying to crow. He began to giggle. After all, this fable about the Wesleyan chapel was, in his opinion, a very good one. He thought it the best that he had ever heard. It would stand on its merits.

"There was once a lady who wrote for some lodgings," he began.

The other children stared as if their eyes would drop out. But Peter's boldness was too much for them. They began, in spite of themselves, to giggle too, all but Rosamund, who had found a handkerchief and was mopping her eyes.

Ellen's expression changed from wood to marble. And then it became confused. Its severity was disintegrated. The spectacle of her son, with his dancing eyes, his audacity, his thin neck and his high, childish giggles, had broken her down. She could not frown on him, whatever he said. And there was no harm in this little *jeu d'esprit*, though it was undoubtedly very vulgar, and she ought, really she ought, to keep a straight face if she could. She drew her mouth down, looked flurried, shook her head, but they all saw that she was trying not to laugh.

"Really, children! Really! How can you be so vulgar? I don't think that's amusing."

"Oh, mother! Oh, yes, you do! You're laughing!"

"*Very vulgar.* How you could have the face to tell me such a story . . . come along! The boats are waiting."

They all trooped after her as she led the way out of

the night nursery. Neither then nor afterwards did they discuss this incident, but not one of them ever forgot it. And they felt very comfortable, without knowing why, as if they were on surer terms with the world.

The only comment made was a long nose pulled by Peter, behind his mother's back, at the indignant Rosamund.

19

THE picnic was being a success.

The sandwiches sufficed and the kettles boiled and Maude was able to say complacently:

"I always begin by making a list, even down to teaspoons."

They took photographs of each other, sprawling in the heather; the kind of groups which are amusing to rediscover after twenty-five years. These children, so dowdy-looking in their sailor suits and long holland smocks, would some day find it impossible to believe that aunts and mothers, dressed like that, could ever have been quite human. Such hats could only have been worn by women without taste, without passion and without a sense of humour. Only a snapshot of Dick, in profile, kneeling over the picnic fire, remained timeless and Ellen kept it for ever afterwards in a small silver frame on her dressing table.

It was their first picnic without Elissa, and for some of them this fact alone was a relief and a source of pleasure. For others, who knew of the little intrigue behind it, there was an undercurrent of excitement, so that they all seemed to be in particularly high spirits. And it was a pleasure to see Dick so much himself again. He seemed at last to have shaken off the lethargic depression which had weighed upon him for the last weeks. Louise, radiant at having secured her own way, felt that now at last she had got them all into harness.

They lunched close to the lake, for the little children

could not walk far and there were heavy baskets to carry. But afterwards all those who felt inclined to do so would explore the glen while the two nursery-maids packed the hampers, washed up and guarded the babies.

"Though it will be a very hot walk," said Louise, turning dubiously to Ellen, "shall you come or would you rather stay down here?"

She was so well satisfied that she was even prepared to make some concession to Ellen's condition.

Ellen, infected by the general exhilaration, laughed a little.

"Stay with my leetle vons? No, thank you! I'd rather get away from them."

A swift shock ran through the company. Ellen was a good mimic; she had a gift of verbal parody which was wasted upon so unsatirical a nature. Louise had often grudged it to her. This time her butt was obvious: Elissa never spoke to Ellen without some reference to the "leetle vons," implying that so good a *Hausfrau* could have no other interest.

They felt as though Balaam's ass had spoken. Was this malice? Was it innocence? How much did she know, and had she heard of the incident on the bathing beach? A few of them laughed uncertainly. Guy Fletcher swallowed a greengage stone, and only the guileless Gordon protested.

"Oh, I don't think Elissa's accent is as pronounced as that."

They kept themselves from looking at Dick.

"Time to get off," cried Louise, hurriedly dealing with an awkward moment. "We've got to get to the top and back before tea. Rosie, you'll have the tea kettles boiling by half-past four, won't you?"

"Eat a lot of bread! Eat a great lump of stale bread," said Maude to the choking Guy.

Singly or in groups they struggled off. Dick and Gordon, who walked quickly, soon got far in front. The children ranged all over the glen. So that Maude and Louise, walking slowly behind with Ellen, were able to return to the engrossing topic.

How much did she know?

"My dear, you know what we've done?"

Ellen now learnt of the note which they had left behind for Elissa. She was surprised and uncomfortable, and sorry that she had laughed at Elissa's accent. It must have sounded ill-natured.

"But what is the matter, Louise? Are you vexed with her about something?"

"Did . . . didn't Dick tell you what happened yesterday?"

"No. What?"

Maude made a warning grimace, but Louise ignored it. She was too eager to see what Ellen would say. She gave the facts and Ellen blushed.

"How . . . horrid!"

"That's what I felt. I don't wonder Dick . . . said nothing about it. He must have been disgusted."

Ellen walked more quickly. Her lively spirits had begun to fail her. She had enjoyed the beginning of the day so much, and getting away from the island, and seeing Dick look almost well again. He had said something that morning about his paper for the Hunterian Society, and it was clear that his mind was beginning to swing back towards his work. She had almost been able to believe that the threatened storm would never break, and that the weeks of leisure and

sunlight on the island were going to cure him. This
labour of living through it would not go on much
longer.

But now it all closed in on her again. Of course he
had not told her about Elissa on the bathing beach. He
never told her anything. They slept every night in the
same room, but there might have been a seven-foot wall
between them. And it was getting to be too much for
her, this continual strain. She had got them all to accept
her version of his moodiness, she had kept them off him,
she had read books to keep herself from worrying, and
she had abstained from prayer. But if it went on much
longer she would have to tell somebody.

Her body did not help her. It was languid, not her
own. Wherever she went she seemed to be a troubled,
doubting mind creeping cautiously along with a cumbrous
body attached to it.

"If Dick doesn't speak to me soon I can't bear
it . . . I *must* know what he is thinking . . . what he
means to do . . ."

At last she got away from Louise and Maude and the
dangers which seemed to lie behind their simple prattle.
They were wanting to suggest some horrid reason why
Dick had not told her. But it could never be worse than
the real reason. She hurried forward to the safe company
of Barny and Guy Fletcher, who were a little way in
front and who waited for her.

"She knows," said Louise. "It's quite obvious."

"Quite," agreed Maude.

"Thank heaven I've got rid of Elissa!"

The Haunted Glen was a bare and stony place. Seen
near to, it was more sinister and less majestic than it had
appeared to be from the island. The steep screes of

stones, which made such a deep trough in the landscape, had no beauty in themselves. They rose gauntly,
on either hand, to a parapet of crags. The vegetation among the boulders grew sparser. It was strange
that there could be enough soil to nourish the few
shrivelled thorn trees which crouched, here and there,
among the stones, like watchers overlooking the path.
The oldest and the largest stood almost at the head of
the glen, as if to bar the way.

A curious silence and oppression filled the hot, stony
trough. There was no longer the grateful sound of
running water, for the little stream which trickled down
the glen had disappeared underground. There were no
echoes. The air was too opaque. The sound of boots
on rocks, and the voices of the climbers, were immediately effaced by silence.

It was stiflingly hot. The sun poured down and
quivered on the stones. It seemed as if the thorn at the
head of the glen was as far away as ever. It became an
effort to go on. Even the children stopped chattering
and drew closer together. Yet nobody admitted to any
mental discomfort. They complained of the heat, but of
nothing else. Even the imaginative Louise could not
bring herself to suggest that their progress was being
resisted, though she said so afterwards.

Dick and Gordon had got up to the last thorn and sat
down in its shade to wait for the others. But their faces
had no repose, like the faces of men who snatch a
moment's grateful rest on the hillside. They looked
precarious and watchful.

"The lake is very ugly," said Dick.

They could see the whole of it, a kidney-shaped piece
of dull grey steel lying far below them, solid-looking,

with no reflections. The island, in the middle, was dark and small. It did not float. It was a tuft of earth flung at random on to the flat, steely surface. And the mountains, rising up everywhere, were shapeless, uninteresting. It was as if all meaning had suddenly gone out of the landscape.

"What's that headland out there to the right?" asked Dick.

Gordon got out his map and they both bent over it. Here was the same kidney-shaped lake with the lump of turf flung into the middle of it. And here in a mesh of contour lines was the Haunted Glen.

There was a plop! Something hairy and repulsive fell out of the tree on to their map, on to the island. It writhed obscenely. Both men started away with a cry of disgust, almost of fear, as if their nerves had suddenly been caught on the raw. And then they looked very much ashamed of themselves, for it was only an enormous caterpillar. Dick threw it away into the grass.

The others, when they reached the tree, did not want to rest there in the sultry glare. To get to the top of the glen was their only desire. They toiled on, and Ellen, who was getting tired, came last with Dick.

"Sure you ought to go any further?" he asked.

"Oh, yes. I want to get to the top. I want to see over the other side."

"It won't be so bad coming down."

"No, it will be downhill."

"Like an arm?"

"No, thanks. The path is too uneven."

He was looking the more exhausted of the two. The sweat was pouring down his face.

"I seem to be in filthy condition," he said.

The children got to the top first. They danced about on the skyline and waved their arms. A wind, unfelt by the climbers below, a gentle breeze, fluttered their garments. One by one each of them crested the ridge, and each, feeling the soft, reviving wind, came once more to life. They were out of the glen, on a long slope of heather all in bloom. Before them were blue ranges of hills, valleys which they had never seen before, the gleaming waters of a chain of little lakes; a varied and noble scene, full of softness and colour, beheld in that miraculous clarity which comes before rain.

Their toil over, they flung themselves down on the heather, drawing in long breaths of the balmy air. Louise, relaxed, said at once:

"That place *was* haunted."

"Don't say so yet," exclaimed Guy. "Remember, we've got to go back."

"It's most extraordinary. Not a bit what I would have expected. I would have thought that we would feel there was more than we could see. But I had an impression there was less. As if what we saw was hollow. Everything *shrank* . . ."

Dick and Ellen reached the crest, and drew in their breath quickly as they saw the new hills. They were together in a swift sense of conquest and repose.

"Not bad," said Dick, with a nod at the view.

"Oh, I'm glad I came all the way up!"

"After that wretched island . . ."

The fresh wind gave her power. She could speak.

"Why don't you go away, Dick? You don't like it. I shouldn't stay if I were you."

"Over there?"

Receiving the overture calmly, he nodded towards

the genial valleys and the little chain of lakes. She had not meant over there, particularly, but any place would be better than Inishbar.

"I might," he said. "I will. But there's my paper . . ."

"I shouldn't bother about your paper if I were you until . . ."

She paused. She was afraid of going too far. But he accepted even this.

"Until I've quite got over all this nervous exhaustion. I expect you're right. But wouldn't Louise take offence? I couldn't stand a scene with her."

"Oh, I'll explain. You just go and say nothing about it, and I'll explain after you've gone."

"Will you? All right. I'll go . . . quite soon . . . I'll go over there and walk up into those mountains. It would do me a lot of good to be alone for a bit."

She left it at that, for she was terrified of saying too much and the effort of speaking at all had left her breathless. They went on to where the others were sitting and flung themselves down into the heather.

Ellen could not take her eyes off these new mountains. They stirred in her an emotion which she could not understand, a sense of something coming, something which was going to happen. She was filled with hope.

She watched the dappled shadows of clouds travel across clear slopes, far, far away. And her mind, her soul, seemed to expand, to travel far away, too, into the airy spaciousness of the valleys and the hillsides, and the little gleaming lakes where the soft wind whispered in the reeds. She heard that whispering wind more clearly than she heard the voices talking all round her. Perhaps the long climb, and the emotional tension between herself and Dick, as they stood at the head of the glen, had made her feel a little faint. She felt herself grow cold: her senses became more and more confused.

She could not understand what the others were saying, yet she listened to the symphony of their voices, catching at a word here and there. Words flowed past her like leaves on a current, leaves spinning on towards a weir. She was rushing towards it herself, but the words shot past her.

Frightened of a caterpillar.

A caterpillar, a caterpillar . . . the syllables were like little stones skipping down a hillside. And Gordon's neat voice said: *The Powers of Darkness.* Another leaf spun by towards a thunder that was close. Guy said *the Powers of Darkness* again, on a dragging note of alarm which was smothered in a laugh from Maude.

Was Dick frightened? Frightened of a caterpillar?

Out of their laughter came something about Scotchmen. *They all believe in the devil; it's a legacy of the Shorter Catechism.* Catechism . . . caterpillar . . . catechism . . . the little stones came skipping down. Dick's voice, nervous and taut, cut through the clatter of it. *I did, but I've forgotten.* Caterpillar . . . catechism . . . forgotten . . . the quick words came spinning past, and after them five august monosyllables, tipping slowly over the edge of the weir . . . *the chief end of Man.* . . . Somebody was asking a question.

"What is the Chief End of Man?"

Ellen went over the weir into silence, as Dick answered:

"To glorify God and to enjoy Him for ever."

The coming thing had happened.

She had been waiting to hear this, and she heard no more.

For in that moment she had been overthrown by the occurrence of absolute faith, by a conviction of the presence of God, of His eternal existence, a fact so tremendous that all other facts, everything else in her consciousness became small . . . small . . . diminished into nothing.

"God is there," she thought, clutching at the heather. "God is *there* . . ."

Not any God that she had ever pictured to herself; not yet to be known or understood, but there, infinite, the cause and end of her own existence. To be enjoyed, not here but *there*, in a region where the words "for ever" become a possible conception: an enjoyment too strenuous for the human mind, a hope only to be perceived in revelation.

The last echoes of that revelation rolled away into the sky.

The dissolved world reassembled itself into a vision of mountains and lakes, and voices of people talking in the heather. The moment had come and gone.

She was again imprisoned in time and place and the body of Ellen Napier, and she returned to that habitation desolately, as a stranger. The long, untrodden track of her life still lay before her and the burden of earthly care which she must carry. But she still felt that she had nothing to do with all that, that she had been with God, who had nothing to do with it either, who had willed her to live for this moment only, and who was at the end, at the other side of all the things which she might have to pass through.

She was growing smaller. She could not compass that

thought any more. But she knew that it had been. She had known something. She would know it again. The assurance of it would never leave her.

She was alone, lying in the heather.

Gordon was saying:

"What is sin?"

They were still amusing themselves by trying to find out how much Dick could remember of the shorter catechism. But Dick laughed and shook his head. He could not remember any more.

20

EVEN after sunset the air was sultry. There was no cool-
ness, indoors or out, and the full moon, blazing down
upon the castle courtyard, seemed almost hot. From far
away the least noise travelled for miles in the breathless
night, and on the island they could hear the voices of
people going along the lake road, and the tinkle of little
streams in the glens, so soft as scarcely to be sound at all.

Dick came out of the drawing-room and stood in the
deserted courtyard, which the moon had painted sharply
in silver and black. He had listened for a little while to
Guy Fletcher and Barny playing sonatas for piano and
violin, but he was too restless to stay anywhere for long.
He had thought that it might be cooler outside. The
furnace heat of the day still seemed to stream up from the
baked flagstones and when he sat down on the parapet
of the well it was quite warm.

His desires returned continually to that moment when
he came out at the head of the glen and felt the breeze
which came from those unexplored valleys and hills. It
had seemed to blow right through him, through his sick
brain and heavy heart, and he found himself standing
upon the frontiers of recovery.

But he could not recapture the purity of that first
impulse. Now it seemed that he had been thrown into
a mood of disturbance and change, and that was all. It
was better than the deadness which had held him for so
long. There was exhilaration in it. There was the need
to be strenuously active. He had said, going up the glen,

that he must be in filthy condition. But he was not. Anybody would have sweated, clambering up that airless funnel. This fortnight of idleness and sunshine had restored his vigour. Without knowing it he had amassed a lot of energy during those two weeks and now that energy made him restless.

The constriction of the island exacerbated this mood. He paced the courtyard like a caged beast and sat, fuming, upon the edge of the well where he had first sat by the side of Elissa Koebel.

He would sit by her side no more, if he could help it. For he was no longer safe. He realised that as soon as he got back to the island. There was not a tree or a stone that was not drenched with her personality; he must think of her continually, even when she was not there. He had lived for a fortnight in her company, aware of the nature of her appeal but immune, secure in his inability to respond to that or to any other stimulus. But to-day, at some time in the course of the day—he could not determine exactly when—his immunity had deserted him. His thoughts were no longer negative. They were positive—extremely positive—and he was sensible of an inherent, a satisfying rightness in them which counter-balanced any warning which his reasoning self might choose to give. It was right that he should have made up his mind to go away and walk in the Ardfillan mountains. And it was right that afterwards . . . oh, yes, he was almost sure of it, afterwards, he was going to be able to snap his fingers at Thring. And in the same terms it was right that he should find himself, for the first time, think-ing of Elissa with a certain lustful vigour. It was im-possible to separate the ingredients of recovery: he was a sound man again, or nearly a sound man, and that was as it should be. His spirits had been raised, by some mysterious and vital spell, until he scarcely knew what to do with them. On getting back he had taken Guy and Kerran for a swim. He swam three times round the island and only left off swimming because it was supper-time.

But Elissa was another reason for immediate departure. It would not do to see much more of her. She had been quite right, that first day, when she made him understand that he must either capitulate or run away. He would run away. He would pack up and go at once.

"Like a fool," he thought ruefully, pausing for a moment before the forbidden, but alluring alternative.

For he knew too much about her not to feel that he was missing the chance of a lifetime. She talked too much, but he thought that he would know how to shut her mouth. With such a temperament . . . but then he was a man of principle, although he could not remember more than the first dozen answers of the shorter catechism. He did not think that a husband, the father of a family, could do anything except run away. Being susceptible he had run away on several other occasions, both before and after he married Ellen. Nor was this the first time that he had called himself a fool.

After debating his position for more than twenty minutes, he did actually go up to his room in the tower and change his boots. He tossed a few things into his haversack, more because it was something to do than because he really meant to be off that night. But he toyed with the idea of going over to Killross and staying at the inn there. To-morrow morning, very early, he could send a fisherman up with a note to tell them that he had gone. In this way he could slip off, while his mind was still made up. Ellen would get his note as soon as she woke. She would understand and she would be glad. When next they met their trouble would be over.

But when he had carried his haversack down to the landing stage he changed his mind. It was too late to arrive at Killross and demand a bed. It was past eleven. He doubted if there would even be one at the tiny inn. He might walk all night, which would be a good way of working off this superfluous energy, or he might stay one more night at the castle and get away early to-morrow before anybody was about.

Flinging his haversack into the boat-house, he wandered back irresolutely towards the castle. It seemed as though a better plan was forming itself somewhere in the back of his mind, but he could not think what it was. He could hear the piano and the violin still at it in the drawing-room and this time he went up on to the gravel terrace, outside, to listen. Strolling up and down past the windows he could see them all in there, Gordon and Kerran intent over a chessboard, Maude's needle going in and out as she smiled to herself, and Barny's long nose bent so low over the piano that he might almost be going to strike an extra note with it. Guy stood with his back to the windows. Only his square head and square shoulders were visible. He played with clumsy movements, but the music which came from the violin under his chin was sweet enough. Half lying on a sofa, just opposite the second window, the tired Ellen had almost gone to sleep. She was looking pale and spent after her exertions of the day. And, like a shadow, Louise moved uneasily up and down, pacing through the candlelight.

Dick leant with his elbows on the sill, looking in through the third window at Guy and Barny and Maude with her needlework. They were engaged in the intricate coda of a last movement, thumping their way to a final, triumphant chord. There was a pause, and the silence of the night outside seemed to rush into the listening room. Guy touched his strings softly, tuning them, and Barny turned over some music. Nobody spoke. But Dick could hear faint noises from the people he could not see, a yawn from Ellen, and Kerran saying *check!* Louise, in her pacings, did not come into view. He felt safe there, unobserved. Guy and Barny, intent on their music, Maude with her needlework, not one of them had looked up and seen him.

"What am I going to do?" he kept wondering. "What do I *want* to do?"

Suddenly they began playing again, launching into the night a sharp, high note which flowed on into a long, shapely phrase, down and then up again. A little phrase and another long one balanced the melody, and then Barny had it and the notes of the piano came tinkling down, like crystal drops, while Guy see-sawed away on his G-string. Dick stiffened at the sound, as he came suddenly to grips with the other plan which had been floating about somewhere in the back of his mind. What had brought it to life he did not know, but it had sprung into complete being with that first high note. He was thinking:

"Not to Killross . . . to her house. I could go on to Killross afterwards. I would send up a message from Killross to-morrow. Nobody would know. I'll go to her first, and then to Killross . . ."

It was almost as if he had her already in his arms. He tried to push the idea away from him, but his resistance was weakened by his insidious conviction of rightness. The possibility, the practicability, of spending a night with Elissa fell upon him like a raging fire. And he had only one slender weapon: the knowledge that he would, in retrospect, feel ashamed of himself. At the moment he was not in the least ashamed.

"I should be a fool if I didn't."

He felt no surprise, only triumph and exaltation, when he heard a light step in the gravel behind him, and knew that she had joined him at the window. It was as if his own desire had brought her there. Without looking round he moved a little and made room for her at his side. They stood, for a minute or two, looking at the unconscious players and at Maude bent over her needle.

The music flowed on. Before the first movement was over the two watchers had vanished from the window. He drew her into the shadow of the trees. He had been quite right. Now that she had gained her point she did not talk. They went without a word down to the shore and the boats. It was not until they were far away, over the water and out of earshot of the music, that he broke the silence:

"If you had not come to me, I should have come to you."

Afterwards he could never make up his mind if this was true or at what moment the battle had been lost.

21

ELLEN started awake in a panic, aware that something had terrified her. A moment later she knew what it was, even before she had identified the hissing noise outside as torrential rain. The early morning twilight was torn up by a blinding glare and a crack of thunder which sent her scurrying down under the bedclothes with her hands over her ears. She hated thunder.

When the reverberations had died down, and there was only the drumming of rain, she peered timidly over the blankets towards Dick's bed, wondering if she would have time, before the next peal, to jump out and climb in beside him and hide her face on his shoulder. That was what she always did when it thundered in the night. Any remembrance of estrangement between them was driven clean away by panic.

But Dick's bed was empty and smooth. He had not slept in it. Her heart began to beat very fast. He had fallen into the lake and was drowned. He had taken a moonlight swim and had been seized with cramp. He was not there because he was dead.

She would not have immediately concluded this if she had not been so frightened at the thunder. For the moment she was quite unable to reason. She was beside herself. Jumping out of bed she threw on a dressing-gown and flew up to the room above, where Kerran and Guy were sleeping.

"Kerran! Kerran!" she cried, hammering on the door. "Are you there? Are you awake? Do come out . . .

it's Ellen . . . just a minute . . . Kerran!"

A tousled Kerran appeared.

"Oh, Kerran! I'm so frightened. Dick's never been to bed. He's never come in. I'm afraid something must have happened to him."

"Dick? What . . . where . . ."

"He's never been to bed. I woke up just now and he wasn't there. I can't think. . . . Oh!"

She hid her eyes from another flash, and Kerran, who knew how she hated thunder, put an arm round her to soothe her.

"Come in for a minute, while I put on a dressing-gown. Guy won't mind."

He drew her into the room and made her sit on his bed while he hurriedly put on a mackintosh and a pair of waders. Guy, just awake, rubbed his eyes in astonishment.

"He wasn't there when I went to bed," narrated Ellen. "Or when I went to sleep. The thunder woke me up. Oh, Kerran! He's dead."

"When did you last . . ."

"Oh, I can't think. I can't remember. Not since after supper when you and Barny were playing. I was so sleepy. Oh, but Maude saw him in the garden after that! She saw him outside the window with Madame Koebel."

"*Did* she?" exclaimed both men. And Kerran added: "But was Elissa Koebel over here last night?"

"I didn't see her. Maude saw her. She saw them looking in through the window. Weren't you there when she . . . oh no, it was when we were going to bed. So Dick must have been in the garden then."

There was a short pause while both men dismissed an instant suspicion. It was *not* possible.

"Perhaps he decided to sleep out," suggested Guy. "It was so hot."

"But he'd have come in when it began to rain."

"Perhaps he's been locked out."

"Oh, yes," said Ellen hopefully.

"It's very likely," agreed Kerran. "Just wait, Ellen, while I go and see."

Guy, who had put on a dressing gown, came down with her to the door of the tower, and they both stood watching while Kerran ran through the sheets of rain towards the gate-house. The thunder was growing fainter, and the flashes less blinding. The rain poured steadily down in the struggling light of early morning.

Kerran reappeared in a moment and shouted across the court that the gates were open. They had, in fact, never been locked since the night of Guy and Dick's arrival. Then he vanished again, and Ellen thought she had better put on a few clothes. She went up to her room and had just huddled a coat and skirt over her nightdress when Kerran came knocking at her door.

"I ran down to the boats. To see if he'd gone over to the mainland. But they're all three in the boat-house."

"So that he must be on the island. Or . . . or . . ."

"My dear Ellen . . . don't meet trouble half way."

He had just said the same thing to Guy, who, on hearing that no boat had been taken, had insisted upon raising an alarm.

Ellen's flurried mind darted hither and thither. It seized on a new idea.

"Or he *could* have gone in Madame Koebel's boat. She must have come in a boat and gone in a boat, as she didn't come in. Perhaps . . ."

There was another knock at the door. This time it was

Maude, who had been roused by Kerran's shout in the courtyard, and who had seen, from her window, his hurried visit to the boat-house.

"Excuse me, but what's up? Is anything the . . ." She had seen Dick's empty bed as soon as she got into the room, and her eyes snapped. "Oh! what's happened to Dick?"

"That's just what we don't know," said Kerran. "He seems to have vanished last night."

"Sleeping out, probably," said Maude with great presence of mind. "I don't wonder. Barny wanted to. It was so hot."

"But in this rain . . . surely . . ."

"It came on so suddenly. If he was some way away, on the beaches at the other side, he may have crawled into shelter under a boulder or something. I expect we shall have him back in a minute or two."

"Do you really think so?" asked Ellen, doubtfully.

"My dear, what else *could* have happened? You go back to bed and I'll fetch you a nice cup of tea. You look perfectly blue."

Maude hurried Kerran out on to the stairs and as soon as they had got out of earshot she said:

"Whatever's to be done?"

"I expect you're right. I expect he is sheltering . . ."

"You don't think I really thought that? It's as plain as a pikestaff what's happened. He's gone off with that woman. I knew he would."

"Oh, no, no," cried Kerran, who had thought so himself when Ellen made her suggestion about Elissa's boat, and had quickly tried to unthink it.

"Of course he has. I saw them in the garden myself last night, peeping in through the window. And I thought to myself we were in for a scene, because, you know, Louise said she wasn't to come to the island any more, and said it on Dick's account. I just took no notice. When we went to bed I asked Ellen if she'd seen them, and she said she hadn't. I wondered what they could be up to, for they hadn't come in."

"Ellen herself suggested that he might have gone off in Elissa's boat."

"Oh, did she? Then she must have put two and two together. How many people know?"

"Guy and I and you. That's all."

"Then we'd better hold our tongues till we see what happens. He may come back, any minute. I don't suppose he meant to be caught out like this. They thought nobody could see them. He'll come back with some story of having slept out, you see. . . . Let's find Mr. Fletcher . . ."

They had got to the door of the tower again and now they saw Louise and Gordon and Guy, all huddled up in nightclothes and mackintoshes, struggling through the rain towards them. For Guy, who really believed that Dick must be drowned, had gone to rouse his hosts.

"Well, then—the fat's in the fire," whispered Maude.

The panic spread. They were all arguing and exclaiming at once when Ellen came running once more down the stairs.

"It's all right," she said breathlessly. "It's *quite* all right. I can't think how I can have been so stupid. His haversack's gone. He's taken his things. I know what he's done. It's all right. He's gone for a walking tour in the Ardfillan mountains!"

How she could have been so stupid she did not know. For she had promised to stand the racket and to smooth it over if he disappeared all of a sudden. And what she had done was to make his odd behaviour seem more odd than ever. But she had not expected that he would go so soon, and the thunder, waking her up like that, had put yesterday's conversation out of her head.

Now they were staring at her in the most unbelieving way.

"To the Ardfillan mountains?"

"Did he say he was going?" asked Maude.

"No—I mean, yes. I mean, he said he was going some time. He said so yesterday. I'm sure that's what he's done, now I see that he's taken his haversack. I'm so sorry, so very sorry, to have made all this fuss."

"But the boats . . ." began Gordon.

"Somebody must have given him a lift."

She was making a mess of it.

She was not smoothing it over at all. Just when things were so very nearly going right she had almost given him away. She wondered how much Kerran had guessed at what was in her mind, when she came rushing up to him that morning. She must try and put a better face on it.

"He . . . he often goes off like this without warning," she asserted.

Which was not true. He had never done such a thing in his life before, and they knew it. Her voice had an over-emphasis which sounded false even in her own ears, and she realised that, if she was really going to lie, she might just as well say that he had mentioned the plan; so she added:

"As a matter of fact, I think he must have told me, only I didn't understand . . ."

But it was no good. She was a poor prevaricator. The more she asserted that everything was all right, the more likely they were to suspect that she was hiding something. She had better leave it alone.

"Anyhow," she added, "I'm not going to worry about him any more. I'm only so sorry to have been so stupid."

"But," said Gordon, "who could have given him a lift, at that time of night?"

Ellen looked even more flurried. She did not know how matters stood between Louise and Gordon about Elissa, or if Gordon knew of Elissa's visit the night before. She turned helplessly to Maude, who interposed:

"There were fishermen going down the lake very late last night. I heard them. Really quite a lot of little boats go past . . . Do go up to bed, Ellen, and let me make you some tea."

Ellen was only too thankful to go. As soon as she had disappeared up the stairs Louise exclaimed:

"What on earth are we to make of all this? Do you believe what she says? Any of you? She seemed to be making the whole thing up as she went along, first of all saying he hadn't mentioned it and then saying that he had. She never could tell a lie. But what is she hiding?"

"I think," said Kerran hastily, "that's her business. She's evidently not worrying about his personal safety, and we shall know in a day or two what's happened to him. The best we can do is to accept her story."

"Most certainly," said Maude. "There's the servants and children to think of. We must put as good a face on it as we can, for as long as we can."

"Don't talk as if he'd eloped or done something disgraceful," began Louise irritably.

But the expression on the faces of Kerran and Maude brought her up short. She gasped and turned very pale.

"You don't think . . ."

"I'm afraid it's so," whispered Maude. "She was over here, over on the island last night. I saw them together in the garden. Ellen knows."

Kerran interposed:

"Don't you think the less said the better. He may come back at any moment, and it's no business of ours what explanation he makes to Ellen. It's not five o'clock now! He may come back."

"But he won't come back," said Maude. "He's taken his haversack. The whole thing was intended."

Gordon chimed in plaintively:

"But I don't understand! What are you talking about? Who was here last night? What does Ellen know?"

Louise turned on him with the triumph of one who is at last proved to have been in the right.

"Your friend," she said bitterly. "Your friend Elissa Koebel."

22

NOTHING would make Gordon believe it. He even went so far as to assert that Ellen's version must be the true one. Elissa might have taken Dick across in her boat, but there was no great harm in that. If, as he now learnt, she had that afternoon received a cruel note from Louise, he could quite understand why she had stayed in the garden and why she had not come in that night.

"Then why did she come here at all?" asked Louise.

"She has friends here, who are more loyal to her than you are."

"Oh! has she?"

"I expect she came to say good-bye, poor woman."

He felt that he understood it all exactly. She had stolen across, not meaning to speak to any of them but just to look in, once more, through the window at the friends she had lost. The thought was very painful to him, and his voice shook a little as he tried to convince Louise.

"Do you think so?" she asked coldly.

This was one of her most effective retorts, and it never failed to exasperate her opponent.

"I certainly think so. But in any case I am going over to Elissa immediately, to apologise and disclaim any part in your very callous treatment of her. She will perhaps be able to tell me if she did see Dick last night and if she rowed him across."

"Oh, no, Gordon! No! You mustn't do that!"

"And why not?"

"Well, supposing . . . well, suppose Dick was there."

Gordon made no answer. He could not trust himself to speak. But it seemed to him, as he set off through the rain towards the boat-house, that he could not bear being married to Louise much longer.

She poisoned everything. The dishonesty of her mind tainted the whole of their companionship. For years he had endured it, admiring her beauty, her vivacity and her quick wits, and telling himself that all women are morally inferior, even the best of them. It was not her fault that she had the lie in the soul, she had been born with it. It was not her fault that he felt degraded, sometimes, at this close tie with a nature which he knew to be false. All married men must feel the same, and in the Golden Age of the world, which he understood so much better than his own time, this fact was generally recognised. Nobody ever thought then of trying to include a woman in the bright garland of friendship. Gordon himself had never thought of it until this summer, when his life had suddenly became irradiated with new happiness.

In Elissa he had found such a woman as he had not supposed to have existed anywhere. Her beauty ravished and soothed him, her sympathy was a stimulation, and she loved truth. She spoke what was in her mind, and her sincerity was as clear as the sunlight. She had drawn him towards his wife, in that brief period of their mutual love, so that they had enjoyed a harmony which they had never known in their lives before.

Now it was broken up. Louise had broken it and it was gone for ever. Not even the unsullied memory was to be left to him. They would not even allow him to mourn his loss. They had driven his friend away and they had filled their minds with evil against her. It was to protect himself and her against their unkind hearts that he set out across the lake, for he must stem this tide of evil and he must prove that they were wrong.

The rain fell in driving sheets and the waves ran so high that he could scarcely steer his boat. However hard he pulled, the next wave swung him round again. He could see neither the shore nor the island and when, after labouring for nearly an hour, he got close in to the mainland he saw that he was still half a mile north of Elissa's cottage. It would be quicker to land and walk along the lake road. He beached his boat and set off at a jog-trot down the track.

He was soaked to the skin, and his heart beat painfully fast. Battling with the cold and the wet, buffeted by the wind, his courage began to fail him. If Dick should be there. . . .

But Dick would not be there. Elissa would be sitting all alone by her warm fire and she would be delighted to see him. He would go in and sit with her, and get himself dry, and their friendship would be safe for ever, so that when he was old he could think tranquilly of those hours when they had all learnt Latin together in the sunlight. Truly he was doing a good deed, struggling along in the rain. Friendship was a thing to be preserved; it had meant more in his life than love or marriage. Some day he must tell Elissa all that he felt about friendship. She would understand. She had understood everything, from the very first, when she caught sight of the sundew in his pocket handkerchief.

The cottage emerged out of the curtain of rain. It had an empty, shut-up look. He knocked two or three times, but there was no reply, and he thought that the noise was muffled by the shrieking wind. At last he picked up a large stone, and hammered with that.

Still there was no answer. No one came. Yet she could not be out in such weather. Standing on tiptoe he peered through the panes of the little window into the untidy living-room. It looked quite deserted and dusty. The ashes were white on the hearth. In the corner he could see the ladder-like stairs to the half-loft where she slept. She must still be up there, asleep. After all it was very early. He looked at his watch and realised that it was still barely eight o'clock.

Yet he needed comfort and reassurance so badly that he could not make up his mind to go away. And it seemed as if there was, at last, some kind of movement in the little house. Someone was stirring.

His heart began to beat thickly.

There was somebody coming down the ladder, not Elissa, but a man, dishevelled, startled, half awake. . . . He did not go to the door. Perhaps he had not heard the knocking. But he came towards the window to look out at the inclement day. For a few seconds he and Gordon stared at each other through the panes, each petrified with horror and astonishment. And then with a faint groan, Gordon took flight. He set off again, jog-trotting up the track towards his boat. Soon the rain hid the cottage and the friendship that had perished there.

A sharp rheumatic stab took him in the back. He slackened his pace to a hasty shuffle, realising that he was in for a bout of lumbago.

"I'm too old," he thought, "to get wet through like this."

His eyes were filled with tears which ran down amid the raindrops on his cheeks. For he felt that he had, in those few seconds, witnessed the ruin of everything that was good and beautiful in the world. It was the triumph of evil, a cosmic calamity, not merely a misfortune to a small group of people. He had lost all that he held most dear, but his own loss was nothing compared with the wound to goodness, to happiness, to innocence.

He found his boat and began tugging away once more towards the island. And the only words which came into his mind were those which Elissa had sung, one day long ago, when they were all still innocent and happy.

Friendships decay . . . he kept thinking in a kind of dreary rhythm as he pulled at his oars. "And *so* may I *follow* with *friendship's decay*. I'm too *old* . . ."

He got back at last, shivering and exhausted, and crept in to Louise. She was kind to him. She made him put on dry clothes and lighted a fire for him in their room. But a time came when he had to tell her.

23

For a few moments Dick stared stupidly at the streaming window-pane where Gordon's face had been. He was still only half awake. Then he remembered that he was in a hurry. It was late. He had slept too late and he must get into Killross so as to send his note up to the island. And then the half-realised horror settled down on him again. Gordon, *Gordon*, had been looking in through the window. Gordon had seen him. Gordon knew. There was no need now to send a note from Killross. They knew. He had been found out.

An impulse seized him to stop Gordon, to say something, he knew not what. He dashed to the door and ran through the rain to the lake-side, but there was no sign of Gordon or his boat. It was too late!

Swearing horribly Dick went back to the cottage. He did not know what time it was, for he had forgotten to wind his watch. He did not know in the least what to do next. His predicament left him stranded, with no plans for the future. For a little while he strove to avoid its full implications and busied himself with wondering how they could have found out, and what had brought Gordon, spying through the window, so soon upon his track. But the fact of being found out was in itself so dire that he could not juggle with these speculations for very long.

He had heard, he had been told, how a moment's folly can ruin a man for life.

Now it appeared that he himself was such a man. His mind went back to yesterday, when he had not been ruined. It travelled from one scene to another as he tried to discover how this thing had happened.

There had been the picnic and the climb up the glen, and the view of the Ardfillan mountains and the decision to go away. But behind all that lay in some earlier time, some point in the last fortnight when he had left off worrying about Thring or feeling that it mattered what Thring would say. He could not remember when it was, and his mind came back to yesterday, the return to the island, the change of mood, the music and the hot moonlight. He saw that he had yielded to temptation. At the time it had not seemed so, nor did he think that it would have seemed so now if he had not been found out. This change in the whole course of his life seemed to have come as suddenly and as irrelevantly as the change in the weather.

"Because I slept too long," he decided.

Indubitably he was ruined because he had slept too long. He had awakened to find himself cut off from everything that he valued in the world, from his wife, his children, his work, from the society and respect of his friends. He had awakened to find Gordon's face, looking in at him, a stupid face, made formidable by its expression of horrified incredulity, the repulsion of a decent man confronted with infamy.

It was very cold in the cottage and he was shivering. During the few minutes when he ran down to the lakeside, the rain had soaked him. On the hearth the ashes of last night's fire lay, white and scattered. He peeled off his wet shirt and knelt down to try and blow the smouldering turf into a flame again, but it was no use.

With a desolate curiosity he began to examine his surroundings, for he had never been inside the house until last night. It seemed as strange to find himself there as to find Gordon's face peering in through the window at him. Into this room he must have come with Elissa, but he could remember nothing of it. He must have been mad. He had come there in the course of a violent dream which had begun in moonlight and changed to the glow of a turf fire on the walls of a house, and ending, not like a dream, in satiety, in darkness, in sleep that had lasted too long.

And then he heard a slight movement, up in the half-loft. Elissa was awake. A little while ago, not more than half an hour, he had awakened, up there, beside her. He had not meant to leave her so abruptly, but he came down to look for his watch, and there, at the window, was Gordon. Since when he had almost forgotten that she was still asleep, while the world came tumbling down about his ears. He wondered how long it would take her to remember last night, and to miss him.

Presently she called him softly:

"De-eck?"

"Yes."

"What are you doing?"

"I'm trying to blow up the fire. It's cold."

"Come up here, please."

He climbed the ladder, still trying to remember when and how he had climbed it before. The half-loft was a little room, and the great curtained bed nearly filled it. Elissa lay, dishevelled, sleepy and warm, among the tumbled sheets, her long hair sprayed over the pillow. She raised herself on one elbow to look at him, and at the sight of his shirtless torso she gave a little exclamation.

"But you are wet!"

"Yes."

"How is that?"

He told her what had happened and she said immediately:

"Then you need not go to Killross this morning, unless you wish."

"I suppose not."

He leant against the wooden bedpost and looked at her. Those strange eyes, so candidly desirous, were all that he could remember of the night. In the firelight he had seen them otherwise, the challenge gone, submissive and tender.

"Mine . . ." he thought, with a sudden wrenching sorrow. "She was mine."

And Elissa, who knew all the moods of love as well as she knew the notes of a scale, did not ask why he sighed.

24

ALL day it rained, and nobody could go out. For the island did not even afford the spartan consolation of a walk in the wet. It was too small, and a journey to the mainland in an open boat appealed to nobody.

Louise and Maude wrote very long letters which were scarcely finished in time for the four o'clock post boat. They had dosed Gordon with aspirin and put him to bed, for his early expedition in the rain had brought on a bad attack of lumbago. Barny discovered an old ping-pong set in one of the gate-houses, and he organised a tournament with the older children, in which Kerran and Guy Fletcher joined. They kept it up all the afternoon, on the dining-room table.

By tea-time the day seemed to have gone on for ever, since most of them had been up that morning at five o'clock. They were in wretched spirits. Recrimination and bitterness were in the air. Louise feared that they were going to blame her for bringing Elissa to the island and when she was not writing letters she was busy taking each one of them aisde, in turn, and pointing out that it was really Gordon's fault, not hers. If Gordon had not made it all so difficult she might have got rid of Elissa in time.

She even called upon Guy Fletcher to agree with her, but he cut her short with less than his usual deference.

"I don't think your sister would care to have her affairs discussed like this."

Louise had so little expected reproof from this quarter that she looked confused.

"Why . . . I . . . of course this is all in the strictest confidence. I know I can rely on you, absolutely."

"It's none of my business. I'd much rather not hear about it."

"Oh, very well. I'm sorry. Do you always receive people in this way if they happen to mention their troubles?"

"I was thinking of her troubles," said Guy, exasperated.

"I see."

If she had not had so much else to make her miserable, Louise would have taken more notice of Guy's open defection. As it was she merely wrote him off as being less nice than formerly, and began thenceforth to notice a number of little things in his disfavour. By the time she got back to Oxford in the autumn she had amassed several entertaining but damaging instances of his priggishness, which went the round of their mutual acquaintance.

Next to Gordon it was Guy who most felt the tragedy of Ellen's situation. Kerran and Barny were buoyed up by their anger, Louise was wandering in a wilderness of personal grievances, and Maude was kept so busy being tactful and smoothing things over that she scarcely had time to think. But to Guy it was an occasion of pure grief. He cared nothing for Dick and his paramour. Their behaviour was evil and he turned from the thought of them with a sickened disgust. It was for Ellen to whom his soul cried out in a voiceless lamentation. He had wakened that morning to see her in his room, so frightened and so lovely, asking breathlessly for help. He knew what she feared. He had not forgotten that walk to Killross. He, too, had jumped to the conclusion that Dick must be drowned, might even have made away with himself. And he had rushed out to waken the Lindsays, feeling that he would do anything in the world for Ellen, and that there was nothing that he could do.

When the truth emerged he could almost have wished that his first guess had been right. That she should have to endure the insult as well as the loss was more than he could bear.

Still there was nothing that he could do for her. But all day he waited about, in case there might be some small service that he could offer. He knew where she was. When she went to her room in the tower he sat in his own room, above, with the door open, so that he might hear her footstep on the stairs when she went down again. If she crossed the courtyard to the keep, he stood by the staircase window, watching to see her return. He knew that she had spent most of the day in the nursery, reading to the older children and helping Muffy to keep the little ones quiet. She seemed to be asking no help of anybody. Her fortitude and her calm became glorified, for him, into something that was almost unearthly.

After tea he got his chance. The rain had stopped for a little while and he asked her if she would like to be taken across for a walk on the mainland. He knew that she had got very tired of the island, even when it was fine.

"I should like to come very much," she said gratefully. "We seem to have done nothing but eat all day."

It was not unpleasant outside, though the hills were sombre and the rain had made the air very chilly. The high wind had dropped and the lough was like a mill-pond, save for the great rings made on its surface by leaping fish. A wrack of angry clouds, sailing down the Haunted Glen, told of storms to come.

Guy had scarcely pulled clear of the shore before he felt

conscious of relief and escape. Once more, in Ellen's company, he had got out of the circle of sad things ill done. It had happened before, when they were in a boat together, coming up from Killross. He felt the oppression, the weight upon his heart, grow lighter. Why this should be he did not know. But he could not sit opposite to her, and talk to her, without beginning to feel that she was not, perhaps, in such deep trouble as he had supposed. She must possess some secret power which he did not understand. Sometimes she frowned a little, as if her thoughts were not entirely pleasant, but her pose, her gestures, were easy and relaxed, and her smile was light-hearted.

"Is she so glad that he isn't dead that she doesn't mind?" he wondered. "It can't be that."

There was a materialism in such an attitude which he would not ascribe to her, for he had already endowed her with every spiritual quality which the ideal woman ought to possess. He preferred to think that she would rather see her husband dead than dishonoured. And yet she looked happier than anyone else on the island, almost as if she had been entirely outside it.

He was quite right. Ellen was outside it. She had been growing more composed all day, though she was still angry with herself for losing her head in the morning. She did not deserve that things should be turning out so well. For they all seemed to have accepted Dick's sudden departure without comment. She was not obliged to go on explaining that everything was really quite all right. Even Louise, whom she had expected to take offence, asked no further questions.

One other thing, an unpleasant little thought, disturbed her. She could have wished that he had not gone away in

s

Elissa's boat, as apparently he had. Any other boat would have been better. It was impossible to ignore the sort of conclusions that Louise and Maude might draw from it. They had hinted at something rather horrid yesterday when they told her that strange tale of Elissa's behaviour on the bathing beach. And Maude's hints had begun before that; they had been dropped at intervals ever since Elissa first came to the castle. She was always foreseeing some catastrophe. First of all it had been Gordon. Did Ellen really believe that two people of opposite sexes could want to sit all day and read Vergil? And then there had been some ridiculous scare about Barny. Kerran and Guy Fletcher, as unmarried men, were both said to be in grave danger. And now it was Dick, for no reason at all except that he had gone across to the shore in her boat.

Still, she had to admit to herself that she would rather some fishermen had taken him across. She had not liked it when Maude told her that they had been in the garden together. She did not like Dick to be alone in gardens with women who took their clothes off in public. No sensible wife could like such a thing. Elissa was not the sort of person who fits well into domestic life, where it is so necessary that people should keep their clothes on. There was that much colouring of truth in Maude's suggestions. Ellen trusted Dick's loyalty as she trusted her own, but still she did not like it. She could not help wondering what they said to one another in the garden, and afterwards, on the lake, and if Dick showed a side of himself to this woman which he had kept hidden from his wife. The thought made her ashamed, yet it stayed with her.

She had seen him, with other women, slip into an easy,

half-mocking familiarity which, as he explained contemptuously afterwards, was the only sort of language that they could understand. There had been nothing of it in their own straightforward courtship, and the sight of that unspoken intimacy, which he could so easily establish with any pretty and provocative stranger, had always given her a faint pang of surprise. But she had never been really uneasy before. She knew the sort of thing which he said to these ladies. She could not imagine what he would say to Elissa.

It was these thoughts which made her frown sometimes, try as she would to shake them off. Yet until she had done so there could be no getting back to that exalted memory of yesterday which seemed to have deserted her. She had allowed herself to become confused by a thunderstorm, a groundless panic and a twinge of unworthy jealousy. But though the exaltation was gone, the conviction remained. She still knew herself to have been in the presence of God, and she still felt that her whole existence must depend upon the return of such a moment.

"I must put these bad thoughts quite out of my mind," she told herself. "I must put them quite away."

It was not so difficult to escape from them, now that she had got away from the island with nice Mr. Fletcher. She liked Guy very much. She liked his seriousness. She felt that she wanted to ask him something, if only she could have been sure what it was. She wanted to tell him what had happened yesterday, and then he might say something which would bring it back.

But that was impossible. When she spoke it was to exclaim at the size of the fish which were jumping out of the water.

Guy agreed that they were very large. Every word that

passed between them was precious to him; yet afterwards he could seldom remember very much of their conversations, which were, indeed, extremely commonplace. It was with Louise that he exchanged views on art, morality and Fabianism. But he would have sacrificed every one of those discussions for the nameless pleasure of hearing Ellen say:

"Look at that fish!"

"Are they jumping out after flies?" he wondered.

"I don't know."

They neither of them knew very much about the habits of fish and they let the question drop. Ellen went on thinking about eternity and Guy went on thinking about Ellen.

Still the rain kept off, so they landed and walked about for a little while on the lake road, skirting the puddles and skipping over the hundreds of little streams which ran down the hillsides into the lake. There was a sound of running water everywhere, for the heavy rain had swollen all the rivulets to double the size that they had been yesterday. Ellen picked some bog myrtle, not because she wanted any, but because she could never resist doing so.

Just as they turned to go back to their boat the sun came out for a few minutes, among the heavy western clouds. Immediately the whole scene became transfused with colour, the translucent hues of a reflection, for moisture had made the air like a mirror. The lake glittered, the grass burned with a green flame, and every puddle was a pool of light.

"This," said Guy, "is worth the whole of a wet day."

Ellen looked round her at the changed world and made no reply. She thought that it was like a sign from God, as if the hills and the water and the very stones beneath her feet shared with her this mysterious existence which was outside time.

"The Chief End of Man," she thought to herself. "Well, that's rather conceited, really. You might as well say the Chief End of Grass."

And then she thought:

"There are two meanings to things. One is here and the other is there. They are quite different."

Her difficult thoughts recoiled upon her. There was no getting any nearer to it than that. She knew it, but she could not think about it.

"But thinking isn't everything," she concluded. "If it was, then only clever people would go to heaven, which wouldn't be fair."

Again she longed to ask Guy, who was clever, if he thought that grass might have a chief end. At last she said, with a breathless rush:

"Do-you-believe-in-the-immortality-of-the-soul?"

"What?" asked Guy, somewhat startled. "Oh, yes. I certainly believe in it."

"No, but I don't mean 'believe.' Do you think about it much?"

"Oh, yes. I think about it a great deal."

"Do you really?"

"Well . . . not as often as I ought, perhaps. But I do think about it sometimes, don't you?"

Ellen solemnly shook her head.

"I find it very difficult to think about it."

They were both silent and embarrassed. Guy could have discussed this point much better with Louise. He was afraid of saying something which might disturb Ellen's gentle orthodoxy.

"We shall know some day, I suppose," she observed piously.

Guy racked his brains for some beautiful and comforting remark, but the moment passed before he could think of anything.

Ellen was preparing to get into the boat. The sound of her words had told her that she would only make a fool of herself if she tried to go on.

"But what shall I do with all this bog myrtle?" she sighed. "I don't really want it."

"Give it to me," said Guy.

"But you don't want it either."

"Yes, I do."

Which had echoes of those conversations between Dick and the ladies who did not understand any other way of talking. Ellen blushed a little. For the first time it occurred to her that nice Mr. Fletcher might be getting fond of her. She wished more than ever that she had not asked him about the immortality of the soul.

Bog myrtle, though aromatic, is a stubby and undecorative plant. Guy carried home his strange posy rather sheepishly and put it into Kerran's tooth-glass in their bedroom. He wished that he had not asked her for it.

25

Letter from Kerran

DEAREST MOTHER,

I need give you no account of this dreadful business, for I understand that Louise and Maude both wrote yesterday. Dick has not turned up, and things look pretty bad. Poor Gordon talks about writing to you too, but I do not know whether he will. He is crippled with lumbago and I told him not to bother. There is nothing to be done until we know what is to happen next.

The official version, to which we all subscribe in public, is that invented by Ellen yesterday morning. Dick has gone for a walking tour in the Ardfillan mountains. As long as Ellen sticks to that I think the rest of us should. How it will end, I cannot imagine.

I hope you will agree with me that it would be unwise for Ellen's friends to interpose at this point. Personally, I should like to go and knock the daylight out of Dick (a bold desire, for he would certainly knock the daylight out of me if I tried), but what good would that do? Ellen must want him back or she would not make these attempts to carry it all off. She bears up wonderfully. But if he comes back it will not improve matters if his brothers-in-law have tried to kick him. Ellen's happiness is the only important consideration.

Gordon has just come in, and I have read this last paragraph out to him. He agrees with me, but he is so stunned by it all that I do not think his opinion is worth much. He minds dreadfully that such a thing should have happened in *his* house. I don't tell him what we all think: that he counts for very little in his house, and that, next to Ellen, we all of us feel most for him. He was really fond of the harpy. He was deceived in her. But then, have we not been deceived in Dick? We thought him a man of character, and it appears that he is not. Even now I can scarcely believe it. To desert such a woman as Ellen, in her condition, too, without the shadow of an excuse, with such cold-blooded brutality! No! Whether they make it up or not, I don't think I shall ever be able to speak civilly to him again.

This is all I have to say about it. I hope Ellen confides in you, for she must suffer deeply in spite of her courage.

Your affectionate son,
KERRAN ANNESLEY.

Letter from Louise

MY DARLING MOTHER,

There is no fresh news. Not a word or sign to-day, and our suspicion that he does not mean to return is becoming a certainty. Gordon feels it very deeply. He feels that it is his fault. If he had not opposed me when I first wished to break with Elissa one might have staved off this catastrophe. But it is no use crying over spilt milk. What is done is done, and it can *never* be undone.

Ellen takes it very calmly. It is impossible to know what she thinks. Has she written to you? It does not seem to me that she has faced it at all yet, and nobody has the courage to broach it to her. But we cannot go on like this. It will have to be done sometime. Could you possibly come? We shall need you badly, when she comes to realise, as she *must* realise, that this is a *final* break.

One might have staved it off, but there are funda-
mental things behind it that might have made it inevitable,
whatever one did. The truth must be faced. Dick and
Ellen are *not* suited to one another. She does not understand him. You know I have always said this. And now
that he is gone I do not think it likely that he will come
back to her. Elissa is a bad, immoral woman. I hold no
brief for her. But she is much more likely to hold him
than poor Ellen. She is much more nearly his equal,
unfortunately. Because one condemns them I don't think
one has the right to suppose that their love has no
element of greatness and tragedy. It must have. He
would not have left his wife and children, thrown up his
whole career, unless he had loved her passionately.
Gordon says it is bound to have a damning effect on his
professional position.

Do not think I am justifying him. I feel, of course, that
we must all stand by Ellen and see that she gets her rights,
especially the custody of the children. She must not be
soft-hearted about that, for it would not do to let the
children grow up in any way under Elissa's influence.
But she must be made to see that divorce is the only
dignified thing, and you are the only person who can
make her see it. Do you agree with me?

I must stop, though I had a great deal more to say, as
the post boat is coming.

Your loving
LOUISE.

Letter from Maude

DEAREST MAMMA,

I've nothing to add to my note of yesterday. We are
still pretending that nothing has happened. Barny feels it

very much and he is not at *all* well. I am worried about him.

What I say is, we ought to think only of Ellen. She seems to have the situation very well in hand. I admire her TREMENDOUSLY. If I were she I could not keep it up, though I do agree that her attitude is the *right* one. I have always felt that she must have a great many difficulties that we know nothing about. Because you know, Mamma, this sort of thing *must* have happened before. She could never have learned the ropes so well without *some* practice.

Now, Mamma, Louise has already begun to talk about a divorce, but I do hope you won't agree with her. If Ellen thinks that keeping her home together for the children is the most important thing, *why* should anyone want to bully her out of it? She evidently knows the kind of man Dick is and she prefers to put up with it. After all, the *wife* has such a very strong position. I am helping her all I can, inventing convincing details about Dick's walking tour, and I have actually gone so far as to remember that he told ME he was going! May I be forgiven!

But I foresaw it all, you know, before the others, so perhaps I was better prepared for it!

Please do not worry more than you can help. I think it may turn out all right in the end. I have not given up hope!

Your affectionate
MAUDE.

P.S.—I don't think the servants know, but Louise has coughed it all up to Muffy, which I think rather a pity.

Letter from Ellen

MY DEAR MOTHER,

Here we all are in pouring rain, which is very dis-agreeable, for we have nothing to do. It is a good thing we got in our picnic to the Haunted Glen before the weather broke. We climbed up the glen, which was rather ugly—nothing but stones, etc., and very hot. But we got a good view at the top, over into the Ardfillan mountains. Dick has gone there on a walking tour. I am afraid he will get very wet. I wish he had gone sooner.

There is no news except that everybody seems to be very 'dowly.' Gordon has got lumbago. Barny isn't well either, but I think that is just boredom. The children get very impatient and quarrelsome, shut up in the rain. Can you send me some books to read to them? Dick is anxious that I should read classical books to them; he says they can read E. Nesbit, which they prefer, to themselves. What about one of the Waverley novels? Not *Ivanhoe*, or *The Talisman*, or *Woodstock*, or *Kenilworth*, or *Rob Roy*, because we have read them. One of the others, only not *Waverley*, because that is not so interesting for children: the beginning is so long. Which was the one where some-body got starved to death? I think they would like that. Dick says they ought to know their Scott when they are so young that the impression sinks in. He wanted me to read them *Vanity Fair*, but I do not think Peter would care for it. Or what about *Lorna Doone?* Or the *Gladiator?* I wonder if Dick would think they were classics. Anyhow, if you are near a bookshop I should be very grateful if you would send me some.

Your loving daughter,

ELLEN.

26

Emily, the Napiers' nurserymaid, was expert at telling fortunes in tea-cups. Her prophecies always came true, but she had to make them when Muffy's back was turned, because Muffy did not approve of such things.

On the third day of Dick's disappearance, there was a good deal of by-play in the keep at breakfast time. Emily, looking into the bottom of her cup, gave a little squeak:

"Well, I never!"

"Whatever's the matter now?" asked Muffy irritably. "Is a dark stranger going to send you a pea-green elephant for a Christmas present, or what?"

"No, but there's going to be a fatal illness in the house. I've never seen it so plain before. Look there, Rosie."

"Oh, stuff and nonsense. I will not have such nonsense talked in my nursery."

Public opinion was against Muffy, who had been as cross as two sticks ever since it began to rain. The children crowded round to look into Emily's cup.

"A fatal illness!" said Peter. "That means somebody will die, doesn't it, Emily? How soon will it happen?"

"Within three days," said Emily, with gloomy relish. "Sure to. I've only seen it once before so plain and then my stepfather fell off a ladder. He was . . ."

"That's enough about that. I won't have it."

Emily and Rosie were cowed, but Peter continued defiantly.

"Emily said that Rosamund would get a letter and she did. And she said that Mrs. Ames would hear something that surprised her very much . . ."

"Peter, be quiet! I've said we've had enough of it."

"Could a person die of lumbago?" asked Rosamund in a sudden panic.

"Another word of this . . . the first person who mentions tea-leaves or illnesses again will go upstairs."

"All right," said Peter. "But if the things—we mayn't—mention in Emily's cup are right, and somebody does get a fatal what-we-don't-talk-about will they be buried here, or will they have to take the coffin home?"

"Upstairs you go, young man."

"But I didn't . . ."

"You'll go upstairs for impudence and that's all about it."

Peter went upstairs as slowly as he could, and was presently joined by Hope and Charles, who had taken up the game of inventing periphrases for the forbidden topics. They were all in revolt. Muffy had no right to treat them as if they were nursery children, just because they took their meals with the babies. All day they baited her, bringing the conversation back to ill-health at every possible opportunity until she announced that the next offender would be sent to bed. So that nothing could exceed their glee when Maude bustled into the keep, while they were having tea, and said that Barny was ill.

"Ssssh!" shrieked the children. "You mustn't! Muffy says you mustn't!"

"Be quiet, children, I wish you'd come, Muffy. He's got a ghastly pain."

"Got another chill," said Muffy, hunting for her goloshes, without which it was impossible to cross the courtyard.

"No, no. I don't think it's a chill. He was sick this

morning, but that seems to have gone off. And the pain seems to be getting more to one place."

Maude looked white and scared, and her face, without its bright, fixed smile, seemed unfamiliar. The children were sobered. In the fun of baiting Muffy, they had forgotten the origin of this tabu. Now that they remembered, they were frightened. Only Rosamund had the courage to ask if it was appendicitis, like the King had, whereat Maude, suddenly losing control of herself, boxed her ears.

"Serve you right for talking nonsense," said Muffy, as they hurried out of the keep.

Barny lay groaning upon his bed, doubled up and ashy-faced. His eyes looked feverish. He had, as usual, refused to let Maude take his temperature. But when Muffy produced her thermometer he submitted. Nor did he take much interest in their verdict. He was too much occupied with his pain.

One glance at the thermometer was enough to banish the scepticism in Muffy's bearing. She went out with Maude on to the landing.

"I'll get hot bottles and help you to put him to bed," she said. "And I'll tell them to send for a doctor. You go back to him."

"Muffy . . . you don't think . . ."

"With that temperature we'd better be sure."

Maude leant for a second against the wall and closed her eyes. The one thing which she had always dreaded most was really going to happen to her. She had always felt that she could face any emergency but one, and that God, knowing this, would not let Barny get appendicitis in some remote place. A feverish voice called her from the bedroom. She braced herself and went back to him.

"Maude!" He clutched her hand. "Don't go away. Don't leave me like that again."

"That's all right, darling. I won't. You'll be better soon. We'll get you to bed with hot bottles. We're sending for a doctor."

"Maude! Do you suppose I've got appendicitis?"

"No, no, no! It's probably a frightfully bad chill."

"It's exactly in the right place," said Barny, who knew just enough anatomy to ruin his peace of mind. "I'm pretty certain myself. In which case I shall die."

"Nonsense. Wait till the doctor . . ."

"Not a bit of good."

Barny, always possessed by an insatiable curiosity, had a way of picking up information concerning the whole population in any place where he stayed.

"The doctor here is a museum piece. The country people swear by him and there aren't enough well to-do inhabitants to make it worth while for a younger man to come. He happens to be nearly eighty, and is said to drink. I shouldn't think he's ever heard of an appendix. We'd probably get on better without him. *Oh, Christ!*"

He doubled up again and clutched Maude's hand. When the spasm was over she assured him that he could not die because she would not allow it. This seemed to comfort him a little.

Louise came to the door and asked if she could do anything. She said that Kerran was going at once to Killross in search of a doctor.

"It's no use," gasped Barny. "He drinks and he's nearly eighty. A major operation . . ."

Maude was making signs to Louise. She could not leave Barny because he was grasping her hand.

"What?" said Louise stupidly. "I don't understand."

"She's trying to tell you," said Barny, "that you must tell him to bring his tools and chloroform and all that, in case—oh, Jesus Christ!"

"Why?" Louise looked frightened. "What . . ."

"It's such a long way to send for things," said Maude. "He'd better come prepared. If . . . if . . ."

"I'll tell Kerran. I'll catch him before he goes."

When Louise had gone Barny said:

"She thinks this is just another of your scares."

"Let's hope it is."

They both knew that it was not. Maude's mind stood still, appalled. But Barny's lively imagination pranced ahead. He thought of his own death as inevitable, saw Maude a widow, and remembered that he had only been able to save two thousand pounds.

"If only I'd stuck to Gilt Edge," he groaned.

"Oh, Barny, don't!"

"I wish I knew exactly how I stand over my mother's marriage settlement. I know I should have had five thousand pounds out of her jointure on her death, and if we'd had children, of course . . ."

"Barny, please . . ."

"My darling, we've got to face it."

Maude did not call this facing it, and said so. And as she got him out of his clothes and into bed, they had a stimulating dispute as to which of them was taking the more sensible line. He was not nearly so frightened as she was, and that comforted her. He could still dramatise his situation.

When Ellen came up to offer help, he was estimating the possible value of his furniture.

"I just came to tell you," said Ellen, "that I've sent for Dick."

There was a moment's stupefied silence, and then Maude, flushing to a deep crimson, caught hold of Ellen's arm. She scarcely knew what she was doing.

"Oh, Ellen! . . ." she stammered. "Oh, Ellen!"

She wanted to hug Ellen and kiss her. She felt like a drowning man to whom a rope has been flung. If Dick could not save Barny, then nobody could.

"You've what?" demanded Barny, confused between his pain and the effort to remember what his sideboard had cost when it was new.

"Mr. Fletcher is going to fetch him back," explained Ellen. "Gordon can't because of his lumbago. I thought we'd better have Dick here, in case . . . don't you think so, Maude?"

"Oh, Ellen . . . but where . . . how . . ."

"Oh, what I said was, he'd better go over to Killross and ask at the inn. All the country people go in there, and everything is known that happens for miles round. Any stranger gets noticed in those parts. You can't walk half a mile without a dozen people seeing you, though it seems so deserted. Dick can't be very far off. I told Mr. Fletcher if he gives ten shillings to some little herd boy they'll probably produce Dick in a very short time. It's astonishing how quickly news travels."

"And you think he'll come?" asked Maude anxiously.

"Come? But of course he will, when he knows that Barny is ill."

"I don't want him," announced Barny. "I'd rather die."

"Ssshl" said Maude. "Ellen, this is very, very good of you."

T

She hurried Ellen out of the room before he could say any more.

"I don't know how to thank you," she repeated.

"But it's Guy Fletcher you must thank," said Ellen, a little surprised.

"I know. I know. And Ellen . . . you mustn't mind Barny."

Barny was so indignant that he almost forgot his pain.

"I'd much rather die," he kept saying, when Maude went back to him. "I don't want him."

Which cheered Maude up considerably, because it showed how far Barny still was from any real apprehension of death. She had seen people die. She had seen people come to that point when they no longer worry about the price of sideboards or the morals of their relations. Barny was still a long way off dying, even when, after a little while, he changed his mind and began to ask anxiously if Dick had come yet.

27

ELLEN found the Lindsays talking to Guy Fletcher at the bottom of the tower stairs. They all fell silent when she appeared, but she knew that they must be discussing this proposal of hers to send for Dick. And she was a little annoyed that they should still be talking it over. There was no time to be lost, and Guy ought to have gone at once.

"I've just seen Maude," she said quickly, "and she quite agrees that Dick ought to come back."

And then Louise asked the same question that Maude had asked.

"But, Ellen, do you really think he will?"

She found herself getting angry.

"But if it's true that there's no decent doctor in Killross, he must. And in any case, if there has to be an operation . . ."

Gordon nodded solemnly.

"He ought to come. It's certainly his duty to come."

But his tone suggested considerable doubt as to whether Dick would do his duty. Ellen flushed resentfully, and then she grew pale. For this sounded as if they must have guessed a great deal. Did they really think that Dick would refuse to operate?

"I don't know what you're talking about. Barny is ill. He's very ill. If Dick's to do any good we must get him here at once. Are you going, Mr. Fletcher?"

Not trusting herself to say any more, she turned away and went across to the keep. Muffy, having driven all the children upstairs, was busy boiling water for hot bottles. When she saw Ellen she began immediately to scold.

"Now what are you rushing about for? There's nothing you can do. You go and have a lay down—I would."

"I will in a minute. I've sent for Dick. Don't you think that is wise?"

Muffy nearly dropped the kettle she was holding.

"Oh, Miss Ellen!"

This was the last straw. Even Muffy seemed to have gone mad.

"Oh, Miss Ellen, dearie, you don't mean it?"

"Mean it? Of course I mean it. What . . . why do you look at me like that? For heaven's sake what is the matter with you all? Why shouldn't I send for him? What have you been saying about him?"

"Oh dear, oh dear! You'll break my heart. Oh, Miss Ellen, don't go on like this, not with me, for I can't bear it. It isn't as if we didn't all know, my lamb."

"What?"

Ellen's heart sank. She grew whiter and whiter, until Muffy caught her arm, fearing that she might fall. But she was not going to faint. She looked round for a chair and sat down before she spoke again.

"Didn't know . . . what do you know? What are they saying?"

"About . . . Dr. Napier . . . and that lady . . ."

"That lady?" repeated Ellen, in tones of unmistakable astonishment. "What lady? . . . Do you mean Madame Koebel?"

Muffy began to speak and then checked herself. This was sincere. This astonishment was genuine. It had taken Ellen by surprise.

"Madame Koebel? What are they saying, Muffy? Tell me at once."

"That it's her that's come between you . . ."

"Muffy! Who says such a thing? How could anybody be so wicked?"

And this, this indignation was genuine too. A whole number of things broke in upon Muffy's mind at once, and the miserable bewilderment of the past three days began to clear up. Like all the others she had been quite baffled by Ellen's behaviour. Now she saw it all. Ellen did not know. She believed, possibly, in her own story of a walking tour. She had the whole shock of discovery before her.

"What do they say, Muffy? That we . . . that we quarrelled? That he went away because of that? Because of a quarrel?"

"Some such talk," agreed Muffy desperately.

"But you didn't think so?"

"I didn't know, dear. It seemed queer, his going off like that."

They stared helplessly at one another. Each was busy in her mind, rearranging facts, feeling for the truth.

Muffy thought:

"So that's why she's been bearing up so well. She hasn't been worried, all this time, not a scrap. She thinks he's . . . and supposing she's right. Perhaps he really. . . . No! You can't get over what Dr. Lindsay saw, with his own eyes. She's wrong. And she'll have to know it . . ."

And Ellen thought:

"So that's why they've all been so quiet about his going. All of them. But they can't all . . . even Guy Fletcher. When I asked him to go, he must have thought

. . . oh, it's intolerable! Louise made it up. It's too bad of her. I hate Louise."

When at last she could speak, her anger against them all was poured out upon the head of the unfortunate Muffy.

"How can you? How dare you? Didn't I explain? He told me he was going. He doesn't like it here, and no more do I. It's a . . . a horrible place. Louise and Maude made this up. I know. They aren't happy unless they're inventing something or other, and interfering and trying to pretend everything is like a book or something. But you, Muffy! Fancy you believing them! You know us both. You know me and Dick. You couldn't have thought there was anything of that sort between us. How could you? I shall never forgive you, never! Never."

She began to shake and tremble and sob.

. "A husband and a wife, Muffy, a *husband* and a *wife*, when they love each other, they don't . . . they don't quarrel about that sort of thing. They trust each other. I could never . . . he could never. . . . Oh, you're all horrible!"

"Miss Ellen, my lamb, my precious, don't! Don't cry like that. Don't excite yourself. Not now. It's bad for you. It's bad for your baby."

Ellen dried her eyes and controlled herself.

"I know. I mustn't. But how can people . . . Louise is married. Maude is married. They must know that a husband and a wife . . . I mean marriage . . . that kettle's boiling over."

Muffy stopped and filled the stone bottle. Her tears fell on her shaking hands.

"Louise and Maude are very wicked," continued Ellen more calmly. "They don't behave properly to their husbands. I've often thought they don't. But you might have known better, I really think you might."

"But it does happen sometimes," ventured Muffy. "Not all men are true, nor all women either."

"There are bad people in the world, I daresay. But that has nothing to do with it. There are lots of ways that people can be untrue to each other. I think it's being untrue to one's husband to have horrible, vulgar suspicions and quarrels. It's being untrue to be rude to him and speak in a scornful way in front of other people, like Louise does. It's being untrue to complain of him behind his back, like Maude does. I think all that is very bad. I don't think a marriage is a proper marriage when such things are going on."

Muffy straightened herself, and wrapped up the hot bottle in her apron. She saw that Ellen was more indignant at the aspersion on herself than at the tacit accusation against Dick. Her thoughts were so far from any possibility of unfaithfulness that she was merely furious with them all for suspecting her of making a jealous scene.

She did not know what to say, and she decided at last to say nothing. This dreadful business could wait for a little while, until they knew whether Dick was really coming back.

"Don't let's ever speak of it again," concluded Ellen coldly. "I think you've all been letting yourselves get into quite a hysterical state, shut up in this horrid little hole. You take over that bottle, and I'll bring the other as soon as the second kettle has boiled."

She kept up a demeanour of stately displeasure until Muffy had stumped out of the keep, and then she began to cry again. Her rage was stimulated by the terrible fright she had had when Muffy talked about everybody knowing.

For two pins, she told herself, she could have gone and slapped all their faces. The wish to slap somebody was uncontrollable, and when all the children came bawling downstairs the floodgates of her wrath were opened.

"This is a perfect bear garden. A bear garden!"

The children had never heard of a bear garden before, and thought it a good trope. Charles broke into ill-timed laughter.

"Oh!" said Ellen. "Oh, you little plague!"

She slapped every child within reach and marched out of the tower. It was a good thing that Guy Fletcher could not see her.

28

FOR Guy was doing his great act of service. He said, as soon as she left them:

"Since she has asked me I shall go. I'll see that he gets her message."

"It's no use, Guy," protested Louise; "it'll only put you in an odious situation. You can't interfere in a thing like this, and I'm surprised you should want to, considering that you've said yourself it's none of your business."

"Who else can go?" asked Gordon. "I would if I could, but you know perfectly well . . ."

"Nobody can go. It's not necessary. A doctor has been sent for from Killross."

Ellen's calm announcement had exasperated Louise. For three days she had been saying that Ellen must be made to see the truth, and nobody would agree with her. She did not want to admit that Dick would probably come back, if he knew the state of the case, and she did not want to admit that Barny was ill enough to make such an errand necessary. It was not a situation which fitted in well with the facts as she had arranged them.

"If she thinks she can whistle him back on this excuse . . ."

Gordon and Guy both protested. They were sure that Ellen had only been thinking of Barny.

"And we don't even know where they are. What are you going to do? Are you going to the cottage?"

Guy did not know. He had thought vaguely that he might go to Killross and send a message by a third party to Dick. But Louise made small work of this idea.

"How do we know they are at the cottage? I don't expect they are for a minute. They may have gone back to England. And you don't want to spread the news of this business in Killross. Goodness knows there's probably been enough gossip already. No. If you go you'd better go straight to the cottage and find out if they're still there. And I wish you joy of it."

This was a horrible suggestion to Guy, but he had to agree that it was the best course, and that much time would be lost if he sent a message from Killross. Nor had Louise quite finished with him.

"If he won't come? What then?"

"We've no cause to think so badly of him as that," broke in Gordon. "And Guy, you needn't say she sent you. You can say I did. I take the whole responsibility."

Guy looked from one to the other in helpless appeal. He could scarcely believe that he had ever volunteered to go upon so odious an expedition. But a hint of mockery in Louise's eye stiffened his resolve and he said:

"Well, if I'm going I'd better go now."

"There's no time to be lost," agreed Gordon.

As Guy passed out of the gate he thought he heard a laugh from Louise and a sharp word of expostulation from Gordon. He realised what a ridiculous figure he would cut in the tale which she might tell about it afterwards. Disgust nearly stifled him, and it seemed as if even Ellen was hardly worth all that he was enduring for her sake. But he forced himself to go on. He got out a boat and set off across the lake.

There remained Barny's illness. That was real, and that was urgent; he found himself invoking it, now that Ellen's image had begun to fail him. For try as he would, he could not at the moment recall her to her proper place, pacing serenely through the avenues of his thought. He tried to remember all the virtues which he had been accustomed to ascribe to her, and all the beautiful ideas which had been associated with her name. But it would not do. She would not mount her pedestal. She had certain attributes of which he could not approve. If she had remained passively tragic it would have been so much better. But by sending him on this errand, by involving him in this sordid business, she had displayed a certain toughness, an earthy commonsense, which shattered his dream. It was no doubt a practical thing to do, but he wished that she had not done it. She was insensitive, and that was an unpardonable flaw. The ideal woman, whom he had never met, must have at least as much sensibility as he had himself, together with all the tranquil temper which he himself, on account of his sensibility, could never possess. How any one woman was ever to combine those qualities he did not know, but until to-day he had really believed that such a combination might exist in Ellen.

But Barny was very ill. There was no doubt about that. And for his sake it would be wrong to hope that Dick and Elissa might have left the cottage.

It seemed probable that they had not, for he saw, even before he landed, that there was smoke coming out of their chimney. He pulled up his boat and picked his way over the puddles to the door.

But he had to knock twice before anyone came. At last he heard the sound of a chair being pushed back. Steps crossed the room and the door was opened by Dick, who very nearly shut it again when he saw who was there.

"What do you want?" he asked in a very surly voice.

Guy looked past him and said coldly:

"The Lindsays have sent me. Barny is very ill. His wife thinks it is acute appendicitis and there is said to be no doctor in the district. They are all in great distress, and it is suggested that you had better come back to the island at once."

"Appendicitis!" exclaimed Dick, opening the door a little wider. "Barny? He would! Come in a minute . . ."

"No, thank you," said Guy, who would rather have walked into a cage full of cobras.

Dick repressed a smile.

"I'm alone. There's no one here."

"I won't come in, thank you."

"Have it your own way. Why do they think it is appendicitis?"

Guy described the symptoms and Dick made an impatient sound of assent.

"Is there any rigidity?"

"I don't know."

"You don't think it's one of their scares?"

"Hardly. I don't think they would have sent me if they hadn't thought it urgent."

"No. I don't think they would."

Again a grim smile flickered for a moment across Dick's face.

"But how . . ." he began. "Does my . . . does my wife know you've been sent?"

"It was her suggestion, originally," said Guy, with a little hesitation.

"Hmph. I see. I wish you'd come in. This wants considering. Did they tell you not to come in?"

Guy went in, reluctantly, and stood just inside the door. For one moment he had hoped that Elissa was gone for good, but he now saw her slippers sprawling on the floor, and the remains of a meal for two people still on the table. The whole room was squalidly untidy.

"This wants considering," repeated Dick. "What's to be done?"

"I can't see that it does. He is really very ill. It's urgent."

"How do things stand over there? Gordon told everyone that he saw me here, I suppose?"

"Yes. But you are said to be walking, over in the mountains. That is what everyone has agreed to say."

"Oh, I see. That puts a sort of face on it. Who invented that?"

"She did."

"Ellen? Good God!"

Dick was greatly astonished by this, but he did not ponder on it for very long. He returned to Barny.

"I suppose I ought to go."

Guy said nothing. His face suggested that Dick's moral problems were beyond his power to decipher, and that the word "ought" upon such lips was an incongruity.

"I must go," concluded Dick.

His belongings were scattered over the cottage, and he began to collect them and stuff them into his haversack. As he did so he talked, plying Guy with rapid questions and running over all the possibilities of getting hospital supplies in a hurry. For, as he pointed out, he could not in the worst event operate upon Barny with a carving knife.

"I'd better go straight back and have a look at him first. And if I do have to do anything in a hurry you must go down to Killross and telegraph. What is the nearest town? Or could we hire a motor in Killross, do you think? I suppose not. I've always told them that appendix of Barny's might give them trouble. But he wouldn't have it out. Do you see my boots anywhere?"

Guy's curt replies were meant to silence him, but he ignored their tacit reproof and went tramping up into the half-loft to find his boots It was as if he had succeeded in putting aside the whole question of his own misconduct, from the moment that he announced that he must go. He made Guy feel foolish, and it seemed possible that he might, when he got to Inishbar, make everybody feel foolish. He even had the effrontery to come and lean over the balustrade of the half-loft and say:

"Have you got a pencil? I shall have to leave a note to explain where I've gone."

"I'll wait outside," said Guy hastily. "I'll wait down by the boat till you're ready."

Not for anything would he remain a moment longer in the abode of evil. Already he had been contaminated past belief with this hunting for boots and borrowing of pencils. There was moral squalor, for him, in the very chairs and tables, the unwashed dishes and the tracks of mud on the floor. The place was no better than a pigsty, a fit shelter for beasts. He got himself out into the clean, sweet air of the evening and saw a cloaked figure coming along the road which looked very like Elissa. By dint of a somewhat undignified scuffle, he escaped into the birch trees before she got near enough to hail him.

A horrible suspicion had crossed his mind: the fear that Ellen might be going to take Dick back. If she did, he would never, never forgive her. She must forfeit, for all time, her claims to be the ideal woman. He might, with an effort of will, have just allowed her to sacrifice her pride enough to send for Dick simply to save her brother. But more than that he could never permit. The reality of Elissa's cottage, with its dust and confusion, the slippers on the floor, had been too sordid. If Ellen could ever condone this swinish amour, then her memory also must become tarnished.

For twenty minutes Guy wrestled with the threat of disillusionment. He tried to tell himself that such a thing could never be. He tried to recapture that moment when they had walked in the burnished sunlight, by the lake, when she had given him the bog myrtle. For it had seemed to him then that she must be very near to heaven. The expression in her eyes had been heavenly. And she had asked him something, he could not remember, about the immortality of the soul. And he had come to the very edge of self-betrayal. He had thought that he loved her.

A shout from the lake-side roused him from his torment. Dick had come out of the cottage and was waiting by the boat.

29

KERRAN appeared soon after dark with an old gentleman whom he had run to earth at Ballymacrennan, ten miles from Killross. This was no doubt the "museum piece" of whom Barny had heard, and the reports of his age had not been exaggerated. Kerran guessed him to be nearer ninety than eighty, and afterwards insisted that he had not been a doctor at all, probably, but a vet. His brogue was disarming and according to himself he thought nothing of removing an appendix—did it every day of the week, in fact. But Kerran's heart had sunk so low by the time they got to Killross that he slipped off and telegraphed to Dublin for another opinion, while Dr. Moore settled down to an interlude of refreshment in the inn.

"Ah, he'll be all right! Ah, don't worry about him! He'll be as snug as a bug in a rug this time to-morrow. Bridgie, me gerrl, I'll have another double Scotch and the gentleman'll be taking the same. Ah, what's the hurry? Isn't there lashins of time?"

It seemed that Barny was as good as dead, for the patriarch was determined to operate. He had brought with him some chloroform and an immense amount of cutlery, which he displayed on the bar counter and explained to his horrified companion.

Kerran looked at the ancient, bone-handled scalpels, the unwieldy curved needles, all of them blunt and rusty, the stiff-jointed artery clips, and thought of a wood-carving set which he had once had as a boy and which had been left out by accident for six weeks in the rain.

"What are those things in bottles?" he asked timidly.

"Sure, they're sutures," explained Dr. Moore, adding that they were perhaps a wee bit dried up.

"But you won't operate if you think this attack has a chance of subsiding?" pleaded Kerran.

"Ah! Not at all. We'll have it out in the flick of an ass's tail, the way he'll never feel the miss of it."

This, at least, was the account of his adventures which Kerran gave to Guy and Gordon as they sat round the dining-room fire, and when they accused him of exaggeration he insisted that it was all substantially true, though he might have touched it up a little here and there. He had been horribly frightened and had almost begun to hope that the old gentleman might drink himself into a coma before ever they left Killross. But at last they had come on to the island to find that Kerran's worst fears had been groundless, since Dick was already in charge of the case. Their arrival was opportune. Dick, after one incredulous glance at the wood-carving set, had said that it must do, for that he dared not wait any longer. He operated immediately and it seemed, to the three men who waited, that he was taking his time about it.

"If anybody had told me yesterday that I should be ready to fall on Dick's neck to-night I'd have called him a liar," said Kerran.

"It was a great relief," agreed Gordon. "We all thought Barny was dying. Poor Maude! Her distress! I must say I was ready to forgive everything when I heard the children calling out that he had come."

"The children . . . ?"

"Yes," said Guy morosely. "They saw the boat coming and all rushed down to meet us."

"Oh!"

Kerran laughed in spite of himself, but Gordon said gravely that the children should not have been there.

"No. I should think not. It would have been more tactful to keep the little ones out of it. 'No children run to greet their sire's return,' as it were . . ."

"We couldn't help it," explained Gordon in distress. "Nobody thought of the children at such a time."

He disliked Kerran's flippancy and repeated, more than once, that the children ought not to have been there.

"And what then . . ." asked Kerran. "Hark! Is that anyone coming?"

He went to the door. But it was only a maid crossing the courtyard. The light, burning in a window of Barny's tower, could tell them nothing: a canopy of suspense still hung over the castle. Kerran came back, looking at his watch.

"I never knew these things took so long."

Guy remembered that he had thought this himself, not so very long ago. And for the first time that day the significance of the walk from Dunclough to Killross flashed into his mind. The fellow had then been threatening to retire: had declared himself unable to operate any more. But he must have got over all that. Guy was sure that he had felt no doubts of his own ability during that queer interview down at the cottage. In the panic and flurry at the castle he had been cool and firm. He had taken charge of them all. And he had gone off to operate, without proper instruments, without a skilled anæsthetist, without sterilised dressings, as calmly as if he had had all the resources of John's at his command. It was strange. It was disquieting. The Dick of three weeks ago ought not to compare so unfavourably with the Dick of to-night. To Guy it was like an exaltation of evil.

"I suppose," Kerran was saying, "that he'll stay now, anyhow, till Barny is out of the wood; and we take it that the walking tour was a success, if a trifle wet."

Gordon agreed. Their belief in Dick was assured; they quite expected that Barny would get out of the wood.

"But afterwards . . . I suppose the best thing that could happen would be a . . . a . . . reconciliation?"

Guy gave an unhappy start and Gordon shook his head.

"That doesn't depend on us."

"It does in a way. At least we can do nothing, say nothing, to prevent it. If they, Dick and Ellen, seem to have come to some agreement, we can hold our tongues and forget the business as quickly as we can."

"But surely . . ." protested Guy.

Both men turned to look at him in surprise. He flushed and faltered. It was, after all, no business of his.

And then, inexplicably, the canopy of suspense was lifted. They were aware, they knew not how, that the operation was over. The night seemed to shake itself, and an inaudible sigh of relief went over the waiting castle. Steps crossed the courtyard just as all the men leapt to their feet.

"Ah, Louise! How . . . how . . ."

"All right," said Louise.

She came wearily towards the fire. "He's coming round. Dick seems to think he's all right."

"Have a brandy and soda," said Kerran. "It'll do you good."

"Well, then, I think I will."

She made a face as she took the drink, and then she gave them what details she could.

"No. I wasn't there. He had Ellen and Maude and Muffy and that dreadful old man, and he said any more untrained people would only get in his way. But I waited outside, in case they wanted anything. I gather that it was only just in time. Dick said he'd have never done it unless he'd thought so, under those conditions."

"Ellen?"

"Oh, dear, yes! From the way they both behaved you'd have thought he'd just gone out for a walk. Where, by the way, do you suppose that old man is to sleep? We must in decency keep him for the night."

"Under the dining-room table," suggested Kerran. "I expect that's where he generally sleeps."

"He'll want something to eat. They all will. I'd better go and see about it."

She went out again into the courtyard and Guy followed her, nerving himself to make his little speech.

"I think I'll say good-night now, if there is nothing more that I can do. And . . . hadn't I better go to-morrow? I feel I'm probably in the way, while your brother is so ill."

Louise nodded indifferently.

"I'm very sorry you should go so soon. But as things are perhaps it would be better." She added with a touch of malice: "Thank you for all you've done. You seem to have staged a reconciliation."

Guy flushed and turned away from her.

He went across to his tower room and began to pack his things. In a tooth-mug on the window-sill there was still the bog myrtle which Ellen had picked two days ago. He took a sprig of it and put it, after a moment's thought, into a copy of the *Golden Treasury* which he carried about with him. He spent a little while finding the right place,

for he had forgotten the name of the poem. But at last
the remembered words caught his eye:

> " . . . there must surely be
>   The face not seen, the voice not heard,
>   The heart that not yet—never yet—ah, me!
>   Made answer to my word."

His friendship with the Annesleys was over, and he
was never to see Ellen again. Within a year he took a
post in a northern university. He married a vivacious
brunette, much more like Louise than Ellen, and he
continued to worry about evil. Once, on a visit to
London, he caught sight of Dick in a box at the opera,
and was shocked to recognise, in this thickening, middle-
aged man, the handsome villain whom he had known at
Inishbar.

And long, long afterwards he chanced to find some
crumbling leaves of myrtle in a book. He could not
remember how they came to be there, but the words,
when he re-read them, gave him a moment's pang.

They were still so true.

30

ONE by one they all went to bed. Only Dick and Maude watched by Barny's bedside all through the night, and Muffy sat in the keep, listening, in case they should call for her. Lights twinkled a little in the tower windows and went out.

The rain had stopped and the night was clearing. A few small stars twinkled doubtfully through the clouds over the courtyard. Each time that Muffy came to the door of the keep the quality of the darkness seemed to be thinner. The world was swinging over into morning. Yet the transition from night to day happened, as it always does, when no one was looking. She went to the door and it was dark. Ten minutes later it was grey.

Barny, emerging slowly from his drugged quiescence, made a bad patient. He had shown great fortitude before the operation, but none now that he knew it was over. He was very thirsty and they would not give him anything to drink for fear that he might be sick. He kept on imploring them to let him be sick, rather than prolong this torture. Dick had little patience with him, and left him to Maude, who might have been born for such a moment, who could meet Barny's unreasonable reproaches with boundless sympathy, simply because they were unreasonable. She was an excellent nurse. Towards morning Barny began to threaten that he would get out of bed and find himself a drink.

"We must tie him down," said Dick impatiently, "if this sort of thing goes on. You can't hold him for ever."

Maude shook her head.

"He won't," she said. "I've seen them like this before."

"Have you? I'm glad I'm not a nurse."

Barny eyed Dick with malignant dislike.

"Has anybody told you you're a swine yet?" he asked. "If I'm sick it'll be from the sight of you. Why don't you go back to your . . ."

"Hush, Barny dear! If it hadn't been for Dick . . ."

"Thinks I ought to be grateful to him, does he? I'm not. We're going to see that Ellen gets a divorce, and he needn't think that this'll make any difference."

Barny relapsed into weary mutterings about cads and swine and the indignity of having one's appendix removed by a physician-accoucheur. He seemed to take this last very much to heart and feared that it might get known in the Temple.

Maude said to Dick:

"Go down for a bit and smoke a pipe in the courtyard. You must want one and I can manage him alone. I'm used to this sort of thing."

"All right," said Dick. "But don't give him anything whatever to drink. I don't want to start that vomiting again."

"My dear Dick! As if I should."

After the sick room, with its reek of chloroform and antiseptics, the air of the courtyard was like nectar. Dick's footsteps echoed against the sleeping walls with a hollow sound, so that he found himself trying to walk softly. It was nearer to-day than he had thought and the stars were waning in the square of pale sky overhead.

He sat down on the edge of the well and lit his pipe. He was tired, but his mood was chiefly one of satisfaction over a difficult job well done. They had got Barny through it, though he had hardly dared to touch that appendix, fearing it would rupture before he got it out.

"Damned good thing I opened him up when I did," he thought. "But how Thring will laugh when I tell him! Only he'll never believe in the old . . . ; nobody could who hadn't seen him. I wish Clarke had been there. He can imitate a brogue."

He began to think of all that they must do to-morrow, the drugs and appliances that he would need and the steps that he must take to get them quickly. Barny's angry reproaches affected him not at all. Later on there would be trouble, he supposed. He would have to face the consequences of what he had done. But he was not sure what these would be, and, at the back of his mind, there was already a certain confidence in his own capacity to deal with them. To-night he had put through a difficult job successfully and that was quite enough for the moment.

He yawned and saw with amazement how quickly the light was growing. Everything in the courtyard was now visible, though without colour. Muffy's white apron glimmered at the door of the keep and the candle which she held burned wanly. She was calling to him, in an echoing whisper:

"Dr. Napier . . . how is he?"

"Going on splendidly. You can go to bed now, if you like, Muffy. We shan't want anything more."

"Dr. Napier! Can I speak to you for a minute, please?"

She wanted him to come with her into the keep. He left the cool air reluctantly and went into the warm dusk of firelight and guttering candles. Muffy offered him a cup of coffee, which he took mechanically.

"Oh, sir . . . are you coming back to her . . . to Miss Ellen?"

He made a gesture to stop her. He did not want to go into all that yet.

"This isn't the time to talk of it, Muffy."

"I know, sir. But there's something I've got to tell you. I've not had the chance before, but I must tell you at once. You see, sir, she doesn't know."

"Doesn't know?" he asked confusedly.

"Not a thing, poor lamb. The others, they've been putting it about that you went on a walking tour. But Miss Ellen, she believes it."

"Believes . . . believes . . ."

"I'm certain of it. She told me so. I could hardly credit my own ears, but it's true."

"But how can she . . ."

This was important. He must attend to it.

"I don't know, sir. I suppose she just didn't put two and two together, like the others did. And then, you know, Mr. Lindsay went over, but nobody was going to tell her that, stand to reason. We all thought she knew already. We all thought she was just passing it off. But it's not so, sir. She thinks you've been true to her, if I might take the liberty of putting it like that. And she'd kill anyone who said anything different."

Dick struggled amidst his other preoccupations, making the attempt to take this in.

"Are you sure?"

"Sure as I stand here. She told me. She'd had her suspicions of what they were saying, you know, though she'd no notion of the real thing. She thought we had made out that there must have been some difference between the two of you, to make you go off so suddenly.

Some quarrel about that . . . that lady. And she said: 'Never let me hear you suggest such a thing,' she said. She was in a real taking. 'A husband and a wife,' she said, 'is quite above that sort of thing.' I couldn't have believed it myself if I hadn't heard her. So you see, sir . . ."

She stopped and began to twist her apron, looking anxiously into his face.

Dick took some time to see. Fatigue and concentration had made him slow-witted. He found it hard to bring his mind to this extraordinary idea. But, after asking Muffy a few more questions, he began to be convinced.

"It was very stupid of her," he commented, more to himself than Muffy.

She flared up at this.

"Stupid you may call it. I don't. What should she know of such things, so good as she is? It's written in the Bible, Dr. Napier, if you care to look. 'Love thinketh no evil,' it says. It wouldn't come to her to think badly of you, because she looks up to you as a wife should do. If you think that stupid, then I'm sorry for you. She couldn't think evil of you, sir, unless she was to hear it from your own lips."

"I know."

But some women, he thought, just as loving, might have guessed. Ellen's stupidity, Ellen's goodness, her love, how were these things to be disentangled? Had she failed to guess because she was good or because she was stupid?

"So you see, sir . . ." persisted the anxious Muffy.

"Yes, I see."

"But do you? You haven't thought yet. What I mean

is that she's still got it all to go through, worse than we thought, unless . . . unless . . ."

"Unless what, Muffy?"

"Unless you see to it that she's spared."

This was going on rather far for Dick. He was conscious of relief and thankfulness, because Ellen had not suffered. He was even dimly aware of the importance of this news. He knew that he would have been much more moved by it if he had not been so sleepy and so busy. Both his relief and his hope were languid.

"You want me," he said with an effort, "never to tell her? To remain here, and behave as if nothing had happened?"

"That's right, sir. You will, won't you?"

"I don't know, Muffy. That's not a question I can answer now."

"It would kill her if she knew. It really would. She'd never understand. She'd think you couldn't love her."

"Do you think I do?"

"I don't doubt it, sir. But then I'm an old woman. I wouldn't have seen it that way, not when I was Miss Ellen's age."

"No," agreed Dick. "You're right. She'd never understand."

"And there's more than her to think of. There's her baby. The shock . . ."

"I know."

"If she must be told, couldn't you wait . . ."

"But the others? They all know. If I don't tell her, they will . . ."

"Oh, no, sir. They'll do what's best for Miss Ellen. If they see you've come back to her they'll not say anything to upset her. They know she mustn't be upset, same as we do. Least said, soonest mended, they'll think. And it's not known to anyone outside the family barring Mr. Fletcher."

"He won't talk."

"No. He seems a nice gentleman. And they'll have all written to Mrs. Annesley, sure to. But she never interferes. She won't want anything but to see Miss Ellen happy."

Dick surveyed with detachment these possibilities.

It appeared that he was not ruined after all. All he had to do was to hold his tongue. Home, wife, and children were still his, and he might go back to his work in the autumn with an untarnished name. Ellen's relations could not be expected to like him very cordially again, but they would keep their feelings to themselves. He did not much care. He had no great opinion of Ellen's relations. And he would continue to think badly of himself. The episode had done him no credit at all. But even this was a bearable prospect. His opinion of himself could stand a good deal of wear and tear. The passing folly which has not ruined a life can be leniently dismissed.

He had been through a period of nervous disintegration, when the forces which governed his character seemed to be at a standstill. That was over now. He had come to himself. And though he felt remote from any sort of decision at the moment, he knew that his nature, confident, insensitive, and a little unscrupulous, would eventually carry the issue.

"If you should wait till after the child is born . . ." pleaded Muffy.

"I shall do what's best for her," he said. "I'll think over what you've said. You were right to tell me at once. I'm obliged to you."

He looked at his watch and drank up the coffee, which had grown cold. Bidding good night to Muffy, he went back to see how Maude and Barny were getting on.

She watched him striding across the court, looking, she told herself resentfully, as if he'd bought the place. It was broad daylight now, and a glow on the eastern tower told of the approaching sunrise. When she drew back the curtains in the keep it was so light that she could blow out the candles. She washed the coffee things, rehearsing mentally a narrative of these things:

"He didn't seem to feel it as he ought, ma'am, but I think he will do what is right in his own way. He is a hard gentleman. I said to him, I said: 'She doesn't know any more than the babe unborn.' 'Oh!' he says, 'stupid of her.' 'Stupid!' I could have boxed his ears. But it's his nature to be hard, I suppose. And that's the whole truth of it, ma'am. Miss Ellen, she never knew. I said: 'It'll kill her if you tell,' I said. 'She wouldn't understand.' And she wouldn't, would she? Not Miss Ellen . . ."

On the dresser there was a penny bottle of ink and a leather writing case which Mrs. Annesley had given to her at Christmas. She got as far as sitting down at the table and dating the letter which she would have wished to write.

"Dear Madam . . ." she wrote.

But it was too difficult. Her powers as a letter-writer were very limited and the narrative, so fluent in her mind, escaped her when she tried to commit it to paper. She got no further than *Dear Madam*.

Sunlight filled the sky and all the birds on the island began to sing. Muffy chewed the end of her pen for a little while. And then she gave it up. There was no need to write it in a letter. Plenty of people would tell Mrs. Annesley what had happened, how Barny had been taken ill, and how Dick had come back, and how everything seemed to have turned out for the best. Her story would keep. Soon she would be seeing Mrs. Annesley and they would have a long talk, and then she could be sure that her tale would go no further. Mrs. Annesley never betrayed confidences. After all it was not very safe to write things down. You never knew who might read them.

She tore up the sheet, yawned twice, and went to bed.

Epilogue

SUNDAY EVENING

KERRAN was annoyed with Hope for taking so seriously the letters which she had written herself. She read each of them twice, with amused comments, exclamations, and scattered reminiscences, as the fragments of her own forgotten past came back to her. And when she came to her *Stanzas written in Dejection at Inishbar*, she wanted to take a copy of it.

"You can keep it if you like," said Kerran. "Keep all your own letters if you like. And Rosamund's too. I only kept them because my mother did. They have no value in the main story."

"I was a far more imaginative child than Rosamund. Yet there was always this legend that she was an exquisite, sensitive little thing and I was a lump. I resented it obscurely at the time, and now, looking back on it I resent it still more. These family legends are exasperating. They stick and stick. To one's aunts and cousins one remains what one was at ten years old, or what they thought one was at ten years old, till the day of one's death. I can still remember the exasperation . . . of course Rosamund was so much better *produced* than I was. She had very pretty clothes . . . djibbahs with nice embroidery, while I was kept in clumsy holland smocks. And she was brought up to be so much more cultured: Aunt Louise took her about. She went abroad and to concerts and things. She was much more like a modern child. I got plenty of solid teaching, but nobody ever encouraged me to have any æsthetic interests. I had to

do it all for myself. And the mere title of that poem . . .
Stanzas Written in Dejection . . . shows that at least I'd
discovered Shelley for myself. It's pathetic. And I can
remember all those humiliating comments on my legs.
I'm sure Aunt Louise still thinks that something ought
to be done about them."

Kerran got so tired of it at last that he went out for a
short walk, leaving her to finish the letters by herself.
When he came back it was dark, and tea had been brought
into the library. She was sitting on the floor by the fire,
with the bundle in her lap.

"Will you pour out," he asked, "or shall I?"

"You. I always spill, and that annoys you." She got
up. "You want these letters back, I suppose? I mayn't
just show them to Alan?"

"No, you may not. You can keep your own if you
like."

At first she thought that she would. But then she said
that the collection ought to remain complete.

"You say they have no value to the main story. But
they have, in a way. I mean, it gives the entire picture
of the family party. There we all were, children and all,
each living our own lives. The mere fact that there was
a whole group of people, a whole community, living, as
it were, entirely outside the drama, makes one understand
how confused, how piecemeal, the whole thing was.
That's one of the great mistakes one makes, looking back
at things which have happened in the past. One sees the
thing as a whole, and one forgets that the people at the
time did not see it as a whole. One doesn't make allow-
ance for their unawareness, and how things which appear
to be consecutive later were not consecutive then."

"Perhaps you are right," said Kerran, locking up the

bundle in his cabinet. "Help yourself to tea-cake and tell me what you make of it all."

Hope shook her head impatiently.

"I don't make much. It seemed to dwindle out so, at the last. The letters get so dull . . . all about packing up and how soon Uncle Barny could stand the journey. And of course one gets bored by all the repetition."

"It did dwindle out. Your father stayed on the island. It was obvious that he had made it up with your mother. There was no more to be said. Barny's health was the thing which most occupied our minds for the rest of the time."

"Still, I don't feel I know any more than I did before," complained Hope. "These letters tell one everything but the one important fact. They give the bare outline, though some of them are rather contradictory, and they show up the characters of the people who wrote them. But they don't tell me why he did it or what mother thought about it."

"Nobody knew."

"A letter from either of them would have been worth the whole bundle. But he never writes at all and she merely writes about knitting wool and the Waverley Novels. What do you think yourself?"

"I never could make up my mind," confessed Kerran. "Partly because I've had these letters to refresh my memory. The others have all got very definite ideas. You'll remember there were considerable discrepancies in their views, even at the time, and these have widened. After all, our memories are at the mercy of our prejudices. We forget the facts which seem to be irrelevant or incongruous, and what is left is liable to be modified or distorted by what we wish to believe. Your Aunt Louise, who had, as you may have noticed, a certain tenderness for your father . . ."

"Oh, yes! I'd never realised that before. It's most illuminating!"

"Well, Louise believes that it was the one love of his life. She has quite forgiven him and she has almost managed to forgive Elissa. She thinks that he came back to your mother from a sense of duty . . . that the whole thing was a tragedy."

"But father wasn't the man to let his whole life be a tragedy!"

"I agree. Maude believes that this episode was one of many. And Barny did too—as far as I can remember. She thinks that your father was a confirmed libertine and that your mother was merely coping with a situation to which she was very well accustomed. These aren't theories with them any more, they're convictions. I have heard Maude asserting that the affair had been going on, quite openly, for some time before they left the island, and that they were discovered *en flagrant délit* on the bathing beach. Louise has got a wonderful account of all that passed between Gordon and 'poor Dick' when Gordon went over and saw them at the cottage. I can find no evidence in the letters that they had any conversation at all on that occasion, but Louise has it all cut and dried . . . what Dick said to Gordon and what Gordon said to Dick . . ."

"You *must* show them the letters!"

"No, no! Too dangerous. They'd all be at one another's throats in no time."

"We-ell . . ." Hope sipped her tea meditatively. "I wonder if it really happened at all!"

"What?"

The idea had only just occurred to her, but she developed it with a growing conviction.

"My first instinct was to say that it couldn't have happened. That it was impossible. And I'm beginning to wonder if I wasn't right. You all contradict one another in your facts. You all contradict one another in your deductions. I can't help asking myself if you weren't all wrong. I don't believe there's anything in it at all."

"My dear Hope! Some of the facts are undisputed. Gordon saw him at her cottage."

"I daresay. But he didn't see her. Nobody saw her again. How do we know that she was there at all?"

"What was he doing there?"

"I believe she went back to England. The cottage was a sort of annexe to the castle. It belonged to the Nugents, didn't it? Why shouldn't he stay there if it was empty. You all say that it rained for the whole of the three days. I daresay he was waiting for the rain to stop so as to get off on his walking tour."

"No, Hope. It won't do. There's her own account of it to be got over."

"Oh, she was a liar. That's proved again and again. She's quite discredited as a witness. She'd be quite capable of making it all up. I've no doubt it's what she would have liked to happen and she didn't like to admit that she left Ireland without bringing off an appropriate *amour*. I daresay she believes it herself now."

"It won't wash. It's too improbable. It's flat against all the facts."

"Facts are only one kind of truth, and very misleading at that. What I go on is what I know, not all this mass of contradictory statement. I know that these particular

people were incapable of being involved in this particular
story. I know what my father was like. He was not that
kind of man. He could not have acted in that way. He
would not have fallen passionately in love with a woman
like Elissa. He wasn't an uncontrolled, impulsive, tem-
peramental person, and he never liked highfalutin
women. All that soulful humbug . . . he would never
have put up with it. But he would have had to be insanely
in love to do what you say he did: to desert his wife in
that brutally callous way and risk his whole career. He
might have found her physically attractive. By all
accounts she was a most seductive creature, and I don't
know enough about him to be sure that he might not
have been unfaithful to mother, though it would have
surprised me. But he'd have taken care that it wasn't
found out. They must have had plenty of opportunities on the island. It wasn't necessary to pack
up and run off with her quite openly. Besides, if he'd
been really in love with her he wouldn't have allowed
Guy Fletcher to bring him back so meekly. He'd have
gone the whole hog and damned Uncle Barny with the
rest of them. That's my first argument. It doesn't square
with father's character. Nor does it square with
mother's. I've said so all along. She wasn't the woman
to forgive such a thing. She might have reconciled herself to letting him go, but she would never have taken
him back. Or even if she had, for the sake of her children,
there would always have been an estrangement between
them. I lived with them. I know there was no estrangement. She loved him passionately till the day of his
death. She must have convinced herself that there was
nothing in it."

"Well, then, why didn't she say so?"

"How should I know? We can't ask her, unfortunately, for I'm sure Elissa's book would distress her. I've hidden it in my suit-case, and we must do our best to see that she never knows about it. Luckily she doesn't read much. But to return to my argument. You all keep saying yourselves that you can't understand them, how you've been utterly deceived in him, how you'd thought him incapable of such behaviour, and how her attitude is a complete mystery. Well, you were quite right. He was incapable of such behaviour and so was she. He wasn't the man to count the world well lost for a second-rate Diva, and she wasn't the woman to overlook it if he did. He didn't and she didn't. And in your heart of hearts you all knew that they hadn't. That's why the whole thing dwindles out so. You all half knew that it had been a mare's nest, so it was easy to forget it and behave as if it had never happened. Because it didn't happen."

"Don't go on so fast. Let me get my bearings . . ."

"You do agree that there's something in what I say?"

"You're very specious. But I've believed that it happened for twenty-five years, and I can't, in five minutes . . . but I wish I'd thought of it before, though. I shall certainly put it to Louise and Maude. Just as an experiment. It'll make them furious. I shall tell them that you believe it never happened."

"And tell them my grounds."

"Oh, your grounds won't cut much ice. You base your theory on your knowledge of your parents' characters. So do they. Louise knows that your father was an incurable romantic: she's as certain as you are that he wasn't. And she knows that your mother was stupid, selfish, and too cold-blooded ever to grasp the situation. Maude knows that he was a rake and she was a saint. I'm the only person who doesn't claim to know all about them."

"But their convictions are built up on a prejudiced selection of imperfect memories. Mine are quite fresh. I come to the facts for the first time, the contemporary facts, as recorded in the letters. I'm sure I'm right. I may have slipped into a stereotyped view of my father, since he's been dead for some years. But mother . . . it's impossible. There's nothing mysterious about mother. She's a bit of a saint, but not that kind of saint. All her conventions . . . her prejudices . . . she couldn't have been through such an experience without being shaken to her depths. Does she strike you as a woman who's ever been shaken to the depths? Don't you feel that she's always led a rather protected life? Of course she's had trouble . . . Peter being killed, and then father dying. And she faced it with great courage. Her religion helped her. She believes that they have gone to Heaven and that she will meet them again and everything will be all right. She thought that the war was dreadful, but that it was quite right that England should protect Belgium and that Peter was a hero because he had died for his country. She never saw the waste and wickedness of it, as our generation does."

Kerran looked at his watch. When Hope began to talk of "our generation," she was likely to go on all night, and he remembered that she had a bus to catch.

"I don't see what the war has to do with it," he said.

"Only this: that she meets trouble in a pre-war way. She's sustained by all her pre-war convictions and prejudices. She thinks of God as a nice old country gentleman. Her religion is the religion of a person who has lived a sheltered life: who's never been churned up and forced to remake all their values about things. She couldn't have lived through all this Elissa business and remained quite what she is. Her kind of stability isn't possible for our generation, that has had to face up to all kinds of shocks and readjustments. What I mean is that she couldn't have lived through anything so modern. If she had, she'd be more modern in herself."

"Men were faithless, and their wives forgave them, even before the war."

"Yes. But not men who belonged to their period so completely as my father did, or wives like mother. I can imagine it all happening to me and to Alan. Or to our grandparents. But not to mother and father."

"You may be right. I've always said one should ask the young."

"I hope you don't call me young. I'm thirty-six, remember. Show the letters to somebody fifteen years younger and see what they say. But my generation is a very interesting one. We were enough in touch with things before the war to . . ."

"I'm very sorry to interrupt you, Hope, but your bus goes in seven minutes."

"Oh, does it? I must fly!"

She jumped up and pushed the tea table so that slops and milk were spilt on the tray.

Kerran felt glad to get rid of her and her clumsy movements, and the loud voice in which she laid down the law. Her theory had ceased to interest him. He was a little resentful at her summary disposal of the past.

This had happened and that had not happened. This was possible and that was not possible. People who belonged to the Church of England did not mind their sons being killed in the war. Unfaithful husbands were not forgiven in the reign of King Edward. Stability was produced by an absence of shocks.

"Sola! Sola!" he said to himself, as quiet once more descended on his library. "And what does she know about it all?"

ELLEN had not gone to church because she was too busy. She worked in the garden until it was dark and then she packed up some things for Hope to take back to London in the morning: a dozen new-laid eggs, three pots of home-made strawberry jam and some nice broccoli. By the time that she had finished it was too late to get down into the village for evening service, so she sat in the drawing-room and turned on the wireless. While she got on with her knitting she listened to a talk upon the habits of the wood wasp. She had a pair of socks for Michael in hand, and she could listen-in as long as she did not have stitches to count. But when she came to turning the heel she switched the wireless off, as it disturbed her.

For a little while she was entirely absorbed in plain and purl, slip one and knit two together, make one and repeat. But at last the enthralling business was over and she had before her the long, dull strip of plain knitting which was to cover the sole of Michael's abnormally long foot. This was not enough to occupy her mind. She could do it mechanically. And then the silence of the room, the loneliness, so painfully kept at bay, rushed in upon her once more.

She thought, as she always thought in November, that next year she would contrive not to spend the whole winter in the country. She would save up and take a little flat in London, where she could be near the children and go to the theatre sometimes in the evening. She did not like London much, but these long winter nights were very hard to get through. It was so quiet, sitting there with only her needles and the ticking clock for company. The wireless was all very well. It knew a great deal and was more entertaining than any human visitor could ever be, but it had its shortcomings. It did not answer when, at ten o'clock, she would fain have said to someone . . . anyone:

"Well? What about bed?"

Sometimes she thought of asking Maude to come and live with her. It would be kind. For Maude had been left very badly off when Barny died, and she was far from strong, poor thing. But then the children would not have enjoyed coming down to Carey's End in the same way if Maude had been there. It was so nice for them all to have this country house to come to. Whatever she did, she must keep up Carey's End.

And to-night, as she remembered, more cheerfully, she would not be alone. She would have her dear Hope. And next week-end Michael would be bringing a friend. It was only in the middle of the week that she would play with the idea of inviting Maude. And she ought to go up and see if Hope's fire had been properly lighted.

She found it burning brightly but she piled on fresh logs and drew the window curtains. The bed was already turned down because Maggie went out before supper on Sundays. Hope's night-gown lay spread out, and Ellen looked at it admiringly:

"Pretty!" she thought. "How pretty their things are nowadays!"

Her own trousseau night-gowns had lasted for twenty years, and her daughters had laughed at them, with their frills, their high necks and their profusion of Swiss embroidery. When they wore out she had made herself new ones of thick washing silk, and was very proud of them, thinking how unheard-of silk night-gowns would have been in her youth. She had had silk petticoats, which rustled, but everything else had been of linen and long-cloth. This diaphanous and scanty garment of Hope's would not have been considered respectable. Her only criticism was that it was chilly. There would be nothing to curl your toes in if they got cold.

For a time she fidgeted about the room, putting the flowers straight on the dressing-table and rolling up a pair of stockings which Hope had left lying on the floor. She had better slip these inside the suit-case, or Hope might forget them in the morning. Lifting the lid, she was really quite shocked at Hope's untidy ways. With all the empty drawers and shelves in the spare room at her disposal, she ought to have taken the trouble to un-pack rather more. Books, cigarettes, underclothes and an evening blouse lay tumbled together. And it was so like Hope to bring such a large book away with her, when there were plenty of books at Carey's End already.

Ellen picked it up and felt a little disagreeable shock as she saw the title:

The Story of My Life. By Elissa Koebel.

She remembered now that she had seen something, an advertisement or a review or something, in the papers.

Elissa Koebel!

That queer woman who used to come to the island, in that queer summer, long ago, when Barny had appendicitis. She took the book over to the light and turned the pages. The print looked small and uninviting, and she had left her glasses downstairs. In any case she did not suppose that she would care for it. There had been some-thing unpleasant about Elissa Koebel. A silly woman, she was, and more than silly. Not a nice woman. A phrase caught her eye:

"My soul had become a battlefield. I was torn between Byron, Jesus Christ, and Edward Carpenter . . ."

A *very* silly woman.

She put the book back into the suit-case and smiled to herself as she shut the lid, remembering how once she had made Kerran laugh with an imitation of Elissa's accent singing English songs:

> "Birrts in the high hall garden
>   Ven tvilight vas falling,
>   Mautt! Mautt! Mautt! Mautt! . . ."

Oh, that summer on the island! How that moment of Kerran laughing sprang out of a mist of forgotten things! Her smile faded as she thought how long ago it all was, and how little she had kept in her heart of those times when she had been so happy because Dick and Peter were still with her. If she had known that she must lose them, would she not have stored up every trivial moment? The regret for happiness squandered overcame her, the regret which is inseparable from our thoughts of the dead, the remorse for caresses not given, for want of patience, want of tenderness, for the love that can never, never again be told.

She had been worried about Dick. But how foolishly, since he was still alive and with her! And Peter had been a little boy, locked safely away in childhood, the war and early death an untold story. Now they had vanished and her desolate soul cried out to their memory:

"Oh, Dick! Oh, Peter! I loved you."

Peter had made her laugh once. She could not remember much about Peter on the island. But once he had made her laugh when she was trying to scold him. He had always been able to do that. He made her laugh when they were getting ready for a picnic, *the picnic*, the only clear memory which stayed with her, a thing so distinct that she never thought of it in the past at all but as something that was still going on. But it had happened then, that summer on the island. They all climbed up a hot valley to a place where there was a beautiful view. And somebody said: *To glorify God!* . . .

So often and often had she thought of it since. And when she did not think of it she felt it, like an echo, going on and on, through all the clamour and lamentation of the years. If it had not been for that echo she would not have known what to do, now that she was alone. She would have been quite lost.

But she was still listening. She still believed that she must hear those words again, and that their meaning, comprehended for a moment and then lost, would be made plain to her for ever.

"It happened then," she thought. "That summer on the island. A very long time ago. But I remember *that* as if it happened yesterday."

THE END

www.vintage-classics.info

Visit www.worldofstories.co.uk for all your
favourite children's classics